The Crack in the Lens

Darlene A. Cypser

Foolscap & Quill

Contents

Chapter 1
Spring on the Moor

A young man leaned against one of the piles of the pier and watched the passengers disembarking from a steamship. If someone had asked him later in the year, there is little doubt that this young man would have said his life began that spring day in 1871 and ended in the winter some months distant. But his mother would have disputed the former claim, and many, both friend and foe, would come to deny the latter. His true date of birth, by his mother's reckoning, was some seventeen years behind him.

Right now he was wishing his brother Mycroft was here. It would be a grand spot for the game. Even Sherrinford would do. Sherrinford wasn't very good at the game, but it was always fun to best him at it. But neither of his brothers was here and he was left to make his own observations and deductions.

The man coming down the gangplank now was a prosperous owner of coal mines, the young man surmised. He was well-dressed by the standards of the merchant class, but he never quite managed to entirely shake off the coal dust which still coated the soles of his shoes. Would an examination of his fingernails show it there as well?

The coal merchant was followed rapidly by a tall man with sharp eyes and a critical stare. His coat was of good material, but well-worn. The elbows had been patched, and the sleeves, especially the right sleeve, had been worn quite shiny. A wad of foolscap covered with pencil scribblings stuck out of his left pocket. He was a writer, an essayist, the young man concluded. The foolscap was undoubtedly some spontaneous critique of the shipping industry that had come to him on board.

If his brothers had been there one of them would have crept

1

away and asked the men their occupation to confirm their speculations. If he could have managed it, he would have done it himself. But he was in sight of his parents, and his father had decided ideas about the behavior of seventeen-year-old soon-to-be-gentlemen. The young man knew that interrogating strangers was not among them. Even staring at the people coming down the plank was a stretch of what his father considered proper, but he could always claim to be admiring the ship. He knew his father would approve of that.

The third man coming down the gangplank was an old soldier from his walk, a veteran of the Crimean War, perhaps. But the young man's observations were interrupted before he could determine more. His parents were signaling for him to join them. The carriage started off towards home as he climbed aboard.

As the carriage rolled along, the young man stuck his head out the window and observed the countryside. The wind whipped at his cloth cap and threatened to carry it off. He pulled it off and sat it in his lap.

"Sherlock," came the remonstration from inside the carriage.

"Yes, Mother," he said with a sigh and put the cap back on, holding it with one hand as he looked out on the countryside.

"You have to be careful," his mother said.

"Yes, Mother," he replied.

They had been away nearly two years. He was taller and stronger. Yet his mother seemed to feel it her duty to nearly constantly remind him that he had left Yorkshire in the north of England for the warmer climates of France because he had been ill. She sat across from him in the carriage, prim and proper, as always, not a hair out of place despite the sea voyage and the carriage ride from the coast. He knew that as soon as they arrived she would be busy supervising the unpacking, assuring that they would be settled in again as soon as possible, and that everything would be in its place.

SPRING ON THE MOOR

They were not close. He and his brothers had been brought up, as was not unusual for a family of their standing, by a succession of governesses and tutors. He had vivid memories of these, both good and bad, but his mother had always been a distant, fuzzy figure absorbed in the details of the running of the house and the maintenance of the squire's social circle.

His thoughts went back to the view out the window. The countryside seemed little changed. The old road wound its way from the coast skirting the moors. It was mostly dirt except where they rumbled over a stone bridge or came through a village large enough to be cobbled. Mostly it was a brown ribbon winding through the green and gold of the springtime moors, which were broken now and then by the grey or white of a rock outcropping. Here and there long stone walls stretched across the land even onto the rocky moors. Sometimes he could see ruins in the distance, some medieval and some much older. It was an old, old land, and it was his home.

"It looks like a glorious day for a ride upon the moors," Sherlock said.

It was his father, Squire Holmes, who responded to this remark.

"I think that could be allowed this afternoon," the squire said.

"Just make sure you dress warmly," his mother said.

"I will, Mother," Sherlock assured her.

"Here's the gate," Sherlock announced as the carriage pulled into the drive of Holmes Hall of Mycroft Manor.

As the carriage pulled up, the door to the manor house opened. First out was Sherlock's brother, Sherrinford, followed by Thomas, the butler.

"Welcome home, Mother," Sherrinford said as he helped his mother down from the carriage.

"Hello, my dear, I trust you have taken good care of things?"

"I have done my best," Sherrinford said, stepping back from

3

the door of the carriage to allow his father to descend unaided.

"Tessy would like to know what time you would like luncheon, when it is convenient."

"Thank you. I will speak to her."

Thomas bowed to the mistress of the manor as he held the door open for her.

"Welcome back, Father," Sherrinford said turning back to the carriage. The squire walked with a limp and used a cane for assistance, but he was a proud man and never allowed any man to assist him.

"Sherrinford," the squire nodded his head. "There is a crate of books among the luggage. Have the servants bring it to my study."

"Yes, sir. Any other instructions?" Sherrinford asked.

"Be prepared to begin reviewing the ledgers this afternoon," Squire Holmes said.

"Yes, sir," Sherrinford responded.

Then the squire followed his wife into the house.

"Sherlock!" Sherrinford exclaimed smiling broadly and greeting his youngest brother warmly. He slapped his hands on the younger boy's shoulders. "You certainly have grown. You are nearly as tall as I am!"

"Sherrinford! It is good to see you! Have you been behaving yourself?" Sherlock said.

"I haven't had much time to do anything else. It has been a lot more work than I anticipated when you set out. It is a heavy responsibility running a manor of this size especially to Father's standards."

"Yet it was what you were born and bred to do. I suspect you do it quite well," Sherlock said.

"I suppose I shall find out this afternoon if Father agrees," Sherrinford said.

While Sherrinford ordered the other servants to unload the

luggage, Sherlock approached the stable boy holding the head of the carriage horses.

"How is Gale?" Sherlock asked.

"Ah, she is in fine form, Master Sherlock," the stable boy said.

"Very good, saddle her up and bring her around after lunch," Sherlock said.

"Yes, sir."

After lunch the squire and Sherrinford retired to the squire's study to review the books of the estate. Sherlock knew that they would be occupied for the rest of the day, and perhaps several more. His mother was back in the kitchen reviewing the state of the larder with the cook when Sherlock came down from his room. He found his horse, Gale, waiting for him out front as he had requested. But as he walked towards the mare a whirlwind of golden curly hair ran towards him and leapt up at him. Sherlock squatted down and took the dog's forepaws in his hands.

"So you missed me, eh, Sandy? Come on, let's go for a ride."

Sherlock mounted the mare and then with a wry smile he produced his cap from his pocket and planted it firmly upon his head before riding off. At his urging the horse loped along eastward, and Holmes Hall, surrounded by its gardens and orchards, fell behind him. He passed the barns where doves cooed in the rafters, and the meadows where sheep grazed lazily. There were the cottages where the labourers lived, their whitewashed walls bright under thatched roofs and their garths brimming with fresh greens for their dwellers' supper.

Sherlock paused as they came to the crossroad. To the right and left was the road leading to the tenant farms. The manor kept its own lands and employed many men to tend the fields and flocks. Most of the estate, however, was parceled out to tenants. The tenant farms were large, a hundred hectares or more, and the tenant farmers were prosperous men who hired servants and labourers in their turn. But each quarter day they brought their rents, in kind or coin, according to their indenture, to the squire for use of the manor.

There were yeomen farmers in the dale as well, men who owned and worked their own small parcels of land. But the manor dominated the best soil in this valley between the moors, and the yeomen had to scrape along as best they could. Sometimes they took work on the manor lands or on one of the tenant farms while their children and women folk tended their own land.

Sandy barked impatiently. Sherlock looked down at the dog, then sent his horse on, not turning to the right or left but heading straight on toward where the road met the sky.

The "moor road" as most folks called it was hardly more than a path, and it was a rare and intrepid cart driver who sought to follow it. For a sure-footed horse, however, it was fair going and well worth the climb.

As his horse dug her hooves into the rising road, a gust of wind swept down from the moor and ruffled his hair where it curled around the edges of his cap. The wind caressed him with the sweet, wild scent of the moors. He smiled and inhaled deeply and his grey eyes sparkled.

As he rode the land before him fell away until the moors swept out around him with wave after wave of bracken, heather, and bent. Here and there the tangle of green was broken by mock bonfires where the yellow broom had burst into flower.

He patted his horse as she crested the moor. When she was a filly he had named her Gale for she was as swift as the wintry winds that blew the snow about. Few horses in the dale could match her. But now he brought her to a halt and dismounted. He stood rubbing his hand along her sleek brown neck as he watched the woolly clouds drift across the broad blue sky, and their broad shadows slide down from the moors to crawl across the fields and forests of the dale below.

The golden-haired dog now pawed at his boots and yipped.

When Sherlock looked down at her Sandy crouched back on her haunches with her forelegs stretched out, then bounced up and ran around him three times. Then she made as if to run away across the moor, but stopped a few feet away and turned her head back to him and barked. Sherlock laughed.

"Oh, so you want to race, do you, Sandy? Go on then. We'll catch you," he said.

The dog shot off as Sherlock turned and mounted his horse. The dog was just vanishing where the road dipped to cross the gill as horse and rider started out. But the horse lived up to her name as she flew like the wind after the mongrel. In less than a minute they were splashing across the gill and mounting the eastern bank. Then they saw Sandy again in the distance. The road was even here for a stretch and Gale took her head and soon flashed past the yellow streak of fur. Sandy, seeing she was defeated, disappeared into the heath, as if to prove she hadn't been racing at all.

Sherlock laughed again as he reined his horse in. He paused for a minute to consider their course. To the north he could see where the mounds and tors rose above the heather. The tors were large stones. Some stood alone. Others were stacked about as if some giant child had been playing there long ago. But he knew that area had been combed thoroughly by him and his brothers and had been robbed of all its artifacts save one. So he turned instead to the northeast and rode beyond the tors where some relics of "t'owd man," as some of the local Yorkshiremen called them, might still be hidden.

As horse and rider picked their way through the heath, a red grouse suddenly shot up in the air not far before them. The yip which accompanied it left no doubt as to what had flushed it. Sandy soon scampered up next to the horse and began to nose about. Then they turned south until they met the moor road again and followed it westward until it dipped towards the gill crossing. There they left the road and followed the stream northward to the mounds and tors. Sherlock rode to one cluster near the largest boulder, and dismounted. He rolled two smaller stones away. Behind them was a large flat rock as tall as he was which he grasped about the top and pulled down until it lay flat upon the ground before him. This uncovered an opening between the larger stones. He walked across the flat rock and entered the hole.

It was dark inside and the air was stale. He pulled an old pigskin down from the southern wall and slivers of light shot in and illuminated the room. The old stone hut was much larger inside than could be imagined from the outside. The boulders that formed the walls supported the stone roof over seven feet off the ground. That alone would have been adequate quarters for most men, but the floor was also dug several feet below the surface, and even horses could easily be weathered in there.

The floor was made of rock and earth and stretched over thirty feet in either direction, though it could hardly be called square. A fire pit had been dug near the southeast corner by some prehistoric inhabitant. The only "furnishings" were a sleeping mat with a few moth-eaten wool blankets, a water jug, and a short three-legged stool which his brothers had provided long ago.

His brothers, Sherrinford and Mycroft, who were nine and seven years his senior, had played in the hut long before they had brought him up to share their secret. They hadn't built it, but rather they had found it in nearly the same condition as it was in today. They used to tantalize each other by weaving exotic tales about the prehistoric men who must have built it.

The first time Sherlock had been to the hut had been long ago before his first illness. In those days he and his brothers had a governess named Mrs. Green. She had been a shriveled old woman who was very strict with their lessons. She insisted upon proper decorum in their schoolroom. A smirk between brothers at the wrong time could bring a rap from the ruler. But each afternoon she had driven them all out with a wave of her ruler and an injunction that they not return until they had some color in their cheeks. There was no order they more strictly obeyed.

Even in winter they frolicked until supper and brought back the "bright roses of the moor" in their cheeks of which Mrs. Green so highly approved. Those were delightful days for the three young boys; the hut held endless possibilities. Sherlock chuckled as he remembered how he and his brothers would imagine that they were highwaymen lying in wait for travelers on the moor road just over the rise. Once they had jumped out and startled an itinerant tinker who nearly shot their heads off in his fright.

The hut was also a handy shelter from the sudden storms which sprang up on the moors. More than once the three boys had spent the night here telling each other ghost stories as a storm lashed outside.

Then there had come his first illness. Sherlock remembered it clearly. He had caught a cold in late autumn as any nine year old might but sniffles had led to a cough and soon he was bedridden with a fever. Pneumonia, the doctor had said and had suggested a warmer climate.

In those days old Malvary had been overseer. He had been overseer long before Sherlock's birth, when his grandfather had been squire. Old Malvary was one of the few men ever known to argue with the present Squire and win. The Squire had respected old Malvary and left him in charge when he left snowy Yorkshire that winter to travel to the south of France. The Squire and his family visited Montpelier and stayed with French cousins on Sherlock's mother's side of the family while he recovered. Then they had returned when spring was fragrant in the Yorkshire air.

But then Mrs. Green was gone. She had retired and gone to live with her daughter somewhere in the south of England. After that there had been a string of tutors, mostly men, but none of them had stayed very long. Some were strong-willed men who could not tolerate the squire's overbearing ways, and others proved to be unsatisfactory in the squire's eyes.

Then Sherrinford had entered Sidney Sussex College at Cambridge University and Mycroft had followed two years later. His older brothers no longer came to the hut on the moors and no one had been here since he had left for France two years ago.

The north wall of the hut was solid. It was the side of the large boulder visible from outside. To the south and east the walls were made of smaller stones piled up. It was through these that sunlight now filtered, but the light was growing dimmer as the shadows grew and the sun crept towards the horizon. The hut had aired out now and he replaced the pigskin, once more plunging the interior into darkness. Then he left, carefully replacing the stones back over the entrance.

His horse wound her way back to the moor road and he turned her west towards the dale. To the south of the moor road he saw another horse and brought his to a halt. There was no rider on the other horse, but it did not seem to be a stray. There were cloth and leather bundles tied behind the saddle.

Sandy tensed and Sherlock followed her line of sight. The bracken to the east of the riderless horse shivered as a hare sought refuge. A shot cracked and the hare lay still.

A poacher!

Sherlock dismounted and drew his own shotgun from the saddle mount. Sandy had a growl rising in her throat but he patted her head and she was quiet. Beyond the horse he now saw a figure shrouded in a long, grey hooded cloak. The figure stooped and picked up the hare.

"Hullo, there!" Sherlock shouted to the figure.

The figure startled, nearly dropping its prize, then slowly turned to face Sherlock. It was a young woman, her face shaded by the hood, who stood facing him. He took another step towards her.

"What have you there?" he called.

For a moment she looked down at the animal she carried, but then she tossed her head back and shouted, "Who art thou to be asking?"

Sherlock approached her, his shotgun tucked loosely under his arm. His dog followed silently.

"The squire's son," he answered quietly.

Doubt wrinkled her brow and she laughed.

"Thou aren't much like a Holmes. 'Tis for sure thou aren't Sherrinford or Mycroft," she said.

"Sherlock," he said.

"Sherlock?" she asked, then laughed again, "Squire took the sickly lad to France. He's been gone for monny a year."

"C'est vrai, mademoiselle, but the squire has returned and I am indeed Sherlock Holmes," he responded.

She looked at him skeptically. He was about six feet tall and very lean. His chin was prominent and square, and together with his thin hawk-like nose it gave him an air of alertness and self-assurance. It was in that look that he most resembled his older brothers.

"Thou aren't quite the little lad I'd of thought, but like enough I suppose," she said with a shrug.

"Ah, well, that's fine," he said with a smile, "but you have me at a disadvantage now--"

At this she tossed back the hood which had concealed her long black hair and shadowed her fair face.

"Violet. Violet Rushdale," she said.

"Your father is tenant of one of the farms backing the moor," he said.

"Aye," Violet replied, then noticed again the hare she still held. "Thou won't be telling, wilt thou?" she asked holding it up.

"Oh, no. The squire would rather the local folks eat the hares than the hares eat the crops. He mostly worries about roving poachers from other parts who might start with hares and end up shooting livestock."

Sherlock paused and looked at her intently.

"So why is Farmer Rushdale's daughter shooting hares on the moor?" he asked.

She turned away to her horse.

"Thou'st not heard the frosts came early last year? The harvest was poor and monny animals were butchered short of starving for feed. Some of the farms have nowt but porridge for monny a week now," she said tying the hare to the saddle and tucking the gun away.

Sherlock studied her silently. He had heard that what she said was true, but there was more that she was not saying. Not only had she killed the hare with skill, but her hands were coarse and callous, more like those of a farm worker than the daughter of a tenant of the manor. While the tenant farmers were not gentry, they lived fairly comfortably and hired many labourers. Even in far leaner years than this, their daughters did not roughen their hands, or shoot guns, or wander the moors so freely.

"What do you have in those bundles there?" he asked as she mounted her horse.

"Wild herbs. I gather them on the moor and sell them in the village. But I mun be getting back now. My Pa'll be waiting for me. Good day, Master Sherlock." With that she turned her horse and plunged through the heather, not bothering with the moor road.

"Come on, Sandy," Sherlock called to his dog and mounting his horse again, he rode down into the dale.

In front of the stables Sherlock dismounted. As he did so a burly man rode up from another direction. It was the current overseer, Eston.

"Good evening, Master Sherlock. Tis good to have thee back around here. Been out for a ride?" Eston asked as he dismounted.

"Yes. We were relic hunting upon the moor," Sherlock said.

"Aye, well, tis a good thing thou got in a ride today for Cyril says twill be clashy and floudby tomorrow, and thou knowst how it is with him and the weather! Ha, looks like thou'st back just in time for supper. Best hurry along, lad. I'll see to Gale."

"Thank you, Eston," said Sherlock, giving up the reins.

Sandy had already run off to scratch at the kitchen door for scraps. Sherlock hurried up the back stairs of the manor house to dress for supper.

Chapter 2
Holmes Hall

That night the wind rose and wuthered about the old house. Sherlock heard it and knew Cyril's prediction to be true. The next day rose dark and grey and the rain drummed steadily upon the window panes. After breakfast Sherlock returned to his room and glanced about it seeking something to wile away his time.

Since his first bout with pneumonia Sherlock been under the strictest orders that he was not to set foot out of the house when the air was chill or damp. He had chaffed under this as any healthy lad would have, yet the rule held fast, and he had only broken it once. That had been while his brothers had been at the university and he and his parents had lived for two years at the house in Kensington.

Sherlock had attended a day school nearby where he had his first experience with the social pressures that can brew up among a group of school boys. He had also met a birdstuffer named Sherman who had become his friend. It was to help Sherman that he had once defied orders and crept from the house on a wintry night when his mother thought him in bed. It did not remain a secret for long, however, since his encounter that night led to his near drowning in the Thames. He was taken home by a constable shivering and shaking and once again there came that cough and the tightness about the chest and the endless days of fever. But there had been a bright spot in that illness for it had been while he tossed with fever that Sherman had brought to him the tiny puppy that had curled up on his stomach under the blankets and gone to sleep, and he had cherished Sandy ever since.

As Sherlock remembered those days he fingered the small stuffed bird on the mantel that had been his first effort under Sherman's guidance, and the ferret with glass eyes that Sherman had given him as a gift.

A knock at the door brought Sherlock from his reverie.

"Ah, there you are, Sherlock," his mother said. "The weather certainly is dreary today. Perhaps, this would be a good time for you to practice the violin. I would to hate to write to Monsieur Henri that you had forgotten all he taught you! I thought perhaps you could play a piece or two for the guests we will be having next week."

"Has the violin been unpacked yet?" Sherlock asked.

"Oh, I don't believe so. I think it found its way into the crate of books your father brought back from France, which he insists upon unpacking himself. The crate is in your father's study."

"I shall fetch it, Mother," Sherlock said.

"Then come to the sitting room, so that I may hear you play," she said.

"Yes, Mother."

As Sherlock knocked on the door of the study, he could hear his father's raised voice.

"Bah," his father said. "Charity has its place in the community and in the church, but not on the estate. Charity such as this could bring this whole manor down-- Come in."

"Excuse me, Father. Mother asked me to fetch the violin from the crate," Sherlock said.

"Oh, yes. It's over there in the corner," the squire said.

As Sherlock moved stacks of books to free the violin case he heard his father say to Sherrinford, "So tell me why Farmer Rushdale hasn't paid his rent this quarter. He was always one of the more successful tenants."

Sherlock had learned long ago that his father considered the business of the manor to be no business of his. So he silently took up the violin case and left the room. As he closed the door behind him, he heard his brother answer, "That was before his wife passed on." Sherlock's curiosity overcame him and he pressed his ear to the door.

"Cholera took her away not long after you and mother took Sherlock to France," Sherrinford continued. "It took all life out of the man, too. He acts as if he has nothing to live for, except his daughter, and he doesn't do much of a job of that! The man's turned to drink for solace and he's of the most foul humour even on the rare occasions when he's not drunk. He's driven off all the farm hands and the servants. No one goes near the place any more."

"Is the man daft?" the squire asked.

"Like as not, and if it were only him there, he'd have been carted away long ago, but there's his daughter," Sherrinford said.

"Would none of the neighbors take her in?" the squire asked.

"It's not that none offered, Father," Sherrinford explained. "I'd have even suggested that we bring her here, but her father won't have it and the girl won't even consider it. She's the only one who can control the man and she knows if she leaves him, they'll lock him away somewhere. She's quite a spirited young lady."

"Humph. So if the farm is in such a state, how has the rent been paid up to now?" the squire asked.

"The daughter, Violet, sold most of the livestock, some jewelry of her mother's and most of the furnishings from the house, just to keep the roof over their heads. She keeps up the garth near the house, and gleans during harvest. So they can eat, but there isn't much left for her to sell to pay the rent. I don't know how she will come up with the money, but she assured me she would if I gave her time," Sherrinford explained.

"When did she say she would have it?" the squire asked.

"By the first of May," Sherrinford said.

"Hum. Little less than a fortnight away. We'll wait until then, but that leaves fewer days until the next quarter day. Things won't be put off forever. A miracle may save her at Midsummer and Michaelmas. But I warn you, Sherrinford, this matter will come

16

to crisis before Christmas Day," his father said.

Sherlock dared listen no more. He hurried off to the sitting room with the violin and played for his mother.

The rain continued throughout the day. Sherlock was restless. He wandered into the kitchen. Michelle was sitting on a stool eating some biscuits. When she saw Sherlock, she jumped up and brushed herself off.

"Excusez-moi, Monsieur!" she said.

"Asseyez-vous, Michelle," Sherlock said waving her back to her stool. "Finish your meal," he said as he pulled up a stool himself.

Tessy, the plump, jovial cook, who conjured up all kinds of wonders for the manor house table, chuckled.

"Master Sherlock here, used to come visit with me monny a time," Tessy told Michelle. "He'd tell it was for the stories I told, but I'm of a mind twas because of all the sweets I made him. Main fond of them he was," she said with a knowing wink. "Never fattened him up though!"

Sherlock laughed.

"Tis good to see thee out of bed and looking as wick as onny lad, Sherlock," Tessy said.

"Thank you, Tessy. But it's harder having to stay in out of the wet when I'm feeling hale. You know Mother would have a fit if I even suggested going out," Sherlock said.

"Right she is, too, lad. Thou never took a chill well. Always took to thy bed like a tree after the axe, a coughing and moithering us so. No sense risking a chill no matter how thou feel," Tessy said.

"Well, I certainly won't catch a chill in here!" said Sherlock feeling the heat as Tessy secretively checked something in the oven.

Michelle had eaten quietly while Sherlock and the cook chatted. Michelle was a small girl in a dark dress with a white apron. Her long, dark hair was pulled up behind her head and fell in curls down the back of her neck. She was a slim girl with long white fingers which seemed more suited to a keyboard than to a duster. Right now her fingers picked at the last of the crumbs before her as she stole little glances at Sherlock and struggled to keep from blushing. Now, when he turned to her and spoke, she looked down.

"How do you like what you've seen of England, Michelle?" Sherlock asked.

"Oh, c'est bon, Monsieur, very nice." She said in a broken mixture of French and English.

"Ah, the summers you may enjoy, but you have not seen the likes of a Yorkshire winter," Sherlock said.

"I will see. Excusez-moi, Monsieur. I must return to my work," Michelle said giving him a quick curtsey and leaving the kitchen.

"She's quite shy," Sherlock said to Tessy.

"Eh, everything's new to her. The people, the talk-- tis like being born again learning to rules from nowt," Tessy replied.

"She was shy when we found her in France. She's an orphan, you know," Sherlock said.

"She's had a time of it but she'll come 'round," Tessy said.

"Ah, well. Have you seen Cyril today?" Sherlock asked.

"Aye, he was by this afternoon. If it is of the weather thou art thinking, he says twill rain through tomorrow."

Sherlock sighed and leaned his elbows on the table.

"Maybe he'll be wrong."

"Cyril? I canna think on him being wrong about the doings in the sky monny years past. No, if he says twill mist up tomorrow, thou'd best plan on rain. But get thee gone now, lad, so's I can get supper done with."

Cyril's record held, for the next day was as gloomy as the first. The rain no longer pounded but rather drizzled. Yet it persisted throughout the day.

Sherlock spent the morning in his room. He attempted to

read a book, but threw it down. He sat at the window seat staring through the rivulets on the panes of glass. His window looked eastward. Through it he could see fields of wheat, barley, and oats stretching up and down the dale; some backing up towards the moor. The neat green rows gave way suddenly to the chaotic overgrowth of the rocky moor.

The farmers were all looking out gleefully at this spring rain, but to Sherlock the streams of water running down his window were like bars keeping him waiting impatiently inside his cell.

After lunch Sherlock took up the violin in the sitting room again. There was a complex series of changes in this one piece and he wished to perfect it before his mother asked to hear him play again. He tucked the violin up beneath his chin and went to work at it. The first and second went smoothly, the third was a bit hurried, but the fourth.... He winced at the sound as he missed the fourth change. As he made a second try at it, the door to the sitting room opened. Sherlock looked up.

When Squire Holmes entered a room the first thing one noticed was not his limp, but his size. Perhaps in an earlier day he would have been called a giant. He stood well over six feet and resembled a bull both in build and temperament. He loomed over most men with his broad shoulders and a barrel-like chest, and his deep roaring voice could fill a room. His head was huge and his coal black hair and beard grew around it like the mane of a great black lion. There was a stern set to his jaw and the blue-grey eyes that stared out beneath great tufts of eyebrows were cold and critical.

The limp, a reminder of his days in the cavalry, did not detract from his stature, for he carried himself staunchly erect in spite of it, and was all the more a forbidding sight for it. He had no patience for whimsy or weakness, neither in his sons nor in himself. He expected no man to make compensation for him nor was he one to compensate for another man's weakness.

A woman, in the philosophy of Squire Holmes, was altogether a different matter. She was not quite a creature to be understood. But she was smaller and weaker, and yet essential for the continuance of the race. So she must be protected and tolerated in her strange ways.

"How is violin practice proceeding, son?" rumbled Siger Holmes.

"It is humbling, Father," Sherlock replied as he set the violin carefully down on his lap.

"Indeed? Well, we must humour your mother in some things. We'll soon have some more challenging lessons for you. I've found a tutor to prepare you for the university. I just received a letter back from him today. He has accepted the position and will arrive here shortly after the first of May. The man is a mathematical genius. He is just the sort of fellow to give you the solid mathematical background you will need to be an engineer," the squire said. Then without another word he limped out of the room.

His father wished him to be an engineer. Sherlock, himself, had not thought about it much. Sherrinford, as the eldest, was destined to be squire. There was no question there. Mycroft, their father had decided, should audit government accounting books. His brothers had done well enough under Squire Holmes's guidance. 'And most likely,' thought Sherlock, 'so will I.'

Sherlock had known there were times when his father had doubts that anything could be made of him. Six months after Sherlock's near drowning, his family, except for Mycroft, had returned to Yorkshire. Old Malvory had died and the squire had less faith that Eston, the new overseer, could manage the estate alone. Sherrinford had come down from Cambridge University and had to be instructed in the ways of the world, or more precisely, the ways of the manor. The village vicar's assistant, a young don also fresh from the university, had agreed to tutor

Sherlock.

But two years later the old ghost had raised its head and Sherlock had fallen ill again. This time Sherlock had been taken to a specialist, Sir James Smith, who had proclaimed him 'delicate.' The squire had railed against the doctor's diagnosis. No son of his could be delicate. He determined that what the boy needed was toughening. The squire and his wife again rented a house in the south of France. Sherrinford was left to tend the estate. Mycroft was left to his new position in London with the government.

Sherlock and his parents had stayed nearly two years on the Continent. As soon as Sherlock was well enough his father had hired tutors for him not only in the academic subjects, but in fencing and boxing as well. These, the squire thought, would toughen the boy and put an end to these illnesses. The squire's program was counter-balanced by Mrs. Holmes' insistence that the boy learn to play the violin. The spirit, she said, must be strengthened as well as the body. The squire indulged her. The fencing and boxing had given Sherlock a physical poise and self-confidence that he had not had before, and he found as the lessons progressed that he enjoyed playing the violin.

Now his father spoke of making him an engineer again. He didn't know whether he would make a good engineer, but he wished to please his father. There was more need for engineers these days, what with all the factories going up. He had seen some of those factories, dirty places surrounded by dirty little towns. Perhaps a better factory could be designed? Sherlock shrugged his shoulders and picked up the violin again.

Before Sherlock could apply the bow to the strings again, Sherrinford burst into the sitting room. Sherrinford took after his father in build if not in spirit. He was tall and broad with dark, wavy hair like his father, but despite his father's example he was a kind-hearted, jovial sort. Even the two years spent running the manor had not hardened him into the stern businessman his father was.

Now, Sherrinford, who was as a rule a casual dresser, stood before the window of the sitting room more smartly dressed than Sherlock could ever remember seeing him. He nervously checked his attire, tugging at cuffs and collars, as he stared out of the window. Then he ran his fingers up through his hair and sighed.

Sherlock smiled as he saw his chance, and said firmly, "That's ridiculous."

Sherrinford startled, then stood up to smile at his younger brother.

"I hadn't noticed you there," Sherrinford said. "Still up to your old tricks, I see. With Mycroft in London and you in France I'd become accustomed to being alone in my thoughts. How did you know what I was thinking?"

"Oh, come now, Sherrinford. When the young squire-to-be of Mycroft Manor is all dressed up and waiting for his carriage in the mid-afternoon with a worried look on his face, it doesn't take some great detective to determine that he is courting some young woman and needlessly worrying that her parents will not find him acceptable," Sherlock said.

Sherrinford laughed.

"It does sound absurdly simple when you put it that way," he said.

So who is this lucky lady you are courting?" Sherlock asked.

"Amanda Courtney. I don't think you've met her before, but you might remember her brother, Roger," Sherrinford said.

"Oh, yes, fond of racing horses, isn't he?" Sherlock asked.

"Yes, and due to inherit their stables, too," Sherrinford replied with a laugh. "I dare say they'll be breeding a different kind of horse when he takes over."

Sherrinford glanced out the window again.

"Is it really so ridiculous?" he asked.

"What, that her parents might find you unsuitable?" Sherlock responded. "Quite ridiculous! You are a handsome, well-mannered, intelligent man who's destined to become squire...."

"But what of the ages?" Sherrinford asked.

"What of them?" Sherlock asked.

Sherrinford laughed.

"With your smug deductions, I begin to assume that you know everything."

"Hardly," Sherlock responded.

"She was a debutante last season."

Sherlock raised his eyebrows and whistled.

"Now don't you...." said Sherrinford wiggling a finger at his brother.

"I was just thinking that she was closer to my age than yours," Sherlock said.

"But you, sir, have some years of schooling ahead of you," Sherrinford said.

"Quite so, and with no fortune, in no position to take a wife," Sherlock chuckled.

"Too young and saucy, too," Sherrinford said.

"Is Miss Amanda too young?" Sherlock asked.

"Not for me. The question is: am I too old for her?" Sherrinford asked.

"Come, come, Sherrinford. You're not old," Sherlock responded. "You've seen much, much worse matches before. This one sounds brilliant! A lovely young lady from a respectable family, and one of the most eligible bachelors in the county, what more could be asked for?"

"Father and Mother seem to be pleased with my choice," Sherrinford said.

"And no doubt relieved that you've finally gotten around to making it," Sherlock teased.

Sherrinford scowled at him.

"Otherwise," Sherlock continued, "They would have had to arrange something for you. After all it is your duty to produce an heir."

Sherrinford snorted and looked out the window again.

"I love her, too," Sherrinford said.

"And she, you?" Sherlock said.

"I-I-think so...." Sherrinford replied.

"It's settled then! Ask and ye shall receive!" Sherlock exclaimed.

"Ha! What are little brothers for?" Sherrinford said with a laugh, slapping Sherlock on the back. "Well, we'll soon see. I speak to her father today. Wish me luck!" With that Sherrinford rushed from the room.

Left to himself again, Sherlock applied bow to string, in pursuit of perfection.

Chapter 3
The Rushdale Farm

The rain stopped that night. Sherlock woke early to the chirping of the birds. Rising from his bed he watched as the sun climbed over the moor and sent its rays piercing through the ragged clouds. As the sun rose higher its light reached down into the dale, warming the soil and chasing the mists away. With the rising of the mists, Sherlock's spirits rose as well and he was anxious to be out and about.

After breakfast with his family, however, Sherlock spent an hour in the sitting room playing pieces upon the violin as his mother listened before he was free for the day. When the violin was once more resting in its case, Sherlock hurried off to the kitchen.

"Tessy, I'm going out and I might be gone through lunch," Sherlock said.

"Canna keep in another moment, canst thou, lad? Tessy said.

The cook cut off a chunk of bread she'd just taken out of the oven, and a chunk of cheese and wrapped them in brown paper.

"There thou go, lad," she said handing the package to Sherlock.

He stuffed it in his pocket and hurried off. As requested, his horse was saddled and waiting outside the stables. Sherlock mounted and rode out beyond the cottages again to the back crossroads and then south towards the Rushdale farm.

The fence about the Rushdale farm was overgrown with weeds so tangled and thick that they formed a solid wall. Sherlock slowed his horse as he approached the gate which he noticed hung now only upon its lower hinge and had long ago anchored itself in a half open position. The yard was overgrown, too. The grasses and wildflowers stood high. Few had passed this way recently enough to have trampled down the growth.

The farmhouse itself was not much changed. Perhaps the thatched roof needed patching here and there, but he'd seen many a bustling farmhouse which needed it more. These farmhouses were solid and unchanging, at least on the outside.

The sight most telling of the tragic change in this farm was that of the fields which Sherlock could see beyond the house sloping up against the moor. They all lay fallow and empty. No neat, green rows of wheat or oats or barley. No sheep or cattle grazed the rolling meadows.

It was quiet. The normal cacophony of labourers and animals was gone. Compared to the manor it seemed almost deathly quiet and still. The wind's hollow voice sighed through the trees as if longing for what had been. But the only response was that of a few chickens that were clucking in the distance.

Then the stillness was shattered as a shot blasted through the air. Sherlock scrambled off his horse.

"Get off my farm!" a voice shouted. The voice was thick and slurred.

Sherlock focused in the direction the voice had come from but he saw nothing, wait, there, a glint of a barrel in the sunlight and a door open a crack.

Sherlock stretched out his arms.

"I'm unarmed, sir," Sherlock shouted.

"Donna matter to me. Monny a troublemaker come without their guns showing," the voice said.

"I mean no harm, sir. I'm--," Sherlock began.

"Donna' care what thou wanst or who thou art. Just get thee gone afore I blow thy head off."

Sherlock sighed, and summoned up his most commanding voice.

"Farmer Rushdale? Godfrey Rushdale?"

The voice was silent. Then the door creaked open wider and

a grizzled man in a long black coat emerged from the shadow. He wasn't an old man, but a man in his prime who'd gone to seed. He stood there hunched over and squinting like a mole knocked out of his hole. Something like a smirk crossed the grizzled man's face.

"Aye, thou knowst my name. That don't give thee no right casting thy shadow on my land. Now get," Farmer Rushdale said.

"I thought you might need some help," Sherlock said.

"Ain't doing no hiring!" the man said.

"Papa, put that down!" Violet shouted as she came around the side of the house. She went up and took the gun from her father. "Hast thou begun shooting at the squire's sons now? T'will get us in trouble for sure."

"Squire's son?" The man squinted at Sherlock again. "Thought they's a mite older."

"He's the youngest, or so he says," Violet responded.

"Sherlock Holmes, sir," said Sherlock taking a deep bow, "at your service."

"Thou aren't come to evict us, art thou?" asked the man suspiciously.

"No, sir," Sherlock responded.

"Eh, tis well enough," the man mumbled.

"I'll find out what he wants, Papa," Violet said.

"Aye, call me iffen he's trouble," he said as he disappeared into the house again.

"Thou needn't moither with pa-- he's gone back to his brewing, nigh ready he says." said Violet after her father was gone. "Eh, and what wouldst thou be doing here?" she asked Sherlock.

"I heard what happened after your mother died with your father and the farm," Sherlock began.

"So thou camest to see our ruin?" Violet interrupted turning and walking away.

"No, no," Sherlock said earnestly as he caught up with her. "I thought you might need some help. I heard that the rent hasn't been paid, but that you'd promised it by May Day."

"Would greatly help if thou wouldst talk thy father into foregoing it altogether," she said.

"No, there's nothing I could say that would make him do that," Sherlock said. "He's not even pleased that the farm has been allowed to go idle. He thinks it's bad for the whole dale, as well as the manor. He'd rather see a new tenant here."

"Then what help art thou offering?" she asked.

"I've two hands," he answered holding them out, "And a strong back. I might be the squire's son but I do know how to work."

She stared at him for a moment as if to gauge the sincerity of his offer.

"Well enough. I could use a hand. Come around here then," Violet said.

She led him to a back door of the farmhouse, then up a staircase. They walked down a dim bare hall to a room. The room was sparsely furnished but free of dust and dirt. On the bare wooden floor were a richly carved bedstead, a bureau, a small table and chair, and a small chest made of cedar. A lone candle sat upon the mantel above the fireplace. The walls were bare except for the faded flower pattern of the wall paper.

"This is your room, isn't it?" Sherlock asked.

"Aye, and one of the few with onny furnishings in it. But they've got to go now. All accept this chest," she said running her hand over it fondly. "Tis the last of my mother's things and twill be the last to go."

"Where will you sleep?" he asked.

"Oh, I've been saving up feathers against this day. I'll make myself a down bed. I'll get by," she said in her calm, controlled way.

"Are you certain this is what you want to do?" Sherlock asked.

"Aye," she said firmly, then sighed. "Always," she continued bitterly, "I pray twill be the last quarter I'll have to scrape up the rent alone. I hope against sense that Papa'll come to himself again. Last month I thought I'd seen it. Tis for sure he helped me turn over the garth, so I waited, for nowt. Now rent is late. I always hope... but till then I mun do what I mun. Now, art thou helping or not?"

"I'm helping," Sherlock said.

The table and the chair were taken down first and that was easily done. But it was difficult for the two of them to maneuver the bureau and the bed down the narrow staircase. At last they had it all outside and on the wagon.

They did not see Godfrey Rushdale again during all this time. When Sherlock mentioned it, Violet sighed.

"He's brewin'. Aye, when Mama was alive he'd brew his ale and we'd have a gay time with Mama and Papa and all the hands singing and dancing till late at night. Then brewing time was celebrating time. But t'aint anymore. He does nowt else. I don't help him none, but it don't matter. He finds the grain somewhere and makes his mash all himself. I don't like it but t'aint nowt I can do for it. Some of the hands tried to stop him when he first started drinking like that, but he got real mean so's they left. He's never been mean to me but he don't listen neither. Even when he's dried out he's not all there, so what does it matter? I just leave him be and keep him out of trouble, and hope...." She was silent for a moment.

"I'll fetch some water," she said.

Violet vanished around the back of the house and returned in a moment with a bucket of water fresh from the well. She dipped in a tin cup and offered it to him. The water was cool and refreshing, but it was well after noon now and hunger gnawed at him. He dug the paper package out of his coat pocket. He unwrapped the bread and cheese then tore it in half. He held out one half to Violet. She stared first at it, then at him and then at the bread again.

"Thank ye," she said quietly and took it from him slowly.

She sat down on the wagon next to him and ate. Three chickens came clucking along under the wagon to peck at the crumbs they dropped.

Sherlock looked over the contents of the wagon.

"Are you sure you can get enough to pay the rent?" he asked.

"I'm selling the wagon, too."

Sherlock nodded slowly. Her plan made sense. There wasn't much left for her to haul in the wagon, and she could get more for the wagon than for all that was in it. What amazed Sherlock was the careless way she said it, without hesitation or self-pity, like a farmer announcing which crops he planned to sell or a merchant presenting his wares. He knew of no other woman who could face such a desperate situation so fearlessly.

He shot glances at this strange young woman as she sat there on the wagon eating. She wasn't wearing the grey cloak that she had worn on the moor, just a rough white blouse and a faded blue skirt. Her long black hair was not restrained and fell freely about her shoulders in little waves and ringlets. Her skin was flushed from her labours and her hours in the open air had left a few freckles upon those rosy cheeks.

Violet finished her portion and brushed the remaining crumbs from her lap. She disappeared into the barn and returned with the bundles of wild herbs he had seen on her horse two days before. She tucked them in around the furniture in the wagon and went back for more.

"May I help?" Sherlock offered as he followed her into the barn.

"Aye, here," she said giving him an armful. He could see that plants were spread out to dry upon boards and stones inside the barn. Some hung like upside down bouquets from the walls and rafters. But she took them all down and gathered them up in lengths of cloth and bags of leather and packed them into the wagon.

"I'm taking them to Widow Hadley," Violet said as they brought out a load. "She pays me well for what I bring her. It helps pay rent, though I could never pay it with the herb money alone, but it keeps me in candles and shoes."

"What does she do with them?" Sherlock asked.

"Oh, some of them she makes into sweet smelling little things for rich ladies. Some she dries and grinds to use in cooking. Others she 'stills to strong spirits for strange ointments and potions. Some of the village folk buy things from her. Her son, Will, travels to fairs and sells them, too."

"She has old books with drawings of plants and flowers and she shows me what she needs. Some of the plants she wants, I can find growing wild upon the moor. But others like the savory, thyme and boneset only grow by the ruins of the old abbey. Widow Hadley says the monks must have had a physic garden. About once in a month I ride out by the old abbey and harvest what's in season."

Finally Violet brought out a rope and a large tarp and they tied down the contents of the wagon.

"Day's nearly worn out now and I've other chores to tend to afore dusk. But I thank ye for thy help. What's a day's work for two can be struggle for one. I'll ride to wagon to the village tomorrow and do my selling."

Sherlock bid her good day and turned his horse towards home.

Chapter 4
A Visit to the Village

The sun was not yet over the top of the moor the next day when Sherlock confronted Tessy in the kitchen.

"Come on in, lad," she said, motioning him to a stool. "And don't wolf thy breakfast down! Donna' know why thou art sneaking off afore to rest of the house is up."

He looked up to answer her.

"No, gwon, just eat. I'm just talking to fill the air. Said thou'st going to the village. Well, thou art being main mysterious about it. Eh, but thou'st always been one to keep thy own counsel!"

So Sherlock ate on in silence as Tessy babbled while she prepared breakfast for the rest of the house. After breakfast Sherlock hurried out to the stables, pulling on his cap, and buttoning his jacket against the chill morning air as he went. Well he knew what his mother would think, but he also knew that the sun would rise and warm the air before anyone at the house would know he was gone. A stable hand was waiting for him with his horse.

"Hello there, Gale," he said rubbing the horse's forehead.

Behind him he heard a yap, and Sherlock turned to meet a whirlwind of maize and white.

"Good morning, Sandy!" Sherlock said as he squatted down to pet the dog. Sandy jumped up and licked his face. "No, no, silly dog," Sherlock said holding the dog's forelegs for a moment so the dog seemed to stand upright. "So you aren't going to let me go without you? All right, you can come along." Then he let go of the dog and stood up.

Sherlock mounted his horse and rode eastward just as the morning sun broke over the valley. He slowed his horse as they approached the Rushdale farm, but even as he did he saw the wagon heading away in the distance on the road to the village.

As he caught up with the wagon, Violet turned and looked back.

"Eh, sir? What art thou?" she called, "a highwayman come to rob me of my goods?"

"Quite the contrary, m'lady. I am a gallant knight come to escort you to the village," Sherlock said as he drew even with her and doffed his cap.

"I've ridden this way afore without trouble," she replied.

"But m'lady, little do you know what new dangers may await you! And, alas, I haven't saved a damsel in a fortnight, so you'd be doing me a great service if you let me ride along in case the opportunity should arise," Sherlock said.

"Oh, if thou's a mind to, I won't try to stop thee," Violet Rushdale said.

Sherlock rode his horse alongside the wagon. Sandy raced ahead, a curly mop flecked with yellow and white that ranged to the right and left before them.

"'Tis a lovely dog," Violet said.

"Yes. I call her Sandy. A man gave her to me when she was just a pup, a whimpering, little ball of fur." Sherlock chuckled. "Now she's a big, barking, ball of fur!"

"What manner of dog is she?" Violet asked.

Sherlock laughed again.

"Oh, she's just a silly mongrel, a bit of this; a dash of that. Her mother was a mutt with a poor reputation. With that curly coat of hers I'd say her father may have been a spaniel. Beyond that--" he shrugged his shoulders. "She's a very affectionate dog. I thought she might have forgotten me during our two years apart, but no sooner had we arrived then she came charging up, jumping on me and licking my face. Now if I go anywhere without her she sulks in the stables until I come back."

"I have not been to the village since I returned to Yorkshire,"

Sherlock said as they rode on.

"Eh, donna change much. New wee ones come around and some old ones go, but much stays the same," Violet said.

"Is Mr. Morris still there?" Sherlock asked.

"Aye, still watching the church porch. He'll see himself one of these days," Violet responded.

"And the market, same as always?" Sherlock asked.

"Aye, same as always and the village constable with nowt better to do than chase laddies snatching apples," she said.

They laughed and talked more about the village until the steeple of the church appeared in the distance. Violet brought her wagon to a halt.

"I'm thinking we best be parting here," Violet said. "Widow Hadley is a bit queer. She might not deal with me if thou art along. She's afraid folks'll steal her secrets. She doesn't tell me onny more'n she thinks she has to. And Mrs. Ross across the street is such a meddlesome woman, always peeping out her curtains to see who's passing in the street. She already has me in league with the devil, 'cause she thinks Widow Hadley is, but I haven't given her onny more fuel than that. If thou's business to attend in the village, then ride on ahead."

"As m'lady wishes," Sherlock replied giving a short bow from his horse then riding on to the village alone.

The old stone church with its steeple reaching hopefully skyward rose up before him as he rode. Then there was the vicarage tucked neatly beside. Houses and shops lined the road. There was the cobbler's shop, the bakery, and the public house. As he neared Dr. Thompkins' place, he dismounted.

A woman and a child came out on the doctor's porch followed by the doctor himself. Dr. Thompkins was a stocky man with grey streaking his dark hair. He gave the woman some instructions and a reassuring smile and sent them on their way. Then he looked up and saw Sherlock.

34

"Ah, now there's a young man I'd be glad never to see again!" Dr. Thompkins said.

Sherlock smiled.

"Good morning, Sherlock. You are looking well," the doctor said.

"Good morning, Doctor. I'm feeling it, too," Sherlock replied.

"That's good. Everyone out at the Hall is well, I presume?"

"Oh, yes, indeed."

"Your parents are settling back into the quiet of country life after their travels abroad? Eh, but it mightn't be quiet for long," said the Doctor with a sly little grin. "I hear rumours that your brother Sherrinford is thinking of matrimony."

"There's something to that," Sherlock confirmed.

"I suppose we'll hear soon enough. So what brings you to the village?

"Oh, just getting reacquainted," Sherlock said.

"Aye, but it hasn't changed much has it? Well, I'd love to chat but I've got some visits to make. Take care, Sherlock, and good day."

"Good day," Sherlock said.

Sherlock then walked his horse through the marketplace. It was already bustling with villagers buying fruits, vegetables, wool, milk and eggs from the farms, and looking admiringly at the odds and ends on the merchants' tables. Beyond the marketplace was the blacksmith's shop and across from there the wainwright's shed.

Jack Ramsey, the wainwright, was a jovial sort. He was always one for a good conversation. He was a great storyteller and he was always looking for more tales to add to his stock. The man's only fault lay in his tight-fistedness. The villagers sometimes grumbled that he paid less than he ought when he bought and charged more than he ought when he sold.

"Good morning, Mr. Ramsey." said Sherlock as he entered the

shed.

"Morning, Master Sherlock. I heard a rumour that thou wert back. But my, thou hast grown to be quite a man these years gone by! What might I be doing for thee today?"

"Just visiting, if you can spare the time," Sherlock said.

"Eh, perhaps thou'll tell me a bit of thy journeys on the Continent?" asked the wainwright, tucking his mallet away in the pocket of his leather apron and setting the pot on the fire.

Sherlock settled himself on the stool Ramsey offered and told him of their time in the south of France and their visits to Monoco and Italy

"After we left Rome," Sherlock continued, "We traveled by train west to Verona and followed the Adige River north into the Alps. The Alps were beautiful, great grey peaks. Some were still covered with snow in July! It was amazing how the trains wound through the mountains on very narrow roadbeds. At times they looked like caterpillars hugging the rock walls! We saw great forests of towering pines in the Alps and sparkling lakes, and waterfalls where the water plunges from mountain cliffs higher than the moors and falls straight down in roaring frothy torrents to gorges far below."

"We went as far north as Innsbruck before heading west to Zurich. Then we travelled south to Geneva through a valley which would dwarf the dale. The valley was nearly 30 miles wide and over a hundred miles long with the Alps towering on one side and the Jura Mountains shooting up on the other. From Geneva we followed the Rhone Valley south into France again."

Sherlock stopped as a wagon pulled up in front of the wainwright's shed.

"Oh, Mr. Ramsey, I dinna know thou wert busy," said Violet in a startled voice.

"Just visiting, Miss Rushdale. If you have business with Mr. Ramsey, go right ahead," Sherlock said.

"Thank ye, sir," Violet said.

"So what can I do for thee, Miss Rushdale?" Jack Ramsey asked.

"Wish to be selling my wagon, if thou'st a mind to buy it," Violet said.

"Eh, then, we'd best have a look at it," Ramsey said.

Jack Ramsey rose and followed Violet out to the street where the wagon sat. Sherlock followed them both. Sherlock stood and watched as the wainwright looked over the wagon, tugging here and thumping there.

"Eh," said the wainwright thoughtfully, "It's not in too poor a shape, is it?"

"Better'n some at the Hall," suggested Sherlock.

Ramsey looked sideways at Sherlock, rubbed his chin thoughtfully and turned back to Violet.

"Perhaps we can come to terms, Miss Rushdale," Jack Ramsey said.

They bargained swiftly, then Violet led her horse into the shed where Ramsey and Sherlock helped her unhitch the wagon. Violet tucked away the silver she'd received and bid them good day before leading her horse out of the shed.

"I hear them frogs been getting themselves in quite a brew of late," Ramsey said as they resumed their stools.

"That's true enough," Sherlock said. "But you'd hardly know it from Pau or Montpelier. When the news got round last autumn that war had been declared with Prussia, a few adventurous souls ran off to defend the national honour, but for the most part life carried on as usual. Even when the word came that the Emperor had been captured and Paris was under siege, the Provincials were little disturbed. The men argued about the new government over cigars after supper, but the troubles of Paris seemed of little concern until they came crashing in amongst them."

Ramsey's eyes brightened.

"I reckon there's a bit of a tale in that," he said.

"Yes, indeed," Sherlock admitted. "We were just finishing up our breakfast one morning when suddenly we heard some shouting which seemed to be coming from the rooftop. Before anyone could get up, there was great crash in the woods behind the house. We all ran outside toward the sound of the crash. The first sight that met our eyes was a queer one. There were great strips and shreds of paper lying on the ground and hanging from the trees. There was a huge wad of it up ahead in the wood.

"Un balloon!' someone shouted. We all ran forward fighting our way through the paper. Beyond we found a man unconscious on the ground. Above him was a large woven basket hanging sideways from cables tangled in the trees. We took the man up to the house and returned to cut loose the basket. Inside were several bundles of papers and a cage full of pigeons!"

"When the balloonist recovered he told us that he had come from Paris bearing news from the city and dispatches for the national government in Versailles. The pigeons were the means for getting messages back into Paris. It seems that the Parisians had been using balloons to carry people and reports out of Paris ever since the siege. The balloons were manufactured from paper, coated with shellac and filled with coal smoke to set them aloft. Since the balloons weren't steerable it was mere chance that this one hadn't blown in Prussian hands or sailed out over the sea as many of them had."

"Eh, I'd always thought those Paris folks were a mite on the flighty side," laughed Ramsey. "I've enjoyed thy visit, lad, but I mun get back to my work. Good day to thee, Master Sherlock."

Sherlock bid good day to the wainwright, and hurried his horse along the streets of the village. Beyond the village he quickly overtook Violet. Violet looked over at him as his horse fell into stride with hers, but did not say a word. They rode for a few moments in silence.

"Jack Ramsey gave me more for the wagon than I was expecting," she said at last.

"You got your due," answered Sherlock.

"Aye, but Ramsey's not always one to give full worth," Violet said.

"Ramsey's no fool. He'll haggle over the last pence if he thinks he can get it but he's not likely to cheat a poor woman with one of the squire's sons within earshot," Sherlock said.

They rode the rest of the way in silence. At the gate to the Rushdale farm, they paused before parting.

"Thank ye again, sir, for thy help," Violet said.

"You're most welcome, m'lady. If you should ever have need of my services again, just send for me at yon castle," teased Sherlock, his grey eyes twinkling. "Ah, but perhaps we shall meet again upon the moor?"

"Perhaps," responded Violet with a tiny smile.

"You wouldn't mind?" Sherlock asked.

"No, sir," Violet said.

"Very good then, but you must promise me one thing, if we should meet again," Sherlock insisted.

"Eh, what's that?" she asked.

"That you won't call me 'sir' or 'master.' My name is Sherlock," he said.

Violet laughed, and her laughter rang out sweetly and seemed to fill the air like the sound of a bell ringing across the moor. To Sherlock it was the loveliest sound he'd ever heard.

"Then good day to thee, Sherlock!" Violet said as she turned her horse towards her farmhouse.

"Good day," he responded.

Chapter 5
Sherrinford's Engagement

Each day of the following week Sherlock rode up to the moor
in hopes of seeing Violet again. Some days he found her digging
roots along the steep banks of a gill. Sometimes she was picking
buds off the gorse which grew in the high rocky places. When
they met they spoke of the moor. She told him of the plants
she sought and he showed her some of the artifacts he'd found.
Each told the other the little secrets they knew of this wild and
wonderful place.

It was only the moor they spoke of and it was only the moor
they saw. For an hour or so the rest of the world would disappear.
For that short space of time Violet seemed to lay aside the
burdens which awaited her in the dale below and she would laugh
and smile. To Sherlock these were the happiest of times.

But sometimes he did not see her on the moor, and he would
ride over to where the Rushdale farm lay below him, where
he might see her working the garth or feeding the chickens
or hanging out her wash. Then he would watch her from afar,
wishing he could be near her.

Never before had he wanted to be with anyone so much. Even
when they were apart his mind was filled with thoughts of her.
He was always planning and dreaming about the next time they
should meet. Once he jumped the stone fence and rode through
the overgrown fields to within a few hundred yards of where she
worked, before he thought better of it and rode away.

This morning he had another goal to concentrate on, and
with it accomplished he headed back to the manor house. Tessy
spun around as he entered the kitchen.

"Eh, there thou be, lad!" she said.

"Here they are," Sherlock said holding up the birds he'd shot.

"Oh, and fine birds they are! Thank ye, lad. Now just leave them here and scoot. I haven't time to chat today."

The whole house was bustling about. The servants were all dusting and cleaning and moving things. But the busiest person of all was Sherrinford. He had suddenly developed a keen eye for dust motes and the angles of picture frames.

Sherlock stepped to the doorway of the sitting room and watched his brother at work.

"No, more to the right," Sherrinford said. "No, no, back now. There! Now move out this bureau. There is dust on this wall."

Susan did as she was told and began to clean the wall. Sherlock chuckled. Sherrinford turned to frown at his little brother.

"Are you entertaining guests or selling the house?" Sherlock asked. As he did so he heard his father's limping step coming up behind him.

"To Amanda, I am selling the house. The rest I don't care about," Sherrinford responded.

Sherlock turned to face his father in the hall.

"You are correct, Sherlock," said the squire said with his military crispness. "Your brother is going a bit too far. Sherrinford, you are wearing down the servants. This house entertains often enough for them to know their duties. Let them do their work."

Sherlock suddenly found his position uncomfortable.

"Well, if you'll excuse me, Father, I shall take the violin to my room and practice the pieces Mother wishes me to play."

"Very good, Sherlock. We will send for you when the guests arrive," his father said.

The parlour was full of people when Sherlock entered. He knew most of them and exchanged greetings as he made his way across the room.

"Oh, there you are, Sherlock. Come here and let me introduce you," Sherrinford said as he took Sherlock's arm and led him towards the corner of the room.

"Amanda, this is my brother, Sherlock. Sherlock, Amanda Courtney," Sherrinford said.

Before him sat the source of his brother's agitation. She was certainly a beautiful woman. Her skin was fine and fair. Her blond hair had the slightest hint of red where it caught the firelight. Her coiffure held it up and back, emphasizing her delicate white neck. Amanda smiled as Sherlock took her hand, and her deep blue eyes smiled, too.

"Delighted to meet you, Miss Courtney," Sherlock said making a slight bow over her hand.

"Oh, you must call me, Amanda. May I call you Sherlock?"

"Most certainly," he replied.

"Do have a seat. Your father tells me that you will have a tutor coming soon to prepare you for the university."

"Yes, my father feels I should make a good engineer," Sherlock said.

"The boy has a quick mind," Siger Holmes said, "but a more practical bent than his brother Mycroft."

"Indeed," added Sherrinford, "Mycroft can't be bent at all!"

Chuckles played around the little group as Sherrinford avoided his father's scowl. Just then Mrs. Holmes joined the group.

"Siger, dear, it seems everyone has arrived and been introduced. Shall we proceed?" she enquired.

"Yes, dear, we shall," replied the squire as he picked up his cane and rose to his feet.

"Ladies and Gentlemen," he boomed. The hum of conversation gradually died down and he continued, "Friends, my wife and I are quite glad to see all of you again after our long absence from the country. But the renewal of old acquaintances was only part of the purpose for this gathering. There is an important announcement to be made. But I believe I'll allow my son, Sherrinford, to have that honour." With a wave of his hand to Sherrinford, Siger sat down.

Sherrinford stood up. He took Amanda's hand and coaxed her to stand with him. He cleared his throat.

"Ladies and Gentlemen, I am pleased to announce that Miss Amanda Courtney has accepted my proposal of marriage," Sherrinford said.

Murmurs went through the crowd.

"Has a date been set?" a voice asked.

Sherrinford smiled at Amanda and said, "She wishes to have a June wedding."

Murmurs of approval filled the room.

"A toast!" shouted one man jumping to his feet. Others soon took up the shout. The first toast was followed by another and another. The party seemed prepared to go on toasting all night, but the supper bell rang and people began to flow towards the dining room.

Throughout supper Sherlock did his best to keep up his share of the conversation, but his gaze wandered to Amanda, and his thoughts to Violet. His brother had chosen well the future mistress of the manor. She was charming and modest, showing a cheerful interest in all that went on around her. She would be an excellent hostess and a thoughtful mother. But how different was Violet! Amanda was a rose in a crystal vase; and Violet was a wildflower struggling along side the road, all the more attractive for its spirit and persistence!

After supper the party retired to the parlour once more, and Sherlock's mother had him bring forth the violin and play the pieces he had been practicing for her. The crowd listened intently and Sherlock bowed to applause and praise when he was done. Then he sat down next to his brother as coffee was being served. Sherrinford mentioned that May Day was only a few days away.

"Amanda, would you be interested in attending the Festival in the village?" Sherrinford suggested. "The folks hereabouts make quite a day of it."

"Ford, what a lovely idea," Amanda responded.

"Mrs. Courtney, would you care to join us?" Sherrinford asked his future mother-in-law.

"Oh, it does sound like fun. Charles, would you care to escort me?" she asked her husband.

"I'd love to but I have business matters to attend to on that day," he replied.

"Roger?" Mrs. Courtney inquired.

"I'm sorry, mother, I have another engagement," Roger replied.

"Well, what of this young man here?" suggested Charles Courtney waving in Sherlock's direction.

"Well, Sherlock," said Mrs. Courtney, "the lot seems to have fallen to you."

"Madame, I would be delighted!" Sherlock responded with a slight bow.

"Oh, I am so pleased," responded Mrs. Courtney with a more wrinkled version of her daughter's endearing smile. "Then we shall have a chance to get to know each other better, and you can whisper all your brother's faults to me!"

"I shall make a list," Sherlock replied, earning a rueful look from Sherrinford.

May Day was as blue and bonny as ever a day seen in Yorkshire. The village green was full of people talking and laughing, all done out in their gayest spring array. But none were more brightly decked or more in tune with the frolicking spirit of the day than were the milkmaids of the dale, for they considered this their own special celebration.

As the squire's sons and the ladies they escorted entered the gathering, heads turned, and voices tittered as most had their first look at the future mistress of the manor. The whole dale seemed as taken as Sherrinford with his new fiancée. If that had not been obvious from the snatches of gossip Sherlock heard from the crowd, then it was soon made so.

As the procession of milkmaids began to wind its way through the crowd towards the maypole, it suddenly changed course and encircled the little group from the manor. The milkmaids took Amanda by the arms and coaxed her to join them. She hesitated briefly, then with a resigned shrug she allowed them to lead her to the chair beneath the maypole. They crown her queen of the May and dedicated the festivities to her. The crowd cheered in approval and Sherrinford smiled broadly as his country folk honoured his bride to be.

When the festivities had drawn to a close the four of them returned to the manor house cheerfully exhausted. The carriage stopped before the front door, and Sherlock and Sherrinford descended and assisted the ladies. As Sherlock was helping Mrs. Courtney down from the carriage, he heard the front door open, and then he heard his father's voice.

"I have given you fair warning, Miss Rushdale."

"Aye, I mun say thou hast, sir. Good day, Squire."

Out of the corner of his eye Sherlock saw Violet framed in the doorway for a moment before she hurried down the steps and along the path without looking up. His father still stood in the doorway.

"Ah, Mrs. Courtney, Amanda, how was your day?" asked the squire.

"Simply marvelous. We shall tell you all about it once we have freshened up a bit." With that Amanda and her mother disappeared into the house.

"I saw Miss Rushdale leaving just now," said Sherrinford to his father, "Did she pay the rent?"

"She did indeed. Your faith in her was not misplaced, but I

laid the situation out to her," the squire replied.

Sherrinford entered the house with his father. Left alone, Sherlock hurried down the path Violet had taken. She was still there. She held the reigns to her horse, but for a moment she slumped wearily against the wall of the house. When she became aware of his presence she stood up.

"What did he say to you?" he asked, putting his hands on her shoulders as if to hold her up.

"He said he won't suffer the farm to go idle much longer. If Papa doesn't come to himself afore the end of the year, he'll start proceedings."

"He'd evict you and your father?" Sherlock said.

"He said he'd have Papa sent to an asylum if he mun," she said.

"What of you?" Sherlock asked.

"Oh, he was generous there," she said with a touch of sarcasm in her voice. "He said he'd help place me in a position equal to ma station." Then her eyes gleamed defiantly. "I told him I would fight him. I won't have Papa locked up!"

But even as she said the words she saw the hopelessness in them and tears rolled down her cheeks. Sherlock held her in his arms for a moment. Then she pulled away and spoke in her usual controlled manner.

"I'll speak to Papa. Perhaps I can make him understand. Goodbye, Sherlock."

Sherlock Holmes stood there for a moment watching her ride off before he returned to the house.

Chapter 6
The Professor Comes

Three days later Sherlock's glance wandered to the bookshelves that lined the walls of the study. Some were filled with histories of great military battles and intrigues. Others were bursting with tomes on the explorations of dark corners of the world, or contemplations of even darker philosophies. It was his father's study and the books reflected the complexity of the man. The breadth of his interests could not be satisfied nor contained within the farming region in which he lived. Siger Holmes had traveled much during his days in the cavalry before he had become squire. He had been fascinated by the places he had seen and the people he had met. Even as squire of a manor in the far north of England he continued corresponding with scholars in the cities and adventurers in the provinces all over Europe. He invited them to visit his estate or paid them a call when he was traveling with his family. He listened. He argued. He bathed in the mental stimulation until the time came for him to return to his duties.

His primary duty was to the estate, for he was ultimately responsible for its management. It was a duty which had been thrust upon him quite suddenly when his elder brother had died without heir. It was then that Siger Holmes, bringing his new wife with him, had returned to settle in the manor as the new squire. That had been long ago and Siger had always taken his responsibility for the manor quite seriously. Even when he was on the Continent, his hand on the reins could be felt in far away Yorkshire.

Then there were public duties to attend to, not that Siger was any great philanthropist, but the institutions, the church and the like, must be supported. A surplus of hungry, idle peasants tended to lead to an increase in crime and the possibility of uprisings, both things a landowner must always be on guard against.

Of course, there were myriad private duties. Among these last was the proper education of his sons. This was the duty he was presently attending to. The carriage had been sent to the railway station in Thirsk and would soon return with Sherlock's new tutor.

Sherlock's gaze came to rest on his father as Siger Holmes leaned back in the massive black chair behind his desk and began to speak of the man they were awaiting.

"He comes highly recommended and is reported to possess a phenomenal mathematical faculty, as well as being well versed in all the other necessary subjects. Four years ago at the age of twenty-one he wrote a treatise upon the binomial theorem that roused quite an interest in the man and won him the mathematical chair of Westgate University. He recently published a mathematical analysis of the orbital elements of asteroids which has created a stir in some circles. But he has decided to leave his position at that university and has kindly consented to tutor you before going on to seek more prestigious employment," Squire Holmes said.

Sherlock's eyes played over the books again. He wondered why a man would agree to tutor the youngest son of a country squire if such glory awaited him elsewhere. There was little time to ponder the question, for as the thought crossed his mind he heard the carriage rattle up to the front door. When Sherlock glanced out of the window he saw a tall, thin man emerge from the carriage. As the man approached the front door, Sherlock noticed how his pale face protruded forward and slowly oscillated from side to side in a curiously reptilian fashion.

There were voices in the hall, and soon a servant ushered the man into the room. He approached the desk.

"Squire Holmes?" the man asked in a voice so soft that

Sherlock wondered if he might be more fitted to a monastery than a schoolroom.

When Siger Holmes nodded his head slightly, the other bowed and introduced himself.

"I am Professor Moriarty."

"Professor, my son Sherlock," the squire said with a slight wave of his hand in Sherlock's direction as he stood to greet him.

Professor Moriarty loomed over Sherlock by several inches. But his shoulders were rounded and the fingers of the hand he now held out to Sherlock were long and delicate. Moriarty's forehead domed out in a white curve over two grey eyes sunk deep into his head. The eyes themselves had a way of peering and squinting as if they'd spent too long over some treatise. Yet those same eyes seemed to miss nothing and Sherlock could feel them taking him in even as he surveyed the professor.

"I am very pleased to meet you, Master Sherlock," the professor said in a soft, fatherly tone as he shook Sherlock's hand. "I trust you will find our association a pleasant one."

"I hope so, sir," Sherlock responded.

"Well, professor," boomed the squire, "I expect that you'll use the next few days to unpack and settle in. I hope that you can commence work on Monday morning."

"Yes, Yes. That's quite feasible. I assume that you expect me to begin with a few informal sessions with the boy so that I may assess at what level we may proceed," Moriarty said.

"That sounds quite reasonable. The servants will show you to your rooms," the squire said.

At the first session Professor Moriarty asked Sherlock to write out his answers to some questions he had prepared. At the second session the professor reported to Sherlock his assessment.

"You have a good working knowledge of geology and biology," said Moriarty, "as I would expect of a boy brought up in the country. In fact, your understanding of geology is somewhat beyond my expectations. Your trigonometry and geometry are excellent, though I'm somewhat surprised by your weaknesses in other mathematics. I am, however, completely astonished at your near ignorance of astronomy. Your Latin is passable. Your Greek, on the other hand, is pathetic."

So it was decided that for the first few weeks the first hour would be devoted to the study of classical Greek. The remaining time would be devoted to some branch of mathematics or science.

Thus on Wednesday morning Sherlock found himself immersed in declensions and derivations, and he was glad when the afternoon came and he was free to ride out to the moors again.

He had not seen Violet since May Day and he missed her sorely. However, she was not to be found at the usual places on the moor. So he rode over to where the moor overlooked the Rushdale farm. Sherlock did not see her at first, but he waited watching the tiny specks he knew to be chickens milling about in the yard. Then he saw her leave the house and head towards the garth beyond. He waited no longer but rode down and headed across the fields. As he neared the buildings, he angled around behind a small stand of trees. There he dismounted. Sherlock walked to the edge of the trees and called to Violet.

She looked up from the soil she was tending. She seemed quite anxious at the sight of him. She looked first towards the house then ran towards where Sherlock stood.

"What art thou doing here?" she whispered.

"I wanted to see you," Sherlock said.

"Thou munnot come here!" Violet said. "Papa told me he saw thou afore in the fields. He was near off his head. He thinks thou mean to do me harm. Thou mun--"

But she was interrupted by the man himself.Godfrey Rushdale came running from the house waving his fists in the air and shouting.

"Sherlock, go now, please!" Violet urged in a whisper.

"Get away from her thou swine! I've seen thee following and pestering my daughter. Thou manor folks think 'cause thou live in a big house that thou can have whatever thou want," Godfrey raved on as he charged towards them.

"Will you be alright?" Sherlock asked after he whistled for Gale who came galloping around the trees in response.

"Aye. He won't hurt me. I'll see thee on the moor tomorrow. Now, go! Quickly!"

"Should have known thou wert up to no good from the first I saw thou hanging around here!" Godfrey continued as Sherlock mounted his horse and sped away.

Violet ran to her father.

"It's alright, Papa. He's gone," Violet reassured him.

"He'd best be gone for good," her father said still looking off in the direction in which Sherlock had gone. He then turned to his daughter and put his hand on her shoulder. "Oh, Violet, my pretty lass, thou doesn't know about these wily young men, especially the rich ones with nowt better to do then to go about harassing pretty girls." This last he said with a bit of a snarl, but his voice became soft again. "I donna want onnyone to hurt thee, lass."

Then the thought of it made him angry again and he shook his fist in the air. "If he comes around here again, they'll have to carry him back to hall!" he vowed.

Violet shuddered.

Chapter 7
The Lessons of Spring

The next day Sherlock found Violet among the bracken near where he'd first spoken to her. A hare was already tied to her horse, which was nosing about in the ferns seeking the sweet grass beneath. Violet had seen him coming and stood waiting for him.

He dismounted quickly, and took her hand.

"Violet, I'm sorry," he said.

"Thou art lucky he couldn't lay his hand to his gun right away or thou wouldn't have walked away. He said as much after thou'd gone," she said.

"But why?" Sherlock asked.

"Like he said, he saw thee," she explained as they walked along. "After I sold the wagon, he saw us talking outside the gate. He didn't say so at the time. Then he started seeing someone watching the farm from the crest over yonder. It moithered him, but he didn't he know who it was till he saw thee in the fields about a week ago. He about had a fit then, cursing and threatening."

"Then perhaps I should go and apologize--" Sherlock said.

She had walked along looking at the sky as she spoke glancing only occasionally at Sherlock, but she now turned and grabbed his arm.

"No!" she cried. "Thou munnot go near him!"

"I'm not afraid of him," he said.

"I can see that plain enough," she said, a little smile coming to her lips. "Onnyone else around here would have sense enough to keep away from him."

"But surely, you could explain--" Sherlock said.

Now she laughed.

"No, there's no explaining, Sherlock. He still thinks me his own little lass. He'll not go in for sharing. He thinks thou mean to harm me and I'm all he's got in the world."

Then she turned and began to walk along the road again. She gazed off in the distance as she spoke.

"Tis not just thee. Know thou, I got myself a position once as a scullery maid at one of the farms to the south. The pay wasn't much but it was regular and I got fed there as well. I thought to hang on to some of the furniture a bit longer that way, but it dinna last. I tried talking to Papa before I went, but he just answered like I was a li'l girl playing house. 'Sure, lassie,' he said. Well, the first day or so he dinna miss me. Just finished a new batch of brew, but by the end of week he noticed I wasn't around. He looked high and low around the farm. Then he went on a rampage through the dale, wandering around accosting onnyone he met till he ran into someone who knew where I was. Then he came up to the house and made such a ruckus, I had to leave. I never tried again. Who'd hire me on with him on my tail?"

They walked in silence for a moment.

"Then how do you manage to get away to the moor?" Sherlock asked.

"Oh, sometimes he works himself into such a stupor that he doesn't know whether I'm coming or going. But the rest of the time I just tell him I'm riding up to pick flowers on the moor. And I don't stay too long. Sometimes he'll be watching at the window when I ride up, and I rush in and give him a big hug and a bouquet of wildflowers, then everything's fine. I've been making a habit of coming up here to pick the herbs, so he'll think nothing of it so's long as thou stay clear of that ridge over there where he might catch sight of thee."

Sherlock promised he would.

"I tried talking to Papa after what the squire said. I sat down beside him and said, 'Papa, I need thy help.'"

"'What doest thou need my help for, sweet?' he said"

"'The farm, Papa?' I said."

"'Donna moither thy little head about the farm,' he said. 'Papa will take care of it.'"

"'Wilt thou?' ah asked. 'Sure, lass, like always,' he said."

"'But Papa it needs plowing and planting,' I protested."

"'I told thee not to moither about it. I'll get the hands to do it.'"

"'The hands are all gone, Papa.'"

"'They are, aren't they?' he said looking bewildered."

"'And the plow is broke. The fields haven't been plowed in two summers now,' I told him."

"'Well, I've been meaning to--'"

"'Papa, the squire told me he's gonna put us off the farm if we don't get it working again.'"

"'That mun have been quite a sight -- a little girl like thee going up to the big gruff squire.'"

"'Papa, I'm not a little girl onny more.'"

"'Eh?'"

"'See, Papa, I'm a woman now. I'm wearing Mama's old dresses now.'"

"'Ha Ha! That thou art! Won't thy Mama be surprised when she gets back.'"

"'Papa, Mama's not coming back. Mama's dead,' I said and he just stared at me. 'Mama's dead. Dost thou hear me?' I said. He buried his face in his big hands and sobbed."

"'No girl, she canna be,' he said. His whole body shook."

"'I'm sorry, Papa -- But I'm still here and I need thee,' ah said. But I knew he wasn't listening onny more."

"I'm sorry, Violet," Sherlock said.

"'Tis none of thy doing. We'll just keep muddling on as we are and see what comes of it," Violet said. "But being with thee gives me a chance to stop moithering and smile for a space. For that I thank thee. Now let's talk of something else."

THE LESSONS OF SPRING

So on rolled the month of May. Sherlock spent most of his afternoons with Violet upon the moors, and in the mornings he studied under the direction of Professor Moriarty.

As the days passed and lesson followed lesson, Sherlock found no fuel for his early suspicions of the professor. Moriarty was an exacting master; sometimes requiring a lesson be redone several times before proceeding with the next, but no fault could be found with the man. He was not lacking in knowledge or intelligence, nor were his words ever harsh. He was soft spoken and polite in his demands. So polite was he that he soon ingratiated himself with the whole household. Few could refuse him a request and his slightest whim was often fulfilled. The professor even seemed to be able to influence the squire. This development somewhat disturbed Sherlock for he had never seen any man who could manipulate the squire's will. Yet in all other ways Professor Moriarty seemed the sweetest, most gentle of men. So Sherlock put his suspicions to the back of his mind and spent his idle moments instead thinking of Violet.

It was a day in early June, then, as Sherlock prepared to go out upon the moors that he opened a drawer in his desk and drew out a small rock hammer and leather case which had "E. S. Sherrinford" inscribed on the outside. He opened the leather case and grasped the handle inside. Then he gently pulled out a magnifying lens. He looked at it admiringly. It was four inches in diameter and in perfect condition. It had belonged to his maternal grandfather, Sir Edward Sherrinford. The old man had once noticed how Sherlock as a little boy had liked to collect pebbles. His grandfather had told Sherlock what the different colors in the rocks meant and how to sort the rocks and label them, and to keep track of where he found them. Then in his will the old explorer had left Sherlock the rock hammer and the lens so that he might carry on this little hobby. Sherlock had treasured the lens ever since. He carefully returned the lens to its case.

55

The sun was bright and warm as Violet and Sherlock
scrambled down the steep banks of the gill. At the water's edge
they unlaced boots, rolled up trousers, tied up skirts, and were
soon wriggling their toes in the swift running stream.

"Oooh, tis enough to ice the blood!" Violet exclaimed.

"Come on!" called Sherlock, "This way!"

They waded upstream a ways until they came a spot where the
gill had carved its way through a mass of limestone.

"Look at this," Sherlock instructed as they approached the
exposed rock.

"What is it?" Violet asked as she stared at what seemed to be a
seashell half imbedded in the rock.

"It's a type of fossil called a brachiopod," Sherlock explained.

"Oh, here's another, and another! There seems to be a lot of
them," she said.

"Oh, yes. If you were to break apart this stone you would
find thousands of them. They are far too common to be worth
collecting. But there has been quite a bit of water weathering
at this rock since I've been here last so we might find a few
interesting things."

Sherlock took out his lens and his rock hammer. He showed
Violet the many different kind of fossils that were jumbled
together in the rock. Occasionally, he chipped one loose from the
rock and deposited it in his bag. Violet was examining one with
his lens as Sherlock put another away in his pack. Suddenly a
spiral shape under the water caught his eye.

"Hello! What's this? An ammonite! And a fairly good sized
one at that. The stream must have worn it completely out." He
said as he carefully picked it up from the bottom of the stream.

"Here, have a look," Sherlock said as he held it out to Violet.

Violet reached for the fossil. But as she did, the stones beneath
her feet shifted, and she tumbled head long into the stream.

Sherlock quickly dropped the fossil into his pocket and

reached out a hand. Violet tossed her wet locks out of her face as Sherlock helped her up. "Thy glass!" she sputtered, "It slipped from my hand!"

Crouching in the stream, hardly daring to move for fear they would step on it, they searched the rippling water for the magnifying lens.

"Here it is," Sherlock said at last. He fished it out of the stream and held it up.

"Oh. Tis cracked," Violet said.

"It must have struck the rock here near where I found it," Sherlock said pointing to the spot.

Sherlock sat down on the bank and stared at the lens. He'd always been proud of it and had handled it with care. Now the view through it was distorted by the crack.

"I'm main sorry about it, Sherlock," Violet said as she sat down beside him. "But look," she said hopefully, "The crack is only down one part. The rest tis good as new. If thou donna look through the cracked part everything is clear."

Sherlock looked from the lens to Violet. Her brown eyes held a questioning look between the rivulets which ran down from her hair. He couldn't help smiling at her and she smiled in return.

"You are right," he said and packed the lens away in its case.

"Come, there is a grassy spot further on where you can dry out," he said standing and offering his hand. She jumped up and they ran hand and hand along the bank.

"Tis a spot fallen from heaven," Violet said as they lay on their backs in the sunlight. "Even the gill seems to glow a bit rosy."

Sherlock chuckled.

"I've followed most of the streams around these parts. Some of those to the south have more clay and sand. Some are dug in deep like this one and some just flow over the ground after a rain and disappear the next day. But no other stream has that "rosy glow" like this one. Here, I'll show you."

Sherlock went down to the water's edge and scooped up a handful of sand and pebbles. As he held it out before Violet she saw small red fragments glinting amidst the brown and grey stones.

"What are they?" she asked.

"Crystals-- limestone crystals. Up near the source there are so many of them that the gill almost seems to run red like wine. Fewer make it down here, thus your 'rosy glow.' The few that make it beyond the tors are so broken and scratched that you don't notice the color, but take a scoop from the bottom and you're sure to spot some."

"Where do they come from?" she asked.

"I think they must form in an underground cavern that the gill here runs through before coming above ground. The water probably wears some away and washes them out."

"Thou knowst a lot about the rocks on this moor for a sickly lad who spent half his life on the Continent," teased Violet.

"Not half!" he protested with a laugh. "You make me sound the perfect invalid. I spent a good many summers on this moor."

"Look at me," he requested as he took her hand. "Do I look an invalid?"

"No, indeed," she laughed, "as handsome and hardy a lad as ever I've seen."

Then their eyes met.

"And you are beautiful," he sighed, releasing her hand. He gently slid his hands along her cheeks and kissed her.

Chapter 8
A Complaint

As Sherlock and Violet talked in the sunshine on the moor, there was a knock at the door of the squire's study.

"Excuse me, Squire. I trust I am not disturbing you? I would have a word with you, if I may," said Professor Moriarty.

The squire waved the man to a chair and said, "Speak, sir."

"I am sure, sir, that you have noticed that Master Sherlock has been a bit distracted lately," Moriarty said softly.

"Indeed? Has it been interfering with his studies?" the squire asked.

"Yes, sir, it has. You understand that I would not trouble you with this, Squire Holmes, if I did not fear it would interfere with the programme I have set out," the professor said.

"Yes. You have done the right thing. What do you believe the source of this distraction is?" the squire asked.

"I cannot say exactly, but the boy has been spending a great deal of time riding on the moors in the afternoons. He seems to enjoy these little jaunts very much. Perhaps it is the excitement and physical exertion that diminishes his powers of concentration," the professor suggested meekly.

"Well, then I shall instruct my son that he is to spend less time riding on the moors," the squire said.

"Very good, sir," Moriarty purred. "Then we shall have more time to make up the ground we have lost. Thank you, sir."

As the twilight slipped away, Sherlock was at the desk in his room. The specimens he had collected that day were scattered about the desktop, but at the moment Sherlock was not examining any one of them but rather the lens that had been cracked during the excursion. Sherlock looked up as his father knocked at the door and entered.

"You have been collecting rocks upon the moor today, I see," the squire said. "An interesting hobby, but you must put it aside for a while and concentrate on your studies."

"I have been concentrating on my studies, Father," Sherlock said.

"Your tutor says otherwise. He says you are falling behind," his father said.

"His schedule is rather demanding, but I had no idea that Professor Moriarty was dissatisfied with my work," Sherlock said defensively.

"You must apply yourself more strenuously. You are to do no more riding on the moors in the afternoons. There will be additional lessons in the afternoon until you catch up," Squire Holmes said.

Caught off guard, Sherlock suddenly saw his afternoons with Violet being stripped away.

"But surely I am allowed some respite?" he protested.

"You may have Saturday afternoons free," his father said after a moment of thought. "However, I want to hear better reports from Professor Moriarty in the future."

Thus two weeks passed before Sherlock saw Violet again. On the first Saturday he had free he searched for her on the moor, but returned home disappointed. On the following Saturday, no sooner was lunch over than he headed up towards the moors in hopes that he might happen upon her. But he never reached the moor road for as he passed the road to the tenant farms beyond the meadow he heard the squeal of a pig and the answering curses of a familiar voice.

He turned his horse and rode along until he came to where a large pig had decided to sit in a rut by the side of the road. Violet stood over the pig beating him with a stick and cursing at him, but the pig only squealed in response and made no effort to move.

Sherlock dismounted.

"Having trouble?" he inquired.

Violet looked up at him.

"If thou'st just come to stand there and smirk, then thou can be getting on thy way. I've enough nonsense from this porker here," she said.

"Won't budge, eh?" Sherlock said.

"No, he was moving along the road just fine till he spotted this hole," Violet said.

"Where is he meant to be going?" Sherlock asked.

"Farmer Martin's offered to take him from me. I'm sorry to give him up 'cause he'll give heap of bacon. Aye, that's all thou art good for: Bacon!" she reminded the pig and gave him another whack with the stick. "But I need the money. Thou knowst what for. Squire won't take it in kind. 'Here is the indenture your father signed,' he said. 'Rent will be paid in coin.' But Martin's offered me enough for this devil in pigskin that with what's left over from selling the wagon, and my herb money, I can pay rent again. If," she said giving the pig another whack, "I can get this pig to move afore Midsummer!" Violet said.

"I know how to get the rascal to move," Sherlock said.

Violet sighed and said, "Well, I'd be glad to see it."

Sherlock called up Sandy and spoke to the dog for moment. The mongrel then walked up to the pig and gave it a nip in the tail. The pig got quickly to his feet and was soon running and squealing down the road. Sandy was after him like lightning, keeping him on the road and herding him from any new holes he might take a liking to. No more than a yap from Sandy was necessary from then on to get the pig moving.

Sherlock and Violet stood laughing for a moment as the pig had jumped out of the hole, but now they trailed along behind pig and dog.

"I've not seen thee for a while, Sherlock," Violet said softly.

"I'm sorry, Violet, but my father believes I've been riding on the moors too much and not studying enough. I looked for you last Saturday," Sherlock explained.

"Oh!" she said with hopeful surprise. "I was afraid thou wert still angry with me for breaking thy glass."

"Oh, no, Violet. It's my tutor. He's convinced my father that I am not working hard enough. So now except for meals, and some small time with the violin which my mother won for me, I spend nearly all my days at study." He stopped and looked at her. "I'd much rather spend them with you," he said. Violet smiled, and they walked on.

"They do allow me Saturday afternoons free, so--"

Suddenly, Sherlock stopped and pulled her back. A boy appeared to drop out of the air before them. He brandished a crude wooden sword threateningly.

"What are you?" asked Sherlock.

"Oh, Mr. Sherlock! I dinna know twas thee coming along. Beg pardon, Miss Rushdale." The boy blushed and looked down at his wooden weapon. "I was merely playing."

"What's thy name, lad?" Violet asked.

"Beckwith, Ma'am, Jonathan Beckwith," the boy answered. Then he looked at Sherlock, "Perhaps thou knowst my sister, Mr. Sherlock. Pearl is a milkmaid at the manor. Sis is a giddy, gossipy gal. My mum says ah got all in the brains in the family."

Violet laughed.

"There munnot have been much to give out, if thou's a habit of leaping down on unarmed folks coming along," she said.

Sherlock grinned and used his pocket knife to cut down a sapling that was trying to grow up through the fence. He cut it to size and trimmed off the stray branches.

"Perhaps he'd like an armed opponent?" suggested Sherlock as he brandished his stick.

Jonathan's face brightened and he proudly held his weapon high. Jonathan began the engagement with a bold stroke that

Sherlock parried easily. Jonathan pulled back. Sherlock held his ground. Jonathan quickly renewed his attack but wood met wood again and again. No matter what direction Jonathan struck from Sherlock's stick was there to meet his wooden sword. At last Sherlock tired of this defensive play. As Jonathan lunged forward with his sword again, Sherlock brought his stick up with force against the handle of Jonathan's 'weapon.' The crude wooden sword flew up into the air. Sherlock sprang to his left and caught the toy in his left hand while the stick in his right pressed against Jonathan's chest, forcing him back against the fence. Then Sherlock withdrew and saluted his smaller opponent.

Violet applauded.

"I dinna know thou wert such a swordsman, Sherlock," she said.

Sherlock blushed slightly at her praise. Then he shrugged his shoulders.

"I studied fencing in France," he said.

Jonathan's eyes were wide with admiration as Sherlock returned the boy's sword.

"Could thou teach me that?" Jonathan asked.

"Perhaps," answered Sherlock as he tossed aside the stick. "Now tell me, Jonathan, why haven't you found more profitable ways to employ your time? You look like a strong, healthy lad."

"Eh, I do my share of scaring birds, collecting acorns and the lot with the rest of the young'uns about here. But me mum won't let me take more permanent farm work. She tells me I'm too bright for that. She says she'll get me a place at the manor house one of these days."

"Well, I shall mention your name at the Hall," said Sherlock. "In the meantime, I suggest you stop waylaying travelers along the road. Such a habit hardly lends itself to a good recommendation for employment."

"Quite right, sir. I won't do it onny more," replied Jonathan, snapping up straight and tall.

"Now be a good lad and run along and leave us be," Sherlock said, as he and Violet started down the road again.

Jonathan started back towards his own cottage, then turned and ran after them again.

"Thou will teach me, won't thou?" he asked breathlessly as he caught up with them.

"To fence?" Sherlock asked looking thoughtful.

"Aye, sir," Jonathan said meekly.

"Meet me in the yard behind the Hall after tea today."

"Aye, sir!" Jonathan cried jubilantly and ran off waving his toy sword.

Violet laughed. Sherlock smiled at her. How he loved that laugh!

"I shall be free next Saturday afternoon, if you would care to see me then," Sherlock said.

"Surely. We shall have much to talk about," she said, cocking her head to one side and giving him a look he didn't quite understand.

"Shall we meet near the moor road as before?" he asked.

"Aye," she replied, still looking at him oddly.

"Then I shall leave you to your business. Come on, Sandy," he called to the dog that had chased the pig up to the gate of Martin's farm.

"A moment!" Violet called to him as he mounted his horse. "Some fine friend and brother thou art, Mister Sherlock Holmes! Thy eldest brother is to be married with great pomp on t' next coming Wednesday and thou's told me not a word of it! All the dale's buzzing with it and I have to hear it from strangers rather than the groom's own brother. Is it me thou's shunning to talk to about it, or are thou ashamed of thy brother or his choice?"

"Well," began a somewhat startled Sherlock. "I thought perhaps you'd rather not hear about it."

"What little thou knowst, sir! The doings of the folks at the Hall may torment some of us common folk by day, but they fuel our dreams by night. Besides, thy brother's always been kind to me. Art thou to be the best man?"

"No, Mycroft will be coming for the wedding and he shall have that honour. I shall be but a humble usher."

"Well, thou should know I'll be wanting to hear all about it from thee after!"

"Then I'll do my best to remember it all for you," Sherlock responded before riding off.

Chapter 9
Fencing Instruction

Sherlock was good to his word and met Jonathan in the yard behind the manor house after tea that day. He brought with him a pile of strange objects.

"I don't really have the proper equipment for formal lessons, Jonathan," Sherlock said, "but we will make do with what we have."

"Normally a student begins with foils," Sherlock continued, separating the two gleaming epees from the pile. "That's what Monsieur Bencin started me on. But I don't have any foils here. I preferred epees which are a bit heavier. My father bought me this matched set of epees while we were in France. They've been hanging on the wall of my room. That's what we have to work with."

"They're right bonny! Are they sharp?" Jonathan asked.

"No," Sherlock said. "Go ahead and take one. When they've been used sometimes they get spurs and rough spots on them, but we had these filed down before packing them for the trip to England."

Jonathan picked up one of the epees gingerly. He held the hilt in his right hand and ran his left hand past the guard and down the long tapered blade. The blade had three sides but no sharp edges. It ended in a soft cap. The epee was nearly as long as Jonathan was tall. He held it out straight and felt powerful.

"Like a musketeer!" Jonathan said.

"You have read Dumas?" Sherlock asked.

"Aye! I've read *The Three Musketeers* a hundred times," Jonathan confirmed. "Mum said that my pa bought the book for me at a shop in York when I was a wee thing before I could read. She says he never learnt to read himself. That and the Holy Bible are the onny books mum has."

"Did you know Dumas wrote more stories about the musketeers?" Sherlock asked.

"No, I dinna!" Jonathan said.

"I can loan the other books to you if you are careful with them," Sherlock said.

"I'll be main careful!" Jonathan insisted.

Sherlock set the other epee aside and turned to the pile he had brought out with him.

"Here, try on this jacket," Sherlock said. "It is my old one and is too small for me but I suspect it is much too large for you. Yes. Let's cinch it up with this belt. Monsieur Bencin would be horrified, but it will do for our purposes. And put this gauntlet on your right hand."

"Why mun we wear the jacket and the glove?"

"The thick material prevents any accidental piercing or scratching and decreases the potential for bruising. And one more precaution," he said handing Jonathan the second mask.

"Is fencing dangerous?" Jonathan asked.

Sherlock laughed.

"Well, if you have read *The Three Musketeers*, then you know that fencing descends from a martial art where the purpose was to kill your opponent," Sherlock said.

Jonathan gulped.

Sherlock smiled at the boy and continued, "And it wasn't always in the field of war either. Englishmen killed Englishmen with swords in brawls, robberies and duels. Before dueling was outlawed in England nearly a hundred aristocrats per year were dying at each other's hands over 'points of honour.' But killing is not our purpose today."

"For that me and my mum thank thee most greatly," Jonathan said. "If there was killing to be done, I know who t'would be."

Sherlock paused in putting on his own jacket and looked at

Jonathan.

"You said that your mother wanted you to have a position at the Hall," Sherlock said nodding his head towards the back of the manor house which was before them.

"Aye," Jonathan agreed.

"If that is your goal, then there is something else that you should set yourself to learn that would be far more valuable to you than fencing," Sherlock said.

"Wot's that, sir?" Jonathan asked.

"If you hope to work in the manor house, Jonathan, you need to learn to speak the Queen's English. The house staff is expected to speak standard English. The only servant in the household who speaks broad Yorkshire is Tessy, the cook, and she is such a good cook I think they would keep her even if she didn't speak any English at all."

"Then I mun try to learn, though my own mum might not know wot I'm saying!"

"Oh, you don't have to give up Yorkshire. You can speak both, just at different times and to different people. Think of it like learning a foreign language. I speak fairly good French and passable German. My tutor seems to think that I need to learn Latin and classical Greek though I can't think of a call I'd have for using either one. Fortunately, you already understand proper English or we would not be having this conversation. It is just a matter of getting into the habit of speaking it."

"Aye, sir," Jonathan said.

"Yes, not 'aye,'" Sherlock corrected.

"Y-yes, sir," Jonathan said.

"You need to learn is to use "you" and "your" instead of "thou," "thee" and "thy" for the singular. I do not why that is the current standard, but it is. You can listen to the people from the Hall who speak proper English and imitate them. That is far easier than learning something like Latin where everyone who spoke it has been dead for centuries."

"Then why'd thy tutor be wanting thee to learn it?" Jonathan asked.

"Repeat after me: Then why does your tutor want you to learn it?" Sherlock said.

"Then why d-does your tutor want you t'learn it?" Jonathan repeated.

"That is a very good question in any dialect. He says it is required for admission to the university. I don't know why they require it. But let's resume our fencing," Sherlock said.

Sherlock picked up one of the epees. "You hold it like this between the thumb and the forefinger," he said demonstrating.

Jonathan picked up the second epee and tried to imitate Sherlock's hold.

"Don't grip it too tightly or you won't be able to maneuver it quickly. The thick part here near the guard is called the "forte." That means "strong" in French. The other end near the point is called the "foible" which means "weak" in French," Sherlock instructed him.

"The first thing that fencers do is salute each other," Sherlock said.

Sherlock picked up one mask and tucked it under his left arm. Palm up Sherlock swept his right arm up drawing the point of his epee from the ground to level with Jonathan's chest. Then he bent his elbow and drew the epee back until it was pointing skyward before his right eye and then pointed it back towards Jonathan for a moment and brought it to ground again. Jonathan mimicked him.

"Move your right foot over like this. That's it. Now let's get that mask on you properly," Sherlock said and then helped Jonathan put on his mask.

"Then fencers assume the basic 'en garde' position like this," Sherlock continued.

As he assumed the en garde position himself, Sherlock recalled the nearly trance-like state of concentration he had learned from M. Bencin. Feet apart and perpendicular to each other, knees bent, left arm high he raised his sword towards the adversary, and no one and nothing else in the world existed. But then Sherlock mentally stepped back from there to his new role as instructor.

"In theory there are eight basic garde positions in fencing though four of them are used more frequently than the others," Sherlock explained, demonstrating each position and correcting Jonathan's attempts to follow.

"You can use each of these positions to either attack or defend yourself from an attack. You should practice changing between them. Since this is not a duel and these are not sharp, the goal is to make a 'hit' upon your opponent like this," Sherlock said, demonstrating a hit on Jonathan's chest. "You want the blade to flex a little, but don't use enough force on the epee to run through your opponent if these were sharp. They still can still cause some bruising if you hit hard enough. The rules for scoring with an epee are less restrictive than with a foil. You can make a hit anywhere on the body. But no slashing. This is not a saber. Think of it like a rapier with just a sharp point, but no sharp edges. An attack comes from the elbow and the wrist, not the shoulder. Like this. Try it. Yes."

Sherlock remembered how in his first lesson M. Bencin had then invited him to attack. The fifteen year old Sherlock had responded with ineffective vigor while M. Bencin repelled his attacks deftly with an attitude of boredom. Without warning the fencing master had turned the tide and started to attack, scoring hit after hit on the boy who had begun backing further and further away as his master advanced in the flurry. Finally M. Bencin had backed off, saluted Sherlock and told him that he had much to learn. Awed, Sherlock had agreed. Then M. Bencin had taught him to parry and attack properly.

"First you must learn to defend yourself against attacks," Sherlock said to Jonathan. "A defensive movement in fencing is called a 'parry.' In a parry you try to deflect your opponent's attack with the forte or the guard of your epee so he cannot score. There are different types of parries. The simplest is the direct parry where your aim is merely to intercept the adversary's blade and prevent the point from touching you. If I were to attack from the sixth position like this, then you could bring your epee across from the sixth position to the fourth like this. Always make sure that you are moving your opponent's weapon away from your body. One danger of using a downward parry, from the 4th to the 8th position, for example, is that your adversary may then thrust forward under your blade and hit your leg."

"The simplest attack is a straight thrust where there is no opposition. Here now try to attack." Jonathan engaged Sherlock with less boldness than he had in the morning but rather tried to apply what he had been taught. Sherlock easily parried every attempt. When Sherlock attacked Jonathan succeeded in parrying a few direct attacks, but Sherlock still scored easily.

"You learn quickly," Sherlock said. "Let's go again. En garde."

Encouraged by the praise, Jonathan tried harder to get past Sherlock's defenses to no avail. As the supper hour approached, Sherlock began to collect the equipment again.

"Thank ye-you for the lesson," Jonathan said stuttering somewhat as he attempted to choose the right words.

"It gave me a chance to practice," Sherlock said. "We should do it again after tea next Saturday."

"I'd like that very much," Jonathan said smiling brightly.

"Here take the jacket. Perhaps your mother can stitch it up to make it fit better," Sherlock said.

Sherrinford came out of the manor house at that moment.

"Thank th-you, sir," Jonathan said taking the fencing jacket he had been wearing and giving Sherlock a little bow. "I w-will be here next week," he said before running off towards his mother's cottage.

"You seem to have a following," Sherrinford said. "Is that the Beckwith boy you mentioned?"

"Yes," Sherlock said. "Monsieur Bencin would be horrified that I am imparting his wisdom to a cottager, but teaching him gives me a partner to practice with. I had forgotten how much I enjoyed it. I can't see you taking up the sport."

"Oh, no, I enjoy a good hunt when I have the time, but waving pointy objects around is not really my style. But go and get yourself cleaned up for supper. The vicar is coming by and we are going to discuss the details of the wedding afterwards."

Chapter 10
The Wedding

On Monday afternoon the carriage pulled up before the manor house door and a gentleman stepped out. He was tall and broad like Sherrinford but with quite a bit more padding all around. His eyes were a light watery grey and had a far-away introspective look. He had a masterful brow and a firm jaw and his lips curled up into a smile as he descended from the carriage and extended his broad flipper of a hand to Sherlock who awaited him on the porch.

"Greetings, Mycroft!" said Sherlock taking his brother's hand.

"Ah, it is good to see you again, Sherlock. You are looking fit. That professor can't be keeping you in all the time. There's the flush of the moors in your cheeks. And there seems to be an extra twinkle in those mischievous eyes of yours. If I didn't know better-- Ah, but there's the groom himself," said Mycroft as the door opened again.

"Mycroft! It was good of you to come!" Sherrinford said coming forward and slapping his brother on the back.

"Would I miss my elder brother's wedding? No, no, I have a stake in seeing you married and settled into your position. If it weren't for you, I'd have to be going through all this nonsense!" Mycroft insisted.

Sherrinford laughed.

"Ah, but you seem quite pleased at the prospect of marrying this young lady," Mycroft said.

"And quite dizzy, too," laughed Sherlock.

"Dizzy? Really, Sherlock!" scoffed Sherrinford.

"Tell me, Sherlock, you have seen the lady. Are congratulations in order?" Mycroft asked with mock confidentiality.

Sherlock chuckled. "Well, I don't know if he suffers from good luck or good taste, but she is quite a prize. But here comes the lady herself."

The door opened and Amanda stepped out. She was simply dressed in a modest navy blue dress that emphasized her fair skin. Her strawberry blonde curls were tumbling freely about her shoulders.

"Ah, Ford, there you are," Amanda said.

Sherrinford stepped forward and took her arm. "Amanda, this is my brother Mycroft. Mycroft, Amanda Courtney."

Amanda reached out her hand and Mycroft took it.

"It is a pleasure to meet you, Mycroft. I'm glad you could make it up for the wedding," Amanda said.

"The pleasure is mine, Miss Courtney," Mycroft said.

"You must call me, Amanda. We will be family soon," she said.

"I believe Sherlock is correct," Mycroft said. "Sherrinford has found quite a prize, and we are quite honoured to add you to our family tree!"

"I'm quite flattered!" Amanda said.

"Mycroft flatters no one, my dear," said Sherrinford. "He speaks the truth. But let's take our conversations indoors. Come along, Mycroft, the servants will see to your luggage."

Other guests arrived over the next two days until the manor house was brimming. Additional help was hired from the village and the surrounding farms to supplement the household staff.

The morning of the wedding found Sherlock helping grand dames and wizened gentlemen to their seats at the church. Innumerable relatives and all the "best" people in the county had been invited and now filled the pews. The village folk, who were not so privileged, crowded about the church, hoping to press their noses against the stained glass windows for a peek.

The vicar approached Sherlock.

"If there are any more guests I don't know where we'll put

them. How is your brother faring?" the vicar asked.

"Between seating guests and helping to extract my cousin George from the bell tower, which he felt wanted exploring, I've been too busy to check on him. But I'm sure the floorboards must be worn quite through by now," Sherlock said.

The vicar chuckled.

"Well, the bride has arrived and we shall begin soon. Go and tell your brothers to be ready and wait for your sign," the vicar said.

Sherlock opened the door to the small room in the back of the church to a curious sight. Here were his two older brothers, resembling each other in dress and feature. In height and breadth of shoulder they were twins. But never had they seemed so unalike. Sherrinford, the eldest, had a large barrel of a chest and muscular arms, and he was not lacking in padding here and there. But Mycroft was rotund to say the least, as if bulk was drawn to him without his notice. While Sherrinford wandered about the small room pretending to be interested in the workmanship of the builders in crafting the plain walls and simple wooden benches in an attempt to disguise his nervous pacing, Mycroft merely stood in one corner with his eyelids drooping half-down over his eyes, as if to spare him the effort of following his brother's excess activity. Standing there so round and unmoving, he looked like nothing less than a snowman saved from the previous winter.

"Sherrinford, can't you sit down? I believe you have mesmerized Mycroft with your pacing," Sherlock said.

Sherrinford only scowled at him.

"I, for one, would be glad to sit, if there were anything decent in this room to sit upon," observed Mycroft.

"You won't have to wait much longer. The vicar says we will begin soon. I will give you a signal," Sherlock said.

"B-but where is Amanda? Is she here? I haven't seen her!"

Sherrinford exclaimed.

Mycroft chuckled.

"Dear brother, didn't Father instruct you in the etiquette of matrimony when he was moulding you into a gentleman?" Mycroft said. "You are not meant to see the bride until she comes down the aisle."

"She is here, Sherrinford," Sherlock assured him.

At Sherlock's signal, Sherrinford and Mycroft began their march towards the altar. Sherlock took his place with the other ushers and bridesmaids at the rear of the church. A hush fell over the church as those present began to realize that the ceremony was about to begin. As Sherrinford and Mycroft reached the altar rail, the organ sprang into life and the bridal procession began. As the ushers and bridesmaids reached the altar the lines divided, the maids passing to the left and the ushers to the right. Sherlock in his turn came to stand beside his brothers. Next came the Maid of Honour, a cousin of Amanda's, who was quite lovely in her own right. As she found her place along the rail all attention was turned to the bride.

Charles Courtney walked quite proudly towards the altar with his daughter upon his arm, but he might as well have not been there for all he was noticed. For it was Amanda in her queenly promenade which drew every eye in the church. Sherlock heard his brother catch his breath as he beheld his bride in full array. As Amanda reached the altar rail, the two young girls holding her train arranged it neatly behind her and withdrew, and the organ ceased its playing.

"Dearly Beloved," the Vicar's words rang out, "We are gathered together in the sight of God, and in the face of this company, to join together this Man and this Woman in holy Matrimony...."

The vicar was a small person; short, slight of figure and slight of hair. But even the most diminutive of men seems large and important when draped in flowing vestments and stood upon the chancel. His voice was expansive. It boomed and filled the church and could bring you to your knees with repentance or awe in your heart. Whether it was the depth of the man's belief that drove that large voice forth from such a small frame, or whether it was a trick in the construction of the church, Sherlock did not know, but he listened now as that voice spoke loving and gentle words that flooded through the church like sunshine.

"If any man can show just cause, why they may not lawfully be joined together, let him speak now, or else forever hold his peace."

The vicar paused for the space of two heartbeats after this ancient enquiry but Sherrinford's heart must have missed them both, for he blanched and seemed to have forgotten how to breathe. He nearly jumped when the vicar addressed him.

"Sherrinford, wilt thou have this Woman to be thy wedded wife; to live together after God's ordinance in the holy estate of matrimony? Wilt thou love her, comfort her, honour and keep her in sickness and in health; and forsaking all others, keep thee only unto her as long as you both shall live?"

"I will," replied Sherrinford.

"Amanda, wilt thou have this Man to be thy wedded husband; to live together after God's ordinance in the holy estate of matrimony? Wilt thou love him, comfort him, honour and keep him in sickness and in health; and forsaking all others, keep thee only unto to him as long as you both shall live?"

"I will," Amanda answered giving Sherrinford a twinkling smile.

The vicar then addressed the congregation. "Will all of you witness to these promises do all in your power to uphold these persons in their marriage?

"We will," all replied.

"Who gives this woman to be married to this man?" the vicar asked.

"I do," announced Charles Courtney, as he delivered up Amanda's hand and stepped back from the party at the altar rail.

"Thus, in keeping with holy scripture, I would ask you, Sherrinford and Amanda, to join your right hands. And, now Sherrinford, repeat after me: I, Sherrinford"

"I, Sherrinford," Sherrinford repeated, his voice firm and strong. "Take thee, Amanda."

To Sherlock, Sherrinford seemed to relax as he followed the traditional pattern, as if this was now real and final and nothing could ever go wrong again. Tall, and sturdy, suddenly sure of his part, Sherrinford beamed at his bride as he said his vows.

The vicar turned to the bride.

"Amanda, repeat after me: I, Amanda," he said.

Amanda, of course, could not have brightened any for she had been radiant from the moment she had entered the church. She was glorious in her wedding gown and her voice was sweet and loving as she repeated after the vicar.

Then they loosened their hands and Mycroft held out the ring in his broad palm. As vicar took the ring and continued with the ceremony, Sherlock's mind wandered elsewhere... to a lass on the moor.

Chapter 11
Midsummer

The day after the wedding Sherlock was thoughtfully making his way up the front stairs after breakfast. Just as he reached the top landing there was a knock upon the front door of the manor house. Thomas opened the door and Sherlock heard a sweet, clear voice, the broad Yorkshire rolling off her tongue, ask to see the squire. Sherlock paused, half-hidden by the wall, and watched as Violet was shown into his father's study. He was startled when a voice rumbled softly behind him.

"Perhaps your chaffing of Sherrinford is unjustified considering your own interests," the voice said. Sherlock spun around to face Mycroft, who stood in the hall behind him as if he had stood upon that spot for centuries.

"What do you mean?" Sherlock asked, somewhat annoyed that he had not heard Mycroft walk up behind him.

"The young lady below," Mycroft indicated in a low voice as Violet was ushered from the study to the door again.

"What of her?" Sherlock asked.

"You know her, do you not?" Mycroft inquired flatly.

"Yes. She is the daughter of one of the tenants of the manor," Sherlock answered as he began walking down the hall to his bedroom.

"A friend?" asked Mycroft, following Sherlock into his room.

"Yes," Sherlock admitted.

"A close friend or do you always admire her from afar?" Mycroft inquired.

Sherlock blushed.

"Ah!" Mycroft nodded. "I thought as much."

"Mycroft, what purpose is there in this interrogation?" Sherlock said.

Mycroft's broad face spread in a smile. "Oh, just avenging Sherrinford," he said. Then he grew serious again. "But be careful where your interests lead you for you know Father would not be pleased."

"Indeed. He does not seem to be pleased with me whatever I do," Sherlock said.

"You say that with fresh conviction. Is there something of which I am unaware?" Mycroft asked.

"It is this tutor--," Sherlock began, but he was interrupted by a knock upon the bedroom door.

"Excuse me, sir, but the professor is waiting for you," Susan said.

Sherlock glanced at the clock. It read two minutes past the hour.

"I have to go to my lessons," Sherlock said hurriedly collecting his books and his work. "We can speak of this later."

"Any time," Mycroft said. "I am here until Monday morning. I am interested in hearing more about your difficulties with your tutor."

After his exchange with Sherlock, Mycroft observed Professor Moriarty with greater interest. There were still numerous relatives of various degrees about the house to be entertained. The bride and groom had left the day of the wedding. But several of the relatives who had attended were expected to stay into the weekend. So it was not possible to have any tête-à-tête with either the professor or Sherlock. But Mycroft could observe Moriarty's interactions with others.

On Saturday afternoon Sherlock reined Gale in nearly at Violet's feet and dropped to the ground before her breathing heavily.

"I'm sorry," he said pausing to kiss her between gasps. "I have to go right back. They want me to entertain my cousins. But I did not want you to think I had forgotten," he said giving her a hug.

Then he kissed her again.

Violet smiled.

"Tis good to see thee even for a moment," she said.

"I will tell you all about the wedding next week," he said then snatched a last kiss before remounting, waving and galloping off.

"There you are, Sherlock," his mother said as he re-entered the house. "Your cousin George is off having a tantrum in the stables. Could you please find him and keep him busy for a few hours until his parents are ready to leave?"

"Yes, Mother," Sherlock said.

Shortly after tea Mr. & Mrs. Challenger and their son George headed off on their journey homeward. With George now off his hands, Sherlock suddenly remembered another appointment he had made. He found Jonathan sitting in the yard behind the manor house.

"I thought th-you might have forgotten," Jonathan said.

"No, I have been busy trying to control my cousin George. That boy is going to grow into a frightful man some day. Wait here, I will return with the gear," Sherlock said.

When Sherlock returned Jonathan had already donned his fencing jacket which now fit him snugly.

"Ah, that looks much better. Here," Sherlock said handing Jonathan the gauntlet, epee and mask.

"Do you remember the salute?" Sherlock asked.

"Aye-yes," Jonathan said.

The two boys saluted each other and assumed the en garde position. They reviewed the eight garde positions with Sherlock correcting Jonathan's form sometimes. Then they practiced some thrust and parry combinations slowly.

Sherlock remembered the lectures of his maître d'armes, M. Bencin. "Utilisez la tète, pas le bras," he would repeat over and over. "Use your head, not your arm."

"Fencing is more than a physical exercise," Sherlock said

to Jonathan. "It is a mental exercise. You must observe your opponent carefully. You must learn his style, his timing, his strengths, and his weaknesses. A parry or a thrust can only be effective if it is timed properly. If you misjudge you opponent, your efforts will be in vain and he will score. Do not become angry when your opponent scores. It will destroy your concentration. Concentration is crucial. You must pay attention to every move your opponent makes and anticipate his next move."

Jonathan listened carefully to everything Sherlock told him and tried to absorb it as best he could. He'd been taught his letters and numbers at his mother's knee. Never before had he been presented with so much new information in so short a period of time. He was trying to take every possible advantage of the opportunities being offered him by the squire's son and learn everything that was taught to him. He headed home at the end of the hour reviewing all that Sherlock had said.

By Sunday afternoon the last of the relatives had left, and Sherlock and Mycroft found time to speak.

"Shortly after we returned from France, Father spoke again of sending me to the university and making an engineer out of me and he hired Professor Moriarty to prepare me for the university. But since the professor came I think he has begun to doubt that course," Sherlock said.

"Has Father said anything to that effect?" Mycroft asked.

"No, but Professor Moriarty has complained to him that I am not studying hard enough. I am no longer allowed to ride on the moors in the afternoons and must have more lessons instead. Father said that I must apply myself more strenuously."

"It sounds to me like Father still has the same goal in mind," Mycroft said.

"Why would this great professor with this glorious career ahead and behind him want to tutor the youngest son of a country squire? There is something odd about that," Sherlock said.

"That is rather tenuous," Mycroft responded.

"I know. There is nothing definitive that I can point to. But there is something about this professor that bothers me," Sherlock said

"Everyone else seems quite taken by him," Mycroft said.

"I think that's part of what troubles me," Sherlock responded. "He plays the congenial scholar too well. It seems like a mask to me. There is something more below the surface. I just can't quite see it."

"Perhaps you are imagining it," Mycroft suggested. "You have always had a great imagination."

"Sometimes the imagination can interpolate between known data," Sherlock replied.

"Interpolation is one thing. Extrapolation is quite another. It can enter the realm of fiction," Mycroft reminded him.

"Perhaps," Sherlock admitted.

"My observations of Professor Moriarty have revealed nothing more than that he has lived the scholarly life that he claims," Mycroft said.

"I don't deny that," Sherlock responded.

"He seems to be soft-spoken and kind to everyone," Mycroft said.

"He is to me as well, even when he is critical of my work," Sherlock agreed. "Yet there is an undercurrent... something running deep... that he has not yet revealed to even me," Sherlock said.

"I admit that sometimes he seems to avoid questions about his academic achievements," Mycroft said, "but that could indeed be the modesty others credit it as. Without evidence that there is something else--"

"Yes, yes," interrupted Sherlock, "I have no evidence.

Somehow I feel there is a duel going on between us. I think that he knows I feel there is more to him and he sees it as a challenge. If he cannot control me with his ingratiating manner, then he plans to prove he can control my life otherwise. It is a game of wills."

Mycroft Holmes frowned at his brother Sherlock.

"I think perhaps you have been studying too hard," Mycroft said. "I would be careful not to impart these thoughts you have to Father. I think he would misinterpret them."

"As what?" Sherlock asked.

"Paranoid delusions," Mycroft said.

"You don't believe me either," Sherlock said jumping up angrily and pacing the floor.

"It is not a matter of disbelief," Mycroft said trying to soothe his younger brother. "I believe that you believe it, but I also think that you are building your theories on air. It is a capital mistake to theorize before you have data. Inevitably you will twist facts to suit theories rather than theories to suit facts."

Sherlock stopped pacing and looked at Mycroft.

"You are right. As usual, your logic is impeccable. I should not prejudice my conclusions. I will wait and see," Sherlock said.

"Write to me when I am back in London and tell me how things are coming along," Mycroft said.

Chapter 12
A Duel of Wits

Sherlock joined his family for an early breakfast the following Monday. His parents and his brother Mycroft were leaving that morning to journey south to London. Mycroft was returning to his rooms and his employment with the government, and the squire and his wife were going stay a week at the house in Kensington to renew social contacts which had grown rusty during their years in France.

The house at Kensington was a small one used primarily during the London social season. It usually remained closed the rest of the year. The squire was not one to enjoy the dizzy whirl of "the Season," but considered a certain amount of socializing to be among the duties of his position. So he and his wife would make the appropriate calls and appearances necessary to maintain his small social circle, and perhaps, if he were lucky he might encounter some stimulating conversation. Otherwise, he would pay his due and leave as soon as the constraints of etiquette would allow. But Sherrinford and Amanda, being young and lively, were expected to spend several weeks at the Kensington house after their honeymoon. Mrs. Holmes wished to see that all was in order before the newlyweds arrived.

Sherlock and Professor Moriarty would be alone in the manor house except for the servants. Sherlock was not looking forward to that.

It was true that Sherlock was not interested in his studies. He found calculus to be a purposeless struggle and classical Greek to be an unending bore. What of the distance to the moon-- how was that to benefit him? He could not find inspiration in the thought of going to the university or becoming an engineer. They were merely goals his father had set for him. Violet, however, inspired him and overwhelmed him. He ached for her company when he was separated from her and longed to never leave her when they were together. Yes, he admitted to himself that his thoughts did stray her direction occasionally in the midst of his studies. But he felt his lessons did not suffer as a consequence for his mind was so stultified by his studies that it would have wandered somewhere anyway, even if, God forbid, Violet had not existed.

While the rest of the family was away Professor Moriarty increased the length of the lessons, often keeping Sherlock busy from dawn to dusk. On the first Saturday after the squire and his wife had left the manor, Moriarty handed Sherlock some papers to revise shortly before lunch. Sherlock had already sent word to the stables in the morning for Gale to be saddled and ready for him after lunch. Sherlock looked at the papers the professor handed him. Silently he had gathered up his books and left the room. But rather than joining the professor in the dining room for lunch, Sherlock requested that his lunch be brought to his room. He worked while he ate and left the corrected papers on the professor's desk before lunch was over. He was up on Gale's back and headed towards the moor road within minutes of leaving the papers. He found Violet there among the tors. Sherlock dismounted, took her hand in his and kissed it.

"Now wilt thou tell me of thy brother's wedding?" Violet asked.

"Oh, yes. Come here and sit down and I'll tell you all about it," he said drawing her over to a patch of grass before starting the tale. He described the whole ceremony from start to finish.

"And afterwards all returned to the Hall for a bountiful feast," Sherlock said concluding his recounting of the wedding to Violet.

"Twas there goose?" Violet asked.

"Oh, yes, goose and grouse and beef and lamb and puddings and pies. Never has Tessy's fare been more tempting, and Sherrinford, who had hardly touched a fork in the week before had regained his appetite threefold!" Sherlock said.

"And the flowers, did she throw them?" Violet asked.

"Oh, yes, Amanda tossed the bouquet from the steps of the church to the awaiting maidens," said Sherlock playfully. "Her cousin, Elizabeth, caught it and you would have thought it solid gold for how pleased she was of her catch."

"'Twas there a garter, too?" Violet quizzed him.

"Oh, yes, they followed all the local customs," Sherlock responded.

"And did thou race for it?" she asked.

Sherlock said nothing, but smiled at her and drew a ringlet of lace from his pocket.

"Oh, Sherlock, thou hast won it!" Violet said clapping her hands with delight.

"Gale can catch any horse in the county who has less than a quarter mile lead. She left the rest far behind," he said.

"'Tis a bonny thing," she said taking the lace garter between her fingers as he handed it to her.

"It's yours. I won it for you," Sherlock said.

"Violet," Sherlock began softly and she looked up at him, and he lost the words he was going to say. He looked away and began quite casually. "Amanda is very nice and she's quite pretty in a delicate sort of way. But when I saw her coming down that aisle in that beautiful gown--." He paused and looked at her again. "I wished it had been you."

Violet fingered the lace garter absently as she pictured herself in a fine satin gown walking down the aisle of the church on her father's arm. But the thought of her father shattered the daydream. She turned quickly away and crushed the garter in her hand.

"I'm sorry, Violet," Sherlock said when he saw the dark clouds gather over her face. "I didn't mean to--."

But Violet brushed away the clouds.

"It is the stuff of dreams," she said lightheartedly. "But thou mun have more tales from the wedding to tell."

"Yes!" Sherlock said brightly, and they talked and laughed for an hour before he mounted his horse and rode back to the manor house. As he passed in through the back door, he requested that his tea be brought to his room.

When the maid brought it to him, she said, "The professor was inquiring about you earlier while you were out."

"Thank you. I will speak to him later," Sherlock said.

After tea he went out back to fence with Jonathan. They reviewed the prior lessons and practiced positions, parries, and attacks. Then Sherlock showed Jonathan how to do circular and semi-circular parries.

"You wrap your sword around the sword of your adversary with a circular motion that deflects their sword into a new direction," Sherlock instructed him. "That new direction should be away from your body or else a skilled opponent will thrust and score from the new direction."

That evening at the dinner table, Professor Moriarty said, "Dear me, I believe we had some misunderstanding earlier. I expected you back after lunch. I was told that you went riding."

"I am sorry," Sherlock said looking up from his dinner plate innocently. "I expected to have my free time as usual. I thought that you merely wished to have the work completed. I completed it before I left."

"You did indeed," Professor Moriarty cooed. "Well, well, let's not dwell on it."

But the professor further increased the workload and often required Sherlock to rewrite Greek translations several times when the professor felt he had missed some nuance in the text.

"You must admit that your work on the extract from Aeschylus' *Prometheus Bound* was rather below standard. You will need to redo it all before you leave," said Moriarty.

"I do not see what relevance classical Greek has to being an engineer," Sherlock responded with some irritation.

"It is necessary for you to gain admittance to the college at Cambridge University that your father wishes you to attend. You will work at it until you have completed it correctly."

"It is already well into my time for violin practice," Sherlock protested.

"Playing violin has no relevance either to being an engineer or to being admitted to the university. Your father has very exacting standards that I'm obliged to meet. You will work through supper if you do not cooperate."

Sherlock knew he meant it. He applied himself to the translation. When he had corrected his previous mistakes, he handed the paper to Professor Moriarty.

"Ah, much better, my boy. I suppose that the cook has your supper ready by now. You are dismissed. Perhaps if we finish our work on time tomorrow I may dismiss you early," the professor said with a smile.

But the professor began the following day with a long lecture on the history of astronomy. After lunch, he addressed the Copernican model of the universe, including an extensive discourse on *De Revolutionibus*. As the afternoon was wearing thin, the professor concluded and gave Sherlock a series of problems to work.

"Please complete these before leaving," Moriarty said.

Sherlock looked down at the problems before him, then up at the clock.

"It will take hours to do these," Sherlock protested.

"That is correct and if you do not begin them promptly and work diligently it will take longer than that," Moriarty pointed out softly.

"But it is past teatime already. You said you would dismiss me early today," Sherlock reminded him.

"I said no such thing," Moriarty protested. "I said I might dismiss you early if you finished your work. You have not completed your work."

"You arranged it so that I could not complete my work," Sherlock said.

Their eyes locked. They understood each other. No words were necessary.

"I will complete these in my room," Sherlock said gathering up his papers and books.

As he worked over the problems in his room, Sherlock contemplated the situation. Sherlock was quite positive now that Moriarty was playing with him. He realized that he needed to think of it like a fencing bout. He must remain objective and observe his opponent. So Sherlock did all that Moriarty ask of him for the next few days promptly and carefully without complaint. But the professor seemed annoyed rather than pleased.

Chapter 13
The Falling Out

It was close upon mid-day the following Saturday when the professor stood before him shaking his head as he looked over the page of Latin which Sherlock had done that morning.

"Dear me, dear me," Professor Moriarty said softly, his head snaking from side to side. "This translation will most certainly have to be done over again. But there is the luncheon bell. I shall not keep you from your repast, but I expect to see you here immediately after and we will work on this until you get it correct.

Sherlock stared at Professor Moriarty as his hopes of seeing Violet that afternoon were dashed. This time he could not claim that it was a misunderstanding as he had the previous Saturday. Moriarty had been very clear. Sherlock hid his disappointment and reigned in his temper.

"Yes, sir," he responded.

Over lunch Sherlock pondered how to get a message to Violet. He agonized over it as he struggled with the Latin again. His concerns did not improve his work, but at last the professor seemed to accept one version as a passable draft. Still Moriarty kept him on.

"There are these calculations which you did yesterday which need correcting," purred the professor.

As tea time rolled past, Jonathan appeared in the yard below. Sherlock saw him.

"There is something out that window which is distracting you," the professor stated softly. "What is it?"

"It's the boy I've been fencing with. Let me send him away," Sherlock said.

"Do so quickly," Professor Moriarty urged.

Sherlock hurried down the back stairs and grabbed Jonathan by the sleeve.

"Listen," he whispered to the boy. "I can't fence today, but I need you to do me a favor. Take a message to Violet Rushdale. Tell her I can't meet her today because my tutor is keeping me in. Look for her near where the high tors stand by the gill that crosses the moor road." He paused. "If she isn't there--"

"I'll find her," Jonathan responded.

"Good lad. But if you go near her farm keep an eye out for that pa of hers. If he catches sight of you--"

"I'll be out of there faster than thought," Jonathan said.

"Good. Now go on," Sherlock said making the last a bit louder than the rest.

For Jonathan this was high adventure, and he relished his role as he ran off to find the maiden fair.

Despite his disappointment at missing his meeting with Violet, Sherlock attempted to stay detached and continued working without complaint for the next few days. But his efforts were not rewarded. When the squire returned on Tuesday, Professor Moriarty approached him.

"I'm sorry, sir, to disturb you, but if I may have a word," the professor said.

"Regarding Sherlock's progress?" the squire asked.

"Yes, sir, or perhaps more aptly, the lack thereof," Professor Moriarty responded. "I don't know how to put this delicately, Squire, but I am beginning to have doubts that he has the discipline necessary to attend the university."

"Indeed?" the squire said with surprise.

"He is not completing the assignments I give him on time and on at least one occasion he left the lesson early. He is an intelligent boy and I don't believe that he is incapable of doing the work. He is just -- how can I put this delicately?" the professor said meekly. "He is just rather lazy."

The squire's eyes narrowed. He sent for Sherlock and told him of the professor's remarks.

"I'm doing my best, sir," Sherlock said. "I don't believe Professor Moriarty's assessment is accurate."

The squire scowled. He had difficulty believing any son of his could be lazy and yet Sherlock was not like the other two boys. What reason would Professor Moriarty have to lie about it? The professor seemed like an honest and reasonable man.

"Professor Moriarty said that you left one of your lessons early," the squire said.

"No, sir. I completed the work during lunch and left it for him before going riding. It was a misunderstanding. I wrongly assumed that I was still allowed Saturday afternoons off while you were away and I believed that the professor merely wanted the lessons completed before I left. The following Saturday he kept me working until supper time," Sherlock said.

"Because you had not completed your work," his father said.

"Because he made it impossible for me to complete the work," Sherlock said.

"Sherlock, I see no reason why Professor Moriarty should be lying about this," his father responded. "If you are not getting the work done on time then you are not working hard enough."

The squire's fingers made circles on the desk and ended with a tap.

"I think the violin practice will have to be set aside for now as well as your free time Saturday afternoons. Use that additional time to study," the squire said.

"Father--," Sherlock protested.

"This is not a matter for discussion. I don't want to hear any further complaints from your tutor," said Squire Holmes. "Now, we have guests coming this evening. Go and prepare to meet them."

"Yes, sir," Sherlock said.

Sherlock walked up the stairs to his room. Alone in his room he finally vented his anger by pushing all the books and papers off his desk onto the floor. There was some catharsis in that act and he left them lying in a heap. At least with guests coming he would not be expected to study tonight. He changed his attire and waited to be called when he was wanted. While he waited, he sat down at his desk and began writing a letter to his brother Mycroft.

"Dear Mycroft," Sherlock wrote, "I attempted to put away my suspicions of Professor Moriarty and merely apply myself to study. Despite my efforts, the friction between us has continued. While Mother and Father were gone he increased the length and complexity of assignments, requiring me to work from sun to sun to complete them. Even then it is not always possible to complete them to the professor's satisfaction. I redoubled my efforts and rose before dawn to eke out a few more hours of study but to no avail. Moriarty is not to be satisfied. He seemed irritated by my increased diligence and only begrudgingly released me. In fact, Moriarty seems to be secretly delighted when I have been unable to complete an assignment. He greets it with a 'dear me, dear me,' but there is this maddening twinkle in his eye."

"The professor has once again complained to Father and explicitly stated that he does not believe I have the discipline for university work. He even accused me of being 'lazy' to Father and you know how intolerant Father is of laziness. Father now has taken away all my free time. What is to be next? A ball and chain? Or will I merely be bound to the pump wheel?"

"I have tried to be cooperative and I have tried to

avoid direct conflicts, but the war between us continues to escalate. I am at a loss as to how to handle it. Father and Mother are going to a house party in ten days. I expect some new skirmish to occur then.

Sherlock"

The guests that evening were the vicar and a young man who was staying with him.

"Sherlock," the vicar said, "This is Mr. Andrew Goble. Andrew, Sherlock Holmes."

"I am quite glad to meet you, sir," Sherlock said.

"Please call me Andrew," he replied.

"I am considering taking on a curate again and Andrew here has come up to discuss the position," the vicar said to Sherlock. "You and he might have some things to talk over as he just came down from Cambridge University."

"And this is Professor James Moriarty, Sherlock's tutor," the vicar said.

"Always a pleasure to meet an educated man," Moriarty said.

Over supper Sherlock plied Andrew full of questions about the university and Andrew responded with amusing anecdotes as well as factual information. The young men got along well. Sherlock found in Andrew Goble an interesting mix of approachability and authority. In one anecdote Andrew mentioned fencing.

"Do you fence?" Sherlock asked.

"I fenced at school and a bit at Cambridge, but it was just a small informal group with some of the fellows and undergraduates. They don't have a university fencing club," Andrew confirmed. "But I suspect I shan't have much use for it once I am ordained. There aren't many warrior priests these days. Do you fence?"

"Yes, I trained for two years in France. My maître d'armes was Monsieur Bencin. Recently I've just been practicing with a boy from the cottages. Nothing really challenging," Sherlock said.

"I don't have my own gear along or we could have a go, but I'd love to watch," Andrew said.

Sherlock looked over at his father.

"I would, but I'm afraid--" Sherlock began.

"Just this once. But you must concentrate on your studies thereafter," the squire said.

"We usually fence after tea on Saturday," Sherlock said secretly glad to have regained some ground.

"Then you and the vicar must join us for tea on Saturday," Sherlock's mother said to them.

"We would be delighted," the vicar said and Andrew nodded in agreement.

Professor Moriarty was silent.

On Saturday morning Sherlock and the professor met for lessons as usual and they continued with their work after lunch. Professor Moriarty said nothing regarding points won or lost but he did release Sherlock well before tea time.

It was a warm, clear day and Sherlock's mother had tea served upon the front lawn. After tea, the vicar stayed conversing with the squire and his wife while Andrew and Sherlock joined Jonathan who awaited them around back.

"Jonathan has only had a few lessons so far. So we are still practicing the basics," Sherlock explained.

Having his new skills put thus on display made Jonathan nervous. But Andrew Goble quickly put him on his ease, and Jonathan and Sherlock repeated familiar drills. Then Sherlock saluted Jonathan again, assumed the en garde position, and allowed his mind to enter that state of deep concentration he had learned from Monsieur Bencin. He gave no quarter, often parrying Jonathan's attacks before Jonathan even knew where they were going, and he scored with precision.

Jonathan immediately noticed the difference in Sherlock's approach and struggled gamely with his limited skills. He had learned much since their first bout with the sapling and the wooden sword. He now realized that Sherlock had never before shown him his full powers. But he was determined not to be intimidated by it, nor hindered by his admiration. He fought back as best he could.

"Your technique is excellent," Andrew told Sherlock as they removed their masks at the end. "If I do come back up I shall be sure to bring my fencing attire. Perhaps I can prove to be a bit more of a challenge than Jonathan here, though he did well for a novice against a very skilled opponent."

Andrew Goble and Sherlock Holmes parted on good terms that day with hopes that they should meet again. Sherlock and Professor Moriarty seemed to have developed a truce. Lessons proceeded the following next week without incident.

Friday morning Sherlock's parents set out in the carriage to attend a weekend party. They would be returning on Monday. Before leaving, his father reminded Sherlock that he was expected to study diligently during their absence. Sherlock watched them leave with a sense of unease. He felt the professor had just been biding his time until they left. But nothing unusual occurred during lessons on Friday.

Saturday afternoon Professor Moriarty returned the calculus assignment that Sherlock had given him the day before. The professor had made notations on it indicating errors.

"Please correct your mistakes and rewrite the assignment on a fresh sheet of paper," the professor said.

Sherlock began to read the paper. He was puzzled. There were errors on it that he did not remember making. There were also errors that made no sense, and errors that he could not believe that he would have made. He examined the paper carefully. He turned it over and looked at the back and held it up to the light.

"There isn't a problem, is there, Master Sherlock?" Professor Moriarty said in his softest tone of voice.

Sherlock looked up at his tutor utterly speechless. This was beyond anything that he had imagined Moriarty was capable of. He held the paper up close and looked again. In various spots throughout the paper 1s had been changed to 7s and 3s to 8s and 4s to 9s and 7s to 9s. Some letters and symbols had also been changed. The modifications were subtle and only visible under close examination.

"You changed my answers!" Sherlock gasped in disbelief.

"Dear me, what is this?" Moriarty said with seeming concern. "Have you forgotten what you wrote? I must admit that I was surprised by the number of errors, much more than I expected. You seem to be doing some backsliding...."

"You forged this!" Sherlock Holmes said waving the paper in growing anger.

"Oh, come now, Master Sherlock, do you think anyone would believe such a thing?" Moriarty said softly with an irritating smile.

Sherlock knew the answer to that question, but he was too angry to care.

"I will not be manipulated this way!" Sherlock said and left the room clutching the forged document in his hand.

Back in his bedroom Sherlock slammed the door and sat down at his desk to stare at the amazing document again. He examined it more closely with his magnifying lens. Under such an examination the forgery was obvious. The two sets of ink marks were laid down at separate times, the ink colors were slightly different, and the style of the new numbers and letters was close, but did not always match his own.

Sherlock rewrote the entire assignment on a new piece of paper making the corrections necessary and then he placed the forged assignment paper in one of the desk drawers.

The clock chimed and he looked up. It was approaching supper time. He rang for a servant and requested that his supper be brought to his room. He was not going to sit across the table from Moriarty tonight. But as he ate his supper and prepared for bed he wondered whether there was anything he could do about it. He doubted that he could ever convince his father to look at the paper carefully enough to see the signs that it had been written over. Even if he did Moriarty would probably just claim that Sherlock himself had done it and that it was a sign of the sloppiness of his work. Sherlock spent a restless night.

Chapter 14
A Night on the Moors

"But Master Sherlock!" cried Tessy.

"I will be gone all day, Tessy," Sherlock said firmly.

"What of thy lessons?"

"I've had enough lessons this week, thank you," Sherlock said.

"But the professor, he'll tell the squire," she cautioned.

"Yes. I suppose he will. I'll deal with that when the time comes. My parents return tomorrow. Until then I refuse to be manipulated by that man," Sherlock said. "I am going shooting on the moors. I will be gone all day."

He took the bundle Tessy had prepared, and left her standing in the kitchen biting her lip. Sherlock rode along the moor road beyond the gill and down a lesser used fork. Then he broke away and headed south where the brush was thick and the game was good. It wasn't long before he had a brace of birds tied to his saddle. Then he decided to sample some of the food Tessy had provided. He chose a thick patch of bracken, and settled down upon their curly leaves. After having eaten some he lay back and watched the sparrows flitting back and forth across the sky.

He thought of Moriarty. Never before had he met a man who seemed so good and simple on the outside, who was so evil and complex down deep. Now they had reached an impasse. One must give way. Sherlock felt ill-equipped to handle Moriarty alone. He might parry his attacks once and again, but he feared that all the while the professor would be planning the coup de maitre. He wondered where it would all lead, as the wind whistled across the moor and the clouds danced on by. In the warmth of the summer sun Sherlock fell asleep. While he slept, he dreamed. In his dream a waterfall roared past him. He was lying on a ledge next to the thundering gorge and felt the spray wet his face. Then there was a flash of light and he sat up awake. The waterfall was gone, but his face was wet with the falling rain and thunder rolled across the moors.

He mounted his horse and rode west across the moor, reaching the hut as the rain grew heavier. He led the reluctant Gale into the hut out of the thunderstorm. Sandy charged in willingly and shook herself dry. Sherlock lit a fire. Soon the hut was warm and toasty despite the soaking rain outside.

Amidst the droning of the rain and the crashing of the thunder Sherlock heard another sound: the pounding of horse's hooves. Sherlock squinted through a crack in the southern wall of the hut. Sherlock could see nothing through the sheets of rain, but he could feel the rhythmic pounding as the horse and rider grew nearer. Then there above the bridge, was that some motion he saw -- a blur of grey and brown? Before he could be certain, lightning struck the moor. In the glaring light he saw the horse rear up, and the rider fall. He knew that grey cloak and that white faced mare! Violet! He ran from the hut and through the brush to where the crumpled figure lay. She lay face down in the bracken.

"Violet?" he said as he knelt beside her.

There was a low moan. He rolled her over. The pouring rain had soaked her cloak and now streamed through her hair. Her eyes flickered open as he lifted her. Inside the hut, he removed her cloak.

"I'm alright," she said.

"Are you sure? You took a bad fall," Sherlock said

"Twas the lightning; Muffin's easily vexed," Violet said.

Sherlock heard barking outside and suddenly realized that Sandy was gone.

"Where is Muffin? She has the herbs," Violet cried.

"I think Muffin is just outside," Sherlock said as Sandy ran in tugging at the horse's lead.

Despite Sandy's urging, the horse refused to enter the

subterranean dwelling. Sherlock removed his coat and used it to cover the horse's eyes. Then he led Muffin to stand next to his own horse.

Sherlock returned to Violet, who sat shivering on the heather bed.

"But my herbs!" Violet protested. "They will spoil! Twas such a nice crop of savory."

"First we must attend to you. Your clothes are soaked and you will catch your death if you keep them on. Take them off and I will set them by the fire to dry. There are some blankets to wrap yourself in. While you are doing that I shall spread your herbs out to dry."

Then he turned to her horse and untied the bundles from its back. Inside were delicate green plants which he spread out by the fire pit. When he had finished that Violet pushed a pile of clothes towards him and he laid them out around the fire as well. When he turned towards Violet again she sat back against the stone wall behind the heather mat with the blankets wrapped carefully about her. He smiled. He sat down on the stool near the fire pit.

"So what were you doing out in the storm?" he asked.

"I'd gone t' pick herbs by the ol' abbey. Tis no shelter there so when I saw the storm coming up I headed home," Violet said. "Tis a nice little cave here."

"Oh, yes, I've used it before when caught by a storm on the moors," Sherlock said.

Sherlock told her stories of his adventures with his brothers in the hut. Her laughter filled the hut as they passed the time. But the thunder boomed across the moor and the rains still fell as sunset approached.

"Hungry?" he asked, and tossed her the remains of the food Tessy had given him. "That should keep you for a little while until supper is ready." He held up the birds he'd shot earlier.

"Mun I dress for supper?" she asked.

"No, my lady-of-the-lake, your supper shall come to your chamber," Sherlock said with a laugh.

Then he dressed and roasted the birds. When they were done, he offered one to Violet.

"Not as exquisite as Tessy's cooking, but edible nonetheless," he said.

Violet took hers and Sherlock sat down on the stool to eat the other.

It was growing dark outside, but still the rain fell.

"Won't thy family miss thee?" Violet asked.

"They might if they were home," he shrugged. "But my parents won't return until tomorrow. I don't know when my brother and his wife will be back. I'm glad of an excuse not to go home. What of your father?"

"If he should miss me at least the storm will keep him in," she said.

"You'll have to stay until your clothes dry," he said. "Perhaps you should rest. You took a bad tumble."

Violet argued that she was fine, but at last she had to concede that there was nothing else she could do and she curled up on the heather bed. Sherlock watched her for a while. Then he spread out his coat upon the floor between the horses and the fire and fell asleep himself.

Sherlock awoke when something nudged his foot. Gale shook her head and snorted. Muffin kicked at the dirt. Sherlock sat up. The pounding of the rain had stopped. Gale looked towards the door and whinnied.

"Sh, girl, be quiet," he said as he got to his feet. He took the horses outside and looped their reins about a bush.

The night air was crisp and cool. The stars winked and flirted overhead. Sherlock returned to the hut. The air inside was warm and heavy with the scent of the herbs lying near the fire pit. Little was left of the fire. The few remaining embers lit the room with a dull red glow. When those embers died it would grow much cooler.

Sherlock looked across to where Violet lay sleeping. A few locks of her hair had tumbled down over her face and the blanket had fallen off her shoulders exposing part of her back. Sherlock walked over and knelt beside her. He watched her shoulders rise and fall as she slept. Her hair lay in black silky curls against the white skin of her back. Gently he pulled the corner of the blanket up over her shoulder. As he lay it down his hand brushed against her arm. Her skin was soft and warm to his touch. She stirred! Her hand pulled the blanket close as she turned to blink at him. He opened his mouth as if to speak but knew not what to say. It was as if he'd never seen her before. Had her eyes always been such a rich warm brown; her cheeks so smooth and her lips so inviting?

He brushed the hair back from her face and kissed her. Her lips were warm and their heat seemed to fill him. He felt the sweat roll down his back. He ran his fingers across her cheek, through her hair, then down her slender neck. She smiled and his head swam. He kissed her again and again and again....

In the morning the sunlight was trying to force its way through the cracks and crevices in the walls of the old stone hut. Sherlock lay upon the heather mat in a dreamy afterglow as consciousness stole upon him. Slowly, he opened his eyes to behold the bonny lass beside him. Violet lay upon the mat as well, her face away from him towards the wall. Her shoulders rose and fell in the even rhythm of sleep. He gently caressed the locks of her hair which lay before his face, but he did not wish to wake her. He dressed quickly and slipped out of the hut.

The sun sat triumphantly upon the eastern horizon presiding over a royal blue sky. The dale, Sherlock thought, must still be in shadow. But the distant crowing of cocks foretold the day's arrival there as well. Sherlock splashed the icy water of the gill upon his face, but its chill could not chase away the warm sweet glow which hung about him.

Such things happened, he had heard. "Proper" people pretended they didn't, then whispered scandalously of some gent's romp in the hay with a milk maid. But it had never happened to him before. He basked in the sweet foggy remembrance. Yet there grew up slowly in that fog a flicker of doubt.

Sherlock did not care what others might think (and who would know?) but how would SHE feel about it? Would she feel that he, the youngest son of the squire, had merely taken advantage of her? Would she think, perhaps, that all his attention previously had merely been a plot towards this end? He sighed. The doubt consumed the fog greedily. He leaned against the stone that formed the back of the hut and carved at a stick with his knife, as if he could carve away the doubts troubling him.

He heard a sound inside the hut. He didn't know what to do. He whittled at the stick. He certainly had not planned it. He had been overcome by a tidal wave and had gone down with the undertow. She had seemed willing enough at the time, hadn't she?

Sherrinford, who was much less mentally adept, often equated Sherlock's little feats of observation and deduction with mind reading. 'Would that it were so!' Sherlock thought, 'to read her mind now!' Did she know how much he loved her?

But he heard her step. She walked slowly as if looking around. She stopped. He stood up and faced her. He didn't know what to say.

"Violet--" he began.

Then she smiled, and he knew his fears were fancy. She walked towards him. He wrapped his arms around her and hugged her tight.

"Violet, I love you."

"I love thee, too, Sherlock."

And they held each other close as the sun climbed into the clear blue sky.

Chapter 15
Return to the Hall

Sherlock returned to the manor house shortly after dawn reached the dale. He ate breakfast in the kitchen with Tessy.

"The professor was asking about thee yesterday," Tessy said.

"And what was he told?" Sherlock asked.

"That thou'st gone riding," she replied.

"Which is correct," Sherlock said.

"Not trying to tell thee thy business, just letting thee know what I hear," Tessy said.

"Thank you, Tessy," Sherlock said.

Back in his room Sherlock decided to take another look at the forged assignment paper. He opened the drawer. It was gone. The paper was gone. He looked behind the desk, in the other drawers and under the bed. It was nowhere to be found. Someone had stolen it from his room and he had no doubt who that someone was.

Sherlock's parents returned home about midday. An hour later Sherlock was summoned to his father's study. The squire looked grim as Sherlock sat down.

"Professor Moriarty tells me that you abandoned your lesson before you were dismissed on Saturday and failed to come at all the following day," his father began. "In fact, the servants tell me that you were gone from the house all day yesterday and even last night."

"Yes, sir," Sherlock said.

"You do not deny it?"

"No, sir," Sherlock responded.

"Where were you last night?" his father asked.

"I was in the stone hut upon the moors. It began raining while I was shooting grouse and I did not think I should ride back in the rain," Sherlock explained.

"That was wise, given your history," his father said. "I believe it is the only intelligent thing that you have done all summer. But you should not have been up on the moors to begin with. Why weren't you at your studies as you should have been?"

As Sherlock was about to respond to this, there was a knock at the door of the study.

"Come in," the squire called.

Sherrinford entered.

"Excuse me, Father, but there is something I want to speak to you and Sherlock about," he said.

"Ah, I had not known you were back yet from London," the squire said.

"Amanda and I just arrived, sir," Sherrinford said taking a seat.

"What is it that you wished to speak to us about?" the squire asked.

"The Lammas Day Fair is coming up in a few weeks and Amanda would like to go to York with me," Sherrinford said. "However, as you know, much of my time will be taken up by hiring the harvest crews and dealing with the grain and wool merchants. If you would allow Sherlock to come with us, then he could escort Amanda while I am engaged."

The squire tapped his fingers on the desk for a moment.

"I suppose that we should get some use out of him," Siger Holmes said, much to Sherrinford's puzzlement. Then the squire turned to Sherlock and waved his finger at him.

"You are to understand that this is an assignment for you and not a holiday," the squire warned his youngest son. "You are to study hard until then and there are to be no more rebellious acts from you. Any further misbehavior will be punished severely."

"Yes, sir," Sherlock said.

"Sherrinford, I expect you to report to me any unusual behaviour by your brother," the squire told his eldest son.

"Yes, sir," Sherrinford said.

"Sherlock, you are dismissed. Go and meet the professor for your lessons."

"Yes, sir," Sherlock said.

"Anything further, Sherrinford?" his father asked.

"No, sir. Thank you, sir," Sherrinford responded.

The two brothers left the squire's study together. In the front hall Sherrinford grabbed Sherlock's arm and stopped him.

"What was that about?" Sherrinford asked.

"I'll tell you later, but I have to join Professor Moriarty for my lessons or I shall be in even more trouble," Sherlock told him.

That evening after supper, Sherrinford found Sherlock in his room. Sherrinford closed the door behind him and sat down.

"Now explain to me what kind of trouble you are in," Sherrinford said.

"It is Professor Moriarty," Sherlock said.

"What about him? I admit that I haven't been paying much attention to him, but he seems like a decent enough sort, soft-spoken and polite," Sherrinford said.

"On the surface, yes," Sherlock responded, "but it is a facade he uses to manipulate people."

"To what end?" Sherrinford asked.

"I wish I knew. Sometimes I think he does it merely for the pleasure of proving he can. I'm not sure he has any mind to the consequences to those he manipulates. It's all a game to him and winning is all that matters," Sherlock speculated.

"You are painting a rather black picture of your tutor's character," Sherrinford said. "But that is not helping me understand why Father is upset with you."

"Moriarty and I have been fighting," Sherlock said. "He keeps increasing my work trying to make it impossible for me to keep up. Then he complains to Father that I am not being diligent enough. I'm no longer allowed to fence or shoot grouse or do anything else."

"Granted, he's a hard master, but--" Sherrinford began.

"While everyone else was gone he has kept me at work from dawn to dusk right through meals even," Sherlock interrupted.

"Well...."

"He seems to take great pleasure in any mistakes I make and if I do an assignment perfectly, he has started forging errors on my work," Sherlock went on.

"Sherlock!" Sherrinford exclaimed. "You told this to Father?"

"No," Sherlock said. "We had not reached the subject before you came in. But two days ago I walked out on my lessons because of it and I spent all day yesterday on the moors."

Sherrinford whistled.

"Now I understand Father's comments," Sherrinford said. "Rebellious, indeed! What did you hope to accomplish by this?"

"I had no plan," Sherlock said. "I just wasn't going to tolerate it."

"Why would he forge your work?" Sherrinford asked.

"To see how I would react," Sherlock said. "To see if I would just accept it submissively, or perhaps to watch me squirm if I tried to explain it to Father. While I was gone yesterday he stole the paper from my room to make it even more difficult to explain. He knows that Father will not believe me. He sensed early on that Father's faith in me was a tenuous thing."

"Oh, come now, Father has always tried to do his best by you," Sherrinford said.

"He has always felt I was a disappointment," Sherlock said. "Moriarty has done his best to widen that rift whenever he can."

"Why would he do that?" Sherrinford asked.

"Because he knows I see through his facade," Sherlock said. "He knows that I know he is not the man people think he is. If he can discredit me then whatever I may say about it is futile."

"I still don't understand why he would care what you think or

110

why he would be playing these games," Sherrinford said. "How would it benefit him?"

"I think he enjoys the power of manipulating people," Sherlock said, "of bending them to his will whether consciously or unconsciously. If he cannot sweet-talk me into liking him, then he intends to do whatever he can to make my life difficult."

Sherrinford shook his head.

"You don't believe me either," Sherlock said.

"I'm not saying that," Sherrinford responded. "I've been too distracted with my own life to pay him much mind. But if what you say is true, then you might be better off swallowing your pride and just playing along with his games for a few months until you are accepted to the university."

"That is a fine enough plan," Sherlock said. "But I have no idea how far he will take this or how miserable he will make my life until then."

"Well, do your best to stay on Father's good side. You know that he gives me fairly free reign in running the estate, but my powers of persuasion regarding your future are rather limited. But I should let you get back to your studies. At least you will have a few days away from Moriarty while we are in York," Sherrinford said standing up and patting his brother on the shoulder before leaving.

The trip to the fair also meant that Sherlock had to spend some additional time away from his lessons as his Mother checked his wardrobe. No matter how casually they might dress on the estate, the squire's sons must be properly attired in the city.

"Susan, we will need to take those two seams down another half inch. But the rest looks presentable. You grow taller and taller, Sherlock. Soon we shall have to take you down to London for a new wardrobe," Sherlock's mother said. "Here, try on your hat. That looks fine. Now change back to your other things and return to your lessons."

Chapter 16
Lammas Day Fair

A bright August sun presided over a court of fluffy white clouds as the carriage rolled along dusty roads towards the city of York. The road wound southward through the dale and then down other valleys beyond the moors until it reached the River Ouse and followed it south to York.

York was an ancient city. Eighteen centuries before the Romans had built a garrison at the juncture of the Ouse and Foss rivers to defend the northern reaches of their empire. They called the fort Eboracum. A civilian city grew up beside garrison and it rose to be a great river trading center called Eoferwic by the Anglo Saxons and Jorvik by the Vikings. The city of York had survived many political upheavals over the centuries including William the Conqueror's harsh repression of rebellion in the north in 1069, and a siege by Parliamentarians in 1644. York was still surrounded by the stone fortifications built in more turbulent times and travelers to the city had to pass through massive gates called 'bars' to enter the city walls.

As the group from Mycroft Manor approached Bootham Bar at the northern entrance to York, they could see York Minster towering over the city to the east. As the carriage waited its turn to pass through the Bar the bells of the cathedral pealed the quarter hour.

"Oh, the bells are lovely!" Amanda said.

"Yes," Sherrinford agreed, "though I've found sleeping near the Minster to be somewhat troublesome."

Once through Bootham Bar the carriage rolled down the cobbled street called Petergate past the west end of the Minster. The spiked towers and stained glass windows of the cathedral loomed high above them.

"The five narrow windows that you can see above are called the 'five sisters,'" Sherrinford pointed out.

Shortly the carriage turned on Stonegate. This was an old Roman street covered with cut blocks of stone rather than round cobbles. Stonegate was lined with shops built of stone and brick which were gaily decorated for the fair. Near the end of the street the carriage pulled up before an inn.

"Here we are," Sherrinford said as the carriage stopped.

The footman opened the door to the carriage. Sherrinford descended and helped his wife down.

"We will rest up a bit here, and remove some of the dust of the road before proceeding down to the fair," Sherrinford said.

After a light lunch the party boarded the carriage again for the drive across York to the fairgrounds. Traffic on the streets was heavy due to the fair, but that afforded them plenty of time to view the old city. Sherrinford pointed out some features as they drove.

"Ah, perhaps we can visit Knavesmire," Sherlock suggested.

"I think not," Sherrinford said. "Amanda, you must forgive my brother. He has strange tastes in literature. He actually enjoys reading the Newgate Calendar."

"You two have me very confused," Amanda said. "My brother Roger said that Knavesmire was where the race track is."

"Yes, it is," Sherrinford said. "But that's not why Sherlock is interested in it."

"It is where they hanged Dick Turpin, the notorious highwayman," Sherlock explained.

"Oh," Amanda said.

"But the gallows are not there now," Sherrinford said.

"No, they moved the gallows inside the York Castle walls decades ago," Sherlock said.

"Which we have already passed," Sherrinford pointed out. "You had best behave, Sherlock. Remember I'm under an injunction to report any 'unusual behaviour' on your part to Father, though I am not sure how to define 'unusual behaviour' in your case. Ah, this is Fishergate Bar now. We will be there shortly."

Fishergate Bar, which provided passage through the city walls to the southeast, was smaller and less impressive that Bootham Bar to the north. It was hardly more than an archway over the road. A bottleneck of carriages had formed here as well.

"Fishergate Bar was burned in 1489 and was walled up for centuries. When they built the Cattle Market south of here they decided that they needed access again and reopened it," Sherrinford told them.

"Sherrinford's Guide to York," Sherlock teased.

"You do seem to know a lot about the city, dear. Do you come here often?" Amanda asked.

"Sherrinford," Sherlock began before Sherrinford could answer, "being that great man of commerce, travels frequently to York, Leeds, and Manchester, sometimes even as far as London, while us mere rustics--"

"Travel about the Continent," Sherrinford finished.

"Well, yes," Sherlock admitted and the brothers laughed at each other.

"Do you two always tease each other so?" Amanda asked.

"Yes," they answered simultaneously.

Beyond the Fishergate Bar was the Cattle Market where the Lammas Day Fair was held. At the northern end of the Cattle Market there were carriages, wagons, and carts of every size and description. Some were discharging passengers and some were unloading animals. Cattle, sheep and pigs were being herded into stalls and corrals. Hay wagons and carts filled with barrels of water were bringing in supplies for the livestock. The air was ripe with the smells of fresh manure, hay and sweat. Men in worn tweed suits were talking earnestly with men in fine morning coats and top hats. Pedlars of bailing wire and plows were competed for the attention of the men who had come to sell their grain, wool, and livestock. This is where Sherrinford would be conducting his business.

Further south across the Cattle Market, they could see tents, stages, and booths adorned with brightly colored flags and ribbons. Music could be heard mingled in the hubbub of the crowd and the sounds of animals. The carriage pulled down near this area.

"Here is the entrance to the fair," Sherrinford announced as carriage stopped.

He descended and helped his wife down. Before leaving them Sherrinford drew Sherlock aside and handed him a purse of silver.

"There is no sense going to a fair without some silver in your pocket. Amanda has her pin money, but there is quite a bit more in here. Feel free to spend some on yourself, but make sure you indulge that pretty wife of mine."

"You enjoy being married, don't you?" Sherlock said.

"Very much so," Sherrinford replied with a grin.

"Thank you for this," Sherlock said indicating the money.

"Take good care of Amanda. Be especially watchful for pickpockets and other blackguards. Fairs are full of them," Sherrinford warned.

"I will be most diligent," Sherlock assured him.

Sherlock knew that this was why his brother had wanted him along and why his father had permitted it. He was as much a bodyguard as an escort.

"Well, I must be off," Sherrinford said. "There is work to be done. This year looks to be better than last, but I have much dealing to do. Behave yourself."

Sherlock returned to where Amanda and her maid were standing and offered his arm to Amanda.

"Will you accompany me to the fair, m'lady?" Sherlock asked.

"I would be most happy to, kind sir," Amanda responded wrapping her arm around his.

Sherlock and Amanda entered the fairgrounds with her maid following behind. They were immediately surrounded by gaily colored booths where merchants of all kinds had set out their goods to best advantage. Some merchants cried out, hawking their wares and inciting customers, adding to the general noise level. The fair was crowded with all types of people from all stations of life. Tradesmen, labourers, farmers, and gentlemen were all moving in close proximity.

Amanda was wearing a dress of apricot and white striped muslin with a matching hat and ruffled parasol. Her hair was pulled back from her face, tucked under her hat and then cascaded in ringlets down her neck. With her pleasant smile and beautiful blue eyes, she was an outstanding beauty in any crowd. Many a wandering eye turned away with disappointment when they spied Sherlock in his morning coat and top hat by her side, even though they could not see the ring on her finger for her gloves. If she had been unattached she would have been chaperoned by her mother or an aunt, not by a young gentleman.

Jugglers, magicians, and musicians wandered through the crowds seeking to entertain them and garner tips. At a few places there were stages where there were puppet shows, short plays, or other entertainment.

As he and Amanda walked about the fair, Sherlock noticed several small children in rags with bare feet who were weaving in and out amongst the crowds. Some merchants chased them off when they spotted them.

Then Amanda and Sherlock came upon a bare spot of ground between booths where a man had set up a small folding table. The man had a pea and three thimbles. He placed the pea under one thimble, rearranged the thimbles a few times, and then challenged the growing crowd to guess which one contained the pea. The game soon progressed from guesses to wagers. One man won a few bets and then lost one and decided to back off. Another man joined in and won a few games and decided to rest on his winnings and watch. The thimblerigger coaxed others into the game. Sherlock was watching the crowd rather than the game. It was a mixed crowd of high and low, tradesmen to toffs. Amanda touched his arm and he looked over at her.

"It seems so easy to spot. It is the one to the left," she said.

Sherlock whispered in her ear, "No, the middle one."

"You are right!" she said.

"Definitely, the left one this time," she asserted.

"No, the right," he said.

She squeezed his arm.

"Correct again," she said. "You should place a wager."

"I'll do better than that," he said, pushing back his top hat and stepping forward as the thimblerigger was inviting new wagers. He was looking for a young, well-dressed mark. Sherlock knew he fit the part. The thimblerigger encouraged him as he came forward. The first few rounds were simple as the pea stayed put and Sherlock won a few shillings. But he knew his role well and showed increased excitement and increased willingness to wager more as he continued to win. Finally he bet a florin, laying it upon the table for all to see. The thimblerigger once more inserted the pea into the thimbles and slid the three thimbles around each other then tapped each one in turn and invited Sherlock to point out the pea. Then Sherlock frowned and looked puzzled.

"It's not there," Sherlock said.

"What?" asked the thimblerigger.

"You see," Sherlock said, slapping his left hand over the florin and picking it up, as his right hand quickly ran across the three thimbles shaking each one before the thimblerigger could intercede, "I can see through those thimbles and there isn't a pea under any one of them."

"What d'you mean it's not there?" the man said.

"Because," said Sherlock, keeping an eye on the man to his left as he held up his right hand with the pea in it, "it is here."

But before the thimblerigger could object, a signal in the crowd caught his eye and he folded the thimblerig table shut with a slam and hurried off. As he disappeared a constable wandered through the disbursing crowd wishing the ladies and gentlemen good day.

Sherlock offered his arm again to Amanda and they walked on through the fair.

"Why did they all run away?" Amanda asked.

"Because the constable was coming. Thimblerig is a cheat. Mycroft taught me the secret when I was quite small. You need to watch the man's fingers, not the thimbles. He slips the pea out of one and places it under another very quickly. I learned the trick myself, you see."

"And very skillfully!" Amanda said with a laugh.

"They were more concerned about the florin. They wanted it. I used that as a distraction. I was really at a disadvantage with the crowd behind and beside me rather than in front. So it was easiest just to take it out altogether. It was a bit risky because one of the shills was to my left and I've heard that they sometimes carry knives."

"Knives! Do you think he might have attacked you?" Amanda asked looking horrified.

"I think it is less likely with this particular crowd," Sherlock said.

"But you took the risk?" she asked.

"Well, I was trying to impress a pretty lady," Sherlock said with a smile. "Besides I spotted the constable ambling through the crowd a long time before they did. His timing was perfect."

"You said one man was a shill. What is a shill?" Amanda asked.

"A certain number of people in the crowd, four, I think this time, are in league with the thimblerigger. They place bets and stir up interest, but they also protect the thimblerigger. It was one of the shills who spotted the constable and alerted the others," Sherlock explained.

"So that's what you were looking for in the crowd, the shills!" she said.

"That is precisely what I was looking for," Sherlock affirmed.

"You are so clever!" Amanda said.

"But please don't mention this to my father. He caught me doing that once when I was younger and was quite angry with me. He claimed I was creating a spectacle, and that a gentleman doesn't create a spectacle," Sherlock said.

"I've noticed that you have a strained relationship with your father," she said.

"Yes, and it's been a bit rougher than usual recently," Sherlock admitted. "But let's not talk about that. You are supposed to be having fun."

Just then they were drawn by the tempting smell of fresh gingerbread and followed it to a baker's stall. Besides the gingerbread the boards were piled high with scones, biscuits, cakes, and baked goods of every description. Amanda held her folded parasol and her bag in her left hand as she leaned forward under the baker's tent to sample the goods. While she tasted a warm piece of gingerbread that the baker's assistant had just given her, a dirty little hand reached up for the strings of her bag. An inch short of its destination the hand stopped in its course as Sherlock's hand wrapped around the tiny wrist and held it firmly. The boy was quite small and Sherlock feared that his next tactic would be to burst into tears and accuse Sherlock of hurting him. Sherlock took the piece of gingerbread that was being offered to him and thrust it in the child's free hand.

"I suspect you would make faster work of this than I,"

Sherlock said to the child.

The dirty ragamuffin grabbed the cake and immediately bit into it, fearing that it would be snatched away again. Tears forestalled, Sherlock hunkered down to the boy's level and spoke into his ear in a low voice.

"I've a shilling each for you and your two friends who have been following us, if you tell them and the others out there that this lady's off limits," Sherlock told the boy, knowing Amanda couldn't hear what he was saying through the hubbub of the fair.

The child nodded vigorously. Sherlock reached in his pocket and held out his hand with three coins in it and released the child's wrist. The boy immediately snatched up the coins with the newly freed hand and disappeared with cake and coins into the crowd.

"Dirty beggars," the baker said as Sherlock stood up again.

"Sherlock, you are so generous!" Amanda said.

While Amanda had not understood the full import of the incident, she had seen Sherlock give the gingerbread he was now paying for and the three coins to the child.

"Tell that to Sherrinford," Sherlock said with a smile. "They were his shillings!"

Amanda laughed.

"You should know that my brother has given me strict instructions to indulge your every whim and provided me with the silver to do so," Sherlock said as they walked away from the baker's booth.

"That was thoughtful of him," Amanda said. "Ford is a kind and generous man. I am sure he would approve of the shillings as well."

"I have no doubt of it," Sherlock agreed.

"I must remember to thank him for suggesting that you escort me. I am so glad that we have this time to get to know each other!" she said.

"I am very grateful for you rescuing me from my lessons for a few days," Sherlock said. "You are far more charming than Professor Moriarty."

"Sherrinford told me that you were having some difficulty with the professor," Amanda said.

"Oh, I would not want to bore you with my little problems," Sherlock protested.

"We are family now, Sherlock," Amanda insisted. "You must count me as your ally. I do think the professor works you too hard. But then again I've never really had a favorable impression of him."

"No?" Sherlock said with some surprise. "You always seem so attentive to him."

"My mother says that it is the people whom you do not like that you have to work the hardest to be nice to," Amanda explained.

"Ah, perhaps she should write Mrs. Courtney's Book on Etiquette to teach the rest of us that art," Sherlock said.

"She should! She has quite an instinct for those types of things," Amanda agreed.

"But what is it about Professor Moriarty that you don't like?" Sherlock asked.

"I can't really say," Amanda replied thoughtfully. "I just have the impression that underneath he is not really a nice man," Amanda said.

"Interesting," Sherlock said. "We are of like mind on that. But Mycroft and Sherrinford don't see it. You teach me new respect for a woman's impression. I shall remember that!"

Amanda laughed.

Ahead was a jeweler's stall. They stopped and Amanda looked over the wares. She admired some bracelets made like strings of gold roses. She dwelt over them for sometime holding them up against her wrist and smiling, but eventually she passed on. At the other end there were some silver hearts hanging by their chains from the roof of the stall. As Sherlock looked up at them, Amanda laid her hand on his arm.

"Ah, now, Sherlock if you had a ladylove that would be just the thing," she said to him pointing to the hearts.

"Yes?" Sherlock asked.

"Oh, yes," Amanda insisted "As a token of your affection. Have you ever seen the necklace that Sherrinford gave me when we were courting?"

"No," Sherlock replied.

Amanda reached for a chain around her neck and pulled up a gold pendant in the shape of a pair of entwined doves.

"It is beautiful. Yet you keep it hidden?" Sherlock said.

"It is very personal and precious to me. I wear it next to my heart," she said smiling as she tucked it away again.

Sherlock looked up at the hearts again.

"Oh, look at those fabrics!" Amanda said espying another stall. Sherlock followed her as she approached the stall filled with bolts of imported silks and laces. One of the ladies of the booth noticed her quickly and started describing the features of each. Then a man came out of the tent in the back of the stall and saw Amanda.

"Ah, she is the one!" the man said with a foreign accent.

"You are newly wed, are you not?" the man asked Amanda.

"Yes!" Amanda responded with a laugh.

"But this," the said man waving his hand at Sherlock, "he is not your husband, is he?"

"Oh, no, he's my brother-in-law," Amanda explained.

"Just the same we must shoo him away and prepare a surprise for your husband," the man said with a dismissive wave of his hand at Sherlock. "Come, madam, back into the tent here where we have some finished pieces that you must see."

Sherlock started to protest, but Amanda smiled and waved him away as the man and the woman guided Amanda towards the back with her maid following behind her.

"I shan't be far," Sherlock said withdrawing.

Sherlock walked towards the jewelry stall they had been at before, casting an occasional glance at the tent of the clothier's booth. The jeweler approached him as Sherlock looked up at the hearts.

"A surprise for your lady?" the jeweler asked Sherlock.

Sherlock realized that the jeweler may have seen him with Amanda and misunderstood. He did not correct him.

"Yes," Sherlock said.

"Then let me show you something," the jeweler said as he pulled another heart out from below. Unlike the others hanging up it had a name engraved in the front. "You see we can make it very personal. "Like the others, it opens and we can engrave a special message inside as well."

"How long does it take to make one like that?" Sherlock asked.

"My apprentice would work on it back at our shop in Stonegate. He could have it ready by tomorrow morning."

"Could I pick it up at your shop in Stonegate? We are staying at an inn near there."

"Certainly," the jeweler said.

"And the price?" Sherlock asked.

"For you, a special price," the jeweler said and crooked his finger at him. Sherlock leaned closer and the man whispered it in his ear.

"Write down your name, and what you want engraved on the heart," the jeweler said pushing paper and pen towards Sherlock. "I'll dispatch the boy to the shop now and it will be ready by morning."

Sherlock wrote on the paper.

"Could you add one of those bracelets with the gold roses?" Sherlock asked.

"Certainly," the jeweler said. "Here, choose the one that you think she would like best. I will send it along with the boy. You can pay for both when you pick them up."

As he finished with the jeweler Sherlock looked back over at the clothier's booth. There was still no sign of Amanda. As he walked back to it he spied the three ragamuffins in the distance. There were two others with them. All five took off when they saw him looking at them. Then Amanda appeared from within the tent smiling broadly. Her maid was holding a package.

"Ah," said the foreign man, "here is the keeper of the purse!"

"Sherrinford may regret his instructions to you!" Amanda said. "Or maybe not," she said with a grin. "If you could pay the man, Sherlock."

"Certainly," Sherlock said.

He did so and the foreign man retired to the tent with the money. As they left the stall in the distance, Sherlock heard the man's voice say, "Ah, she is the one!" and Sherlock chuckled.

They wandered on until they came upon a puppet show and stopped to watch. As they were leaving after the show ended, a man came running through the crowd pushing and shoving. He was pursued shortly by two others huffing and puffing behind, and shouting "stop!" All eyes turned to see where the first man had gone as the others ran by. Sherlock turned just in time to see one of the following men snatched the package from the hands of Amanda's maid as he ran by. Before Sherlock could react a small child dove in front of the man and two other children grabbed the package as the man fell. As soon as the man was on his feet again, he disappeared into the crowd and left the ragamuffins holding the package.

Sherlock came forward as the first little boy stood up. It was the same boy he had given the gingerbread to. His two friends held up the package.

"Here, sir," one of them said offering the package to Sherlock.

"Are they causing you any trouble?" an authoritative voice

behind Sherlock asked as Sherlock took the package from the children. Sherlock turned to face a constable who had come up behind him.

"No, constable. They were just helping me retrieve this package," Sherlock said turning back to the children.

"Thank you," Sherlock called to the children as they vanished into the crowd themselves.

"Thank you for your concern," Sherlock said to the constable.

"Tis a bit irregular," the constable said. "They're usually doin' the thievin', not the returnin'."

"Well, not this time. Good day," Sherlock said returning to where Amanda and her maid stood.

They continued about the fair enjoying the sights, sounds, and tastes until the women were happily exhausted.

When they rejoined Sherrinford, Amanda said, "I'm glad I had this opportunity to spend time with your brother. He is so charming!"

"Are you trying to steal my wife?" Sherrinford asked in mock sincerity.

"Merely attempting to be an interesting escort," Sherlock said.

"We came upon this game of thimblerig," Amanda began.

Sherrinford looked sharply at Sherlock.

"You didn't!" Sherrinford said.

"I did," Sherlock said with a nod.

Sherrinford scowled.

"He has already warned me not to mention it to your father," Amanda assured him.

"I've done it before so it isn't really 'unusual,'" Sherlock said with a twinkle in his eye.

Sherrinford merely shook his head.

After breakfast the following morning, Sherlock told Sherrinford that he had to go out for a brief errand, but would be back shortly. Sherlock returned in a few minutes with a twinkle in his eye and a bouquet of flowers in his hand. He presented the flowers to Amanda.

"For you," he said with a bow.

"Oh, thank you, Sherlock!" Amanda exclaimed.

"Come, ma'am," Amanda's maid said. "I will put them in your hair for you!"

"Yes, let's do it!" Amanda responded, and the two women retired to Amanda's dressing room.

"Are you up to mischief?" Sherrinford asked Sherlock.

"Are you saying that because I gave your wife flowers?" Sherlock asked looking innocent. "I also picked this up at the jeweler's shop down the road." Sherlock said holding out his hand with the rose bracelet in it. "She was admiring it at their fair booth. I thought you could give it to her later."

"Clever boy!" Sherrinford exclaimed taking the bracelet and tucking it away in his pocket. "I think I shall retain you as a brother."

"I am glad to know that my contract has been renewed," Sherlock said with a laugh. "Ah, here she comes. Let's see if Amanda is ready to return to the fair."

Chapter 17
A Reprieve

It had been good to relax for a few days at the fair, but it made it all the more difficult for Sherlock to resume his role as submissive student. It had reminded him that there were far more interesting ways to be spending his time than enduring his lessons with the professor. But he did his best to keep up with Moriarty's demands while he tried to find a way to see Violet again. Moriarty was keeping him busy for long hours and his only breaks were for sleeping and meals. While the squire would allow Moriarty to work him through tea, they both were expected to attend supper with the family and whatever guests may be in attendance.

Sherlock often found it difficult to enjoy any dinner conversation with Moriarty across the table from him. But this day he had developed a headache during his lesson that had persisted through supper time. Sherlock poked at his food with his fork, but ate little.

"Sherlock, you are looking a bit pale. Are you feeling all right?" his mother asked.

"Just a bit of a headache. Nothing serious, I'm sure," Sherlock responded.

"The poor boy is studying constantly. That can't be healthy," Amanda said, not looking at Professor Moriarty.

"Give me your hand, dear," Sherlock's mother said.

"Ah, it does feel a bit warm. You should go to bed right after supper," his mother said.

"Father," Sherlock said, "May I speak to you first?"

"Yes, certainly," the squire said.

After Sherlock had retired to his room, the squire sent for Sherrinford to join him in the study.

"Do you know this boy that Sherlock was fencing with?" the

squire asked.

"Yes, sir, Jonathan Beckwith," Sherrinford replied

"Matthias Beckwith's son?" the squire asked.

"Yes, sir. Matthias' widow still lives in one of the cottages. Her daughter, Pearl, is one of our milk maids," Sherrinford said.

"The family has a long history with the estate?" his father asked.

"Yes, sir, as you know, Matthias and his father worked for your father," Sherrinford said.

"You have seen them fencing?" the squire asked.

"Yes, Father," Sherrinford said.

"Sherlock wishes an hour per week off of his studies to fence with this boy, for health reasons he says. There is some logic in that. He did well when he was fencing and boxing regularly," Siger Holmes said.

"Do you want my opinion?" Sherrinford asked.

"Yes."

"I think the fencing would be good for Sherlock," Sherrinford said. "He has always been more athletic than Mycroft or I. As you know, Mycroft could survive in one spot for months at a time. I think Sherlock needs more activity. While he did not really seem ill at supper, he certainly is not looking as healthy as he did a month ago. Surely his tutor could spare him an hour a week."

"It is hard to imagine how one hour a week could significantly impact his studies," Siger said thoughtfully. "I will consider the matter further."

A few minutes later Sherrinford entered Sherlock's room at his invitation. Sherlock was lying in bed.

"Was that feigned?" Sherrinford asked.

"I do have a headache. I never claimed anything else," Sherlock responded.

"But I did see your hand under the plate," Sherrinford said.

"Well, yes, when the opportunity arose I took advantage of

it. If Mother had checked further she would have found no fever. But now perhaps I can get a good night's sleep without having to work through the headache. You know Moriarty would never have let me out of doing my lessons," Sherlock said.

"I'm not exactly sure what you said to Father in there, but you seem to have won some points. I think he is seriously considering overruling the professor on this issue," Sherrinford said.

"Moriarty will never be overruled. He will make it seem like it was his idea," Sherlock said.

"Regardless, it's the first time that Father has ever ask my opinion of anything regarding you," Sherrinford said.

"Indeed? Was Moriarty there?" Sherlock asked.

"No. He was not," Sherrinford replied.

"Well, this could be interesting. It would be good to be able to fence again. Right now I shall just be grateful for some sleep," Sherlock said.

"Goodnight," Sherrinford said before closing the door behind him.

The following evening there was a knock at Sherlock's door. At Sherlock's invitation it opened to reveal Dr. Thompkins.

"Doctor, what can I do for you?" Sherlock asked.

"Your parents asked me to take a look at you," the doctor said. "Any complaints?"

"Only that I have too much studying to do," Sherlock said.

"Ah, a common complaint of young men!" replied Dr. Thompkins.

"And none of it seems relevant to the world I live in," Sherlock said.

"Another common complaint," the doctor said. "I think part of it is an attempt to pass down the "wisdom of the ages" to the next generation, but I also think that older men force younger men to study some things merely because it was forced on them -- sort of a rite of passage. However, I have not yet heard of anyone dying from too much Plato."

Sherlock laughed.

"You don't look ill," Dr. Thompkins said.

"I had a headache yesterday evening. That was all," Sherlock said.

"Probably from too much study," the doctor said with a smile.

"I would agree with that," Sherlock said.

"But you don't look as healthy as you did four months ago. Have you been getting any exercise at all?" Dr. Thompkins asked.

"No," Sherlock replied. "I study every day, nearly all day. This tutor insists upon it. I'm not allowed to fence or ride my horse. I was released from my studies for two days to escort my sister-in-law at the Lammas Day Fair, but that has been all."

"Here, let me listen to your lungs," the doctor said taking out his stethoscope.

"Well," Dr. Thompkins said. "I do think it would be better if you were getting some exercise. Your lungs are clear now, but I think you need some activity to make sure they stay that way through the winter."

"I have asked that I be allowed to fence for an hour once a week for that very purpose," Sherlock said.

"I shall tell your father that I think it is a good idea," Dr. Thompkins said as he put away the stethoscope.

"Thank you," Sherlock said.

"Take care, Sherlock, and don't let the studying weigh you down," the doctor said as he left the room.

The following afternoon after he concluded his lessons for the day, Professor Moriarty addressed the matter.

"The squire and I have reviewed your past medical history, which I had been unaware of previously, and we have concluded that perhaps an hour of fencing practice per week would be beneficial. I will be releasing you earlier each Saturday so that you may fence for an hour before tea time."

"Thank you," Sherlock said and gathered up his books and papers.

As Sherlock was passing out through the door, Professor Moriarty said softly, "That was cleverly done."

Sherlock turned back towards the professor.

"Excuse me, sir?" Sherlock said.

"Oh, just talking to myself about this lesson you handed in," Professor Moriarty said. "It is well done."

But their grey eyes met and both knew there was more being said than the words on the surface.

"We will see if you can do as well in the future," Moriarty said.

"I will do my best," Sherlock responded and turned and left the room.

Sherlock stopped in the kitchen before heading to his own room.

"Tessy, do you know Jonathan Beckwith?" Sherlock asked.

"Aye, the lad thou wert teaching with the swords," the cook said.

"Yes. He has a sister named Pearl who is a milk maid here," Sherlock said.

"Aye, I know her well. Threatens to talk my head off each day when she comes by. Never knew onnyone who loved to blather about things she knew nowt so much as that girl."

"Does she come by every day?" Sherlock asked.

"Twice most days. She should be by shortly," Tessy said.

"Good. Could you give her a message to take to her brother?" Sherlock asked.

"Aye, but best make it simple. She's a great one for mixing up details and my memory's not too long these days."

"Just have her tell Jonathan that I wish to speak to him this evening if he could meet me by the back door after supper."

"Aye, tis simple enough."

Sherlock found Jonathan waiting for him near the back door

after supper. He told Jonathan of the new fencing schedule and Jonathan was thrilled to be able to have more lessons.

"You need to be here early so we can get started on time, and there is something else. I want you to talk to Violet and ask her to come and wait behind the shed. What we will do it this...," Sherlock said and explained his plan to Jonathan.

The following Saturday at the appointed time, Sherlock and Jonathan were preparing to fence in the yard behind the manor house.

"Is she there?" Sherlock asked as he handed Jonathan his mask.

"Yes," Jonathan said.

"You know what to do?" Sherlock asked.

"Yes," Jonathan said.

"Then let's make a good show of it," Sherlock said as he saluted his younger opponent.

They started out practicing the garde positions and reviewing previous lessons. Then rather than Sherlock teaching Jonathan a new technique, they saluted each other again and began to bout in earnest. Eventually Sherlock backed Jonathan towards the shadows between the shed and another outbuilding, and they both disappeared for a moment though the clash and slither of the epees could still be heard. Jonathan reappeared on the edge of the shadow swinging his epee and kept appearing and disappearing from view.

In the shadows between the two buildings Sherlock had stopped, rammed the hilt of his epee in a knot hole in the shadows where Jonathan continued to attack it. Jonathan had spoken truthfully. Violet stood waiting in the shadows. Sherlock took off his mask and dropped it to the ground. He took both of Violet's hands in his and kissed them.

"Thank you for coming. I have missed you," he said.

"I've missed thee, too, Sherlock," Violet replied.

"I'm nearly a prisoner here," Sherlock said.

"Most folks think them that live at the Hall can do as they please," Violet said.

"I must bend to my father's will until I can make my own way in the world and that seems to mean satisfying this tutor," he told her.

"Is thy tutor is such a monster?" Violet asked.

"Just a moment," Sherlock said, grabbing up his mask and epee again and actively attacking Jonathan. Sherlock forced Jonathan out into the yard again. Jonathan scored against Sherlock and they stopped for a moment to rest. When they began again, their bout once more led them into the shadows.

"Sorry, but I have to assume that someone is watching even if they are not," Sherlock said to Violet as he rejoined her.

"Thy tutor?" she asked.

"Perhaps. But let's not talk of him. Let me look at you," he said. He cupped his hands around her jaw and looked into her dark eyes.

"You are beautiful," he said and then he kissed her.

"I bought you something at the Lammas Day Fair in York," he said digging a small leather pouch out of his pocket. "I was sent there to escort my sister-in-law, Amanda, which is a pleasant enough duty, but I was especially pleased because it gave me the opportunity to have this made."

He handed it to her.

"Open it," Sherlock urged.

Violet loosened the string on the pouch and reached inside. She pulled out a chain on which hung silver heart. The heart had "Violet" written in script on the front surrounded by scroll work.

"Oh, tis lovely!" Violet exclaimed.

"If you press here on the clasp, it opens," Sherlock said, demonstrating. The front and the back of the heart swung apart on a hinge revealing a hollow middle that bore an engraving reading, "Love, Sherlock."

She looked up at him smiling.

"Here, let me put it around your neck," Sherlock said closing the heart again and fastening it around her neck.

"I'll wear it always," she said as he finished and they kissed again.

"Sherlock?" Jonathan said.

"I have to go," Sherlock said picking up his mask again. "I will send word through Jonathan when we can meet again."

"I'll be dreaming of it," Violet said smiling with one hand over the locket.

Sherlock came back to her again and grabbed one last kiss before donning his mask.

"Goodbye," he said.

Then Sherlock and Jonathan fenced back out into the open. Jonathan scored again.

"You have done well today," Sherlock said, as they were taking off their jackets. "Have you been practicing on your own?"

"I don't believe it is my doing, sir," Jonathan said.

"What do you mean?" Sherlock asked.

"Begging your pardon," Jonathan said, "But I think you were a bit distracted."

Sherlock smiled.

"Yes, yes, I was," he said.

Sherlock and Professor Moriarty resumed their charade. Having won permission to fence again and having determined a way to use that to see Violet, Sherlock did not want to cause any disturbance that would threaten those opportunities. Moriarty observed his student more carefully. He was not fond of being outmaneuvered.

Sherlock met with Jonathan again the following Saturday to fence and again Violet waited in the shadows. This time Moriarty was watching from the classroom window with the curtains partially drawn. He saw Sherlock vanish into the shadows several times. The professor wondered what the boy was up to.

Chapter 18
A Vanishing Guest

Holmes Hall frequently entertained guests. They might be friends or relatives of the family from near or far, or they might be men of science that the squire had corresponded with.

In late August a pair of men came who interested Sherlock very much. One was a French spelunker, Pierre Varappeur, whom the squire had met on the Continent. M. Varappeur was currently on his way to Edinbrough to give a series of lectures. The other man was an English zoologist, Edgar Hastings, with whom the squire had corresponded for several years, but had never met before. The invitation to Hastings to pay a visit had been a long standing one, and the squire was glad of its final acceptance. Their coming had provided Sherlock some relief from his studies for his mother desired that he and Amanda perform a duet for these guests. This required some time for practice for Sherlock had never played with his sister-in-law before.

"I would ask Sherrinford to do it but he really has never taken to the violin," Sherlock's mother said.

Sherrinford agreed. He hated the thing.

Sherlock fell in with his mother's plan, provided she could convince his tutor to allow him the time to practice.

"I don't dare ask," Sherlock said.

So the ladies appealed directly to the professor for a few hours of Sherlock's time. Professor Moriarty showed some hesitation, but agreed in the end.

"I can never deny the request of a beautiful woman," Moriarty said with his smiling face rocking from side to side. "And when faced by two," he continued, looking from Mrs. Holmes to Amanda and back, "I am hopelessly lost."

The performance was held shortly after supper and everyone

was pleased. Thereafter the women withdrew, but Sherlock was allowed to remain for the squire felt that the conversation of educated men might benefit him.

The conversation over brandy and cigars was quite lively. Varappeur's descriptions of the underground caverns of France were fascinating. Professor Hastings was less bubbly than the Frenchman, but as well learned and as devoted to his field of endeavor. While his descriptions of the fauna of the Amazon were no less thrilling than the Varappeur's tales, Hastings was less effuse and the other stole the limelight. But it was not so much the Hastings's field of study or his conversational skills that drew Sherlock's interest, as his words to Professor Moriarty.

When Professor Hastings was first introduced to Moriarty, the man responded, "Professor James Moriarty of Westgate University?"

"I am no longer associated with that university," Professor Moriarty replied.

"But you were, were you not?" Professor Hastings asked.

"Yes, sir," Professor Moriarty responded, but the conversation quickly moved elsewhere.

Sherlock could not make much of this, but after supper the conversation once again meandered in the direct of Professor Moriarty's past career.

"Are you currently affiliated with some other university?" Professor Hastings inquired of Moriarty.

"Not currently, though I have been considering such a position," Professor Moriarty responded.

"But you have definitely severed your relationship with Westgate?" Hastings asked.

"I resigned my position at Westgate because my talents were not appreciated," said Professor Moriarty, much like a parent instructing a rather slow child for the fifth time. "Jealousy spawned childish accusations. I felt it unnecessary to put up with such nonsense."

"Something about a publication, wasn't it?" Hastings asked.

Professor Moriarty looked sharply at the man for an instant, his head gyrating from side to side. Then he smiled and waved his hand. "We don't want to waste our evening with such unpleasant topics, do we? Tell me, where do you plan to take this next expedition that you mentioned?" Moriarty said, deftly rechanneling the conversation.

Sherlock feigned disinterest, but inside he was vibrating with excitement like a hound who has finally found a scent. Here at last was proof! Sherlock knew he must speak to Hastings and hear what more he knew of Professor Moriarty's academic career. He paid little attention as Hastings commandeered a globe in the room and used it to demonstrate his expedition plans to Moriarty, Varappeur, and the squire.

"Does your family mind your long absences?" Moriarty asked.

"Ah," Hastings said, "that is for me an unpleasant topic. We are somewhat estranged."

"That is most unfortunate," Moriarty agreed.

Sherlock found no opportunity that evening to speak to Hastings alone. He spent a restless night. He lay awake, far too excited to sleep, staring at the dim inverted shadows cast upon the ceiling by the fire, contemplating how best to approach the man.

But in the morning all such plans were shattered when the zoologist did not appear for breakfast. The butler presented the squire with a note from Professor Hastings giving his regrets and saying he was called away suddenly.

"Did some message arrive for him late last night?" the squire inquired.

"No, sir," Thomas said.

"When did he leave?" Squire Holmes asked.

"I do not know, sir," Thomas said. "I found this note on the front table this morning. Professor Hasting's room was empty and his bed was not slept in."

"Quite a peculiar man, wasn't he?" offered Professor Moriarty.

"Yes, indeed," said the squire, somewhat puzzled.

"Alors, I fear I have need to bid you adieu today as well," said M. Varappeur. "But I shall do so in a more conventional manner if your man will drive me to the railway station this afternoon."

Sherlock was certain that somehow Professor Moriarty was responsible for the Hastings' sudden departure from the house. After breakfast Sherlock walked up and down in front of the manor house door. Then he got down on his hands and knees and was staring intently at the driveway. Sherrinford came upon his younger brother at this and watched for a few minutes before walking up to him.

"What are you doing?" Sherrinford asked.

"Trying to figure out these footprints," Sherlock responded.

"Footprints?" Sherrinford asked.

"See them?" Sherlock asked.

"Well, yes, of course, I see lots of them. What are you trying to figure out about them?" Sherrinford asked.

"They tell a story," Sherlock said. "See here. These are yours. They show that you just walked over here and stood talking. But now if I were to walk over them this way I would leave my footprints on top of yours. What do we know then?"

"That you have more footprints to look at?" Sherrinford suggested.

"We know that I walked there after you did because my footprints are on top of yours," Sherlock explained. "We can trace the order in which people came and went."

"What is the purpose of all this?" Sherrinford asked.

"A man left this house last night," Sherlock said. "I want to know where he went."

"Why?" Sherrinford asked.

"Because I think he met with foul play," Sherlock said.

Sherrinford laughed.

"You have been reading too many of those penny dreadfuls. A man does not 'meet with foul play' in the middle of Yorkshire," Sherrinford said.

"No, he merely vanishes and no one ever asks what became of him," Sherlock retorted. "I'm serious, Sherrinford! This isn't London or Paris. You can't just walk outside and hail a cab. You know as well as I do that it is a long walk from here to anywhere. It is miles to the village and many times further to the railway station in Thirsk. Did he just set out walking down the road carrying his luggage in the middle of the night? If he did, then he didn't come out this door--"

But Sherlock was interrupted when the front door opened to reveal Squire Holmes and Professor Moriarty.

"Sherlock, you are late for your lessons," the squire said sternly.

"Sorry, sir, I lost track of the time," Sherlock said before excusing himself and rushing up to his room to gather his work. Professor Moriarty followed behind him.

"Sherrinford, you should not be encouraging your brother's whims. He needs to study," the squire scolded.

"Sorry, sir. I will keep that in mind," Sherrinford replied.

That evening after supper Sherlock went out back and spoke to the stable boys. No horses were missing and none had been requested the night before. No strangers had been out to the stable. None of them recalled seeing Professor Moriarty either. Many of the stable hands did not even know Professor Moriarty by sight.

Sherlock borrowed a lantern from the stable and walked around the manor house. He examined the ground carefully around each of the doors and then came back around to the door near the kitchen and entered. The last of the dishes were being put away. Tessy was about to retire for the evening for she would be up well before dawn.

"No lad, I dinna see onnyone last night. But thou knowst I rarely see the guests outside the dining room onnyway," she said.

The maids had seen and heard nothing of Professor Hastings after the house had retired and had not noticed any unusual activity by Professor Moriarty either. Thomas knew no more than he had told the squire at breakfast. Sherlock headed back out to return the lantern to the stable. There he met his brother.

"Now what are you up to?" Sherrinford asked as the two of them walked back to the house together.

"I am still trying to find out what happened to Professor Hastings. According to the stable hands he did not take a horse," Sherlock said.

"So maybe he did walk. He's an experienced explorer in good training. Surely a man who can haul gear through the Amazon basin can carry a suitcase a few miles," Sherrinford said.

"Not unless he had another pair of boots in his luggage. The ones he was wearing at supper were new. Walking that far in a new pair of boots would make even an experienced explorer's feet sore. Besides, I can't find any sign that he exited the house through any of the doors, which suggests either he was carried out or he is still in there somewhere."

"Or that his footprints were covered by someone else's, like mine," Sherrinford said.

"You're right," Sherlock admitted reluctantly as they entered the house. "Perhaps you don't give yourself enough credit, Sherrinford. I think there is a logical streak in there somewhere."

"A very practical streak. I don't try to think up things that I don't have reason to," Sherrinford said.

"Just the same, I may explore around inside the house tomorrow," Sherlock said.

The following morning Professor Moriarty entered the

squire's study looking distraught.

"I am very sorry to disturb you, Squire, but this matter cannot be put off any longer. I am afraid that I cannot continue trying to teach your son. It is rather late in the year and I do not know when I will find another position, but I cannot continue with this," Moriarty said.

"Please, sir, sit," the squire said with a look of concern and motioned the professor to a chair. "Be assured that if we have wronged you, I will allow you to stay on here in this house until you can find other employment. But before we speak of that you must calm yourself and explain."

"Squire, I can work with students who are slow or lazy. It can be a challenge, but it is worthwhile to see them bloom once the inspiration of knowledge strikes them," the professor began, "but Sherlock has become increasingly belligerent and argumentative, even insulting at times. He accuses me of devious plots against him. He has accused me of forging errors in his work. And now, and now he is persecuting me, making enquiries and suggesting that I somehow spirited away Professor Hastings."

As Professor Moriarty had spoken the squire's face had turned red with anger.

"Please hold, Professor," Squire Holmes interrupted. "I will have Sherlock down here," he said as he rang for Thomas and sent him to summon Sherlock.

When Sherlock received the summons, he steeled himself. Of late, a summons to his father's study had not been a welcome experience. His father had only summoned him recently to inform him of some new complaint by his tutor and the last time he had been told that future punishments would be severe.

As Sherlock entered the study he saw Professor Moriarty sitting there looking agitated. What was his game now? What role was he playing? How can you parry a thrust that you cannot see until it strikes? Dealing with Professor Moriarty was like fencing blind.

But far worse was the look on his father's face. He knew that look. His father was not merely disappointed or frustrated, but angry. His father's anger was something that few men stood before unscathed. Sherlock sat as he was bidden with great trepidation.

"Sherlock, have you been arguing with Professor Moriarty?" his father asked.

"Sometimes, yes, but--" Sherlock responded.

"Did you accuse him of plotting against you?" his father interrupted.

"Well, no, not--" Sherlock replied.

"He did not use those precise words, sir," Professor Moriarty interrupted. "But his meaning was clear."

"I am not sure I know what the professor is referring to," Sherlock countered.

"I think the boy knows precisely what I am referring to," the professor rebutted. "He is lying now in an attempt to discredit me."

"I am not lying," Sherlock insisted jumping out of his chair.

"Sit down, Sherlock," his father commanded. "Did you accuse him of forging your work?"

"Yes, sir. He changed the numbers I had written on an assignment to other numbers that were wrong," Sherlock said.

"Sherlock, that sounds preposterous and I will not even offend the professor here by asking if he did such a thing. I cannot imagine why he would," the squire thundered.

"But he did, Father!" Sherlock insisted.

"What would he gain by such a ridiculous waste of time?" the squire asked.

"Father, he is not the man you think he is! He is devious and manipulative--" Sherlock said.

"Enough!" the squire roared.

"You see, sir?" the professor's soft voice whined in the silence that followed. "You see what I have had to deal with?"

"Professor Moriarty came to us with very good credentials and recommendations," the squire said.

"But have you investigated those credentials and recommendations?" Sherlock asked.

"Sherlock, you surely can't deny that the professor here has the learning he claims?" his father said.

"No, I'll have to allow him that. Professor Moriarty is an extremely intelligent and learned man. But why would a man of such talents and accomplishments be interested in tutoring the son of a country squire? Professor Hastings suggested that there was some type of scandal in Professor Moriarty's background and then he vanished from this house!" Sherlock argued.

"You see, sir?" Moriarty interjected.

The squire's eyes narrowed.

"What are you accusing Professor Moriarty of, Sherlock?" the squire said.

Sherlock inhaled and paused.

"I-I don't know, sir. I--" Sherlock said.

"Then I suggest that you stop these wild speculations at once," his father said.

"Sir!" Sherlock protested.

"And you are to cease making inquiries about Professor Moriarty or the whereabouts of Professor Hastings," Squire Holmes said.

"Father, please listen to me!" Sherlock pleaded.

"Silence! I don't want to hear another word from you, Sherlock. I have heard enough," the squire boomed.

Squire Holmes again rang for Thomas and instructed him to summon Sherrinford. This puzzled Sherlock who could not fathom why his brother was being brought into this.

Then the squire turned to the professor.

145

"My sincerest apologies, Professor. I will be good to my word, but you no longer will be required to instruct Sherlock."

"Thank you, sir," Moriarty said.

"You may go now," the squire said.

"Thank you, sir," Professor Moriarty said before leaving a very puzzled Sherlock behind with his father. After Moriarty had closed the door behind him, the squire turned back to Sherlock and spoke.

"If you cannot behave like a gentleman then perhaps you should be treated like a common labourer and earn your keep by the sweat of your brow. It should give you a greater appreciation of the opportunities you are throwing away."

There was a knock at the door and Sherrinford entered.

"You wished to see me, Father?" Sherrinford asked.

"Yes. Sherrinford, you are to tell Eston that your brother, Sherlock, is to work the harvest with the labourers with no special treatment and no pay. It is his punishment for failing to treat his tutor with respect. If I cannot make an engineer out of him at least I can get some work out of him," the squire said.

"Father--," Sherrinford protested.

"Don't," a stunned Sherlock interrupted, reaching up and grasping Sherrinford's arm. Sherrinford looked at him. Sherlock turned to his father.

"May I leave now?" Sherlock said.

"Yes, but you are stay in your room except for work and meals," the squire commanded.

"Yes, sir," Sherlock said standing up and leaving the study.

Back in his room Sherlock threw himself upon his bed. He stared up at the ceiling for a moment and then closed his eyes. When someone opened the door of his room a few moments later without knocking, he said, "Have a seat, Sherrinford," without opening his eyes.

"What was that about?" Sherrinford said.

146

"What Father said: He's finally given up on me," Sherlock replied.

"What prompted this?" Sherrinford asked.

"It seems that Moriarty noticed my inquiries related to Hastings' disappearance and complained of them to Father, among other things. I am the foul-mouthed youth and he the slandered professor. The poor professor will no longer be forced to teach the belligerent and unmanageable student who has defiled his honour," Sherlock said sarcastically.

"Didn't you defend yourself?" Sherrinford asked.

"How could I? Even if Father would have listened, I have nothing that I can prove against Moriarty. But Father didn't listen to me at all. I am a prisoner on the dock prohibited from speaking on my own behalf lest I perjure myself."

"You are starting to sound more and more like those penny dreadfuls," Sherrinford said

"They are more entertaining than Antiphon's speeches. But I haven't read any in many months," Sherlock said. "I think it is my life that is starting to sound like a novel. Too bad Dickens died. I will have to find myself another biographer."

"What are you going to do?" Sherrinford asked.

"As Father said," Sherlock said.

"You'll work the harvest?" Sherrinford asked.

"Yes. I suspect it will be less dreadful than the hours I've spent with Moriarty. Besides," Sherlock said, finally opening his eyes and turning to face his brother, "what would you have me do? Run away from home? I haven't a lot of prospects at the moment. At least he hasn't disowned me, not yet, anyway."

"Let me talk to Father," Sherrinford said.

"No. I don't want to drag you further in to this," Sherlock said.

"Sherlock--," Sherrinford protested.

"Sherrinford, I know that you often tried to protect me from Father's wrath when I was a child, sometimes taking responsibility and punishment for things I did."

Sherrinford smiled.

"Well, sometimes your curiosity got you in over your head and I can't say that Mycroft and I didn't encourage it," Sherrinford said.

"But I am not a child any more," Sherlock responded. "And you and Father are going to have to deal with each other for many years to come. I am not so bound and will probably be leaving here in a few years no matter what happens."

"There was a time long ago," Sherrinford thoughtfully, "when I rebelled against my fate. I dreamed of going elsewhere and doing other things. But then I realized that due to the entail the estate would be mine when Father died no matter where I was or what I was doing. If I was not here to guide it, then the manor would fall into decline and all I knew and loved could fade away. I did not want that to happen. I realized that being squire is like being the father of a large family. Decisions we make regarding the operation of the manor do affect the prosperity of the entire dale. Decisions I make can affect whether a child I don't even know is fed today. It is a heavy responsibility, but I decided that I wanted to head that family and do my best to make sure every child in the dale is fed each night."

"I can think of no one better suited for the task, and I think you will be a fine father of your own family as well," Sherlock said.

Sherrinford smiled again.

"But that's all the more reason not to drag you down with me," Sherlock continued. "You must leave me to my fate no matter where it takes me."

Sherrinford sighed.

"You will always be welcome here when I am squire," Sherrinford said reaching out his hand.

"Thank you," Sherlock said grasping his brother's hand. "But for now tell Eston that tomorrow I'll be where he wants me when he wants me."

Chapter 19
Harvest Time

The harvest was well under way by this time. The corn sheaves were ready to come in and the barley and oats were being cut. Wheat would be ripe for cutting in another week or two.

Eston sent Sherlock to work in the cornfields as a pitcher. Before sunrise the next day Sherlock met the other men in the appointed field. If the farm hands had any thought about the squire's son joining them they held their tongues, and they did not spare him his share of work.

When the wagon rolled up, two of the older men climbed aboard. The younger men gathered the sun dried sheaves from the field and tossed them down the line and up into the wagon where they were caught and stacked by the older men. The older men worked quickly filling the wagon fore and aft and filling the center space last. Then they scampered down from the swaying load and the carter would take off for the rick yard

There was a brief moment of rest before the next wagon rolled up and Sherlock shared the horn of ale that was passed around. He wiped the gritty sweat from his sunburned brow. His arms and back ached but he made no complaint as the next wagon rolled into place and work began again.

In the gloaming of the evening, Sherlock was glad to toss himself on Gale's back and let her carry him home. He was thankful for a bath and clean linens. He knew most of his co-workers had neither. Often he was so tired that he had his supper sent to his room which spared him facing his father or the professor across the table. Then he fell into an exhausted sleep and dreamed of walking with Violet in a forest of giant grain sheaves. Before he knew it, it was time to rise and take his weary body out to the fields again.

For two weeks he was pitching and carting, then Eston came to him one evening.

"Thou'st done well, lad," Eston said. "Now that we've toughened thee up a bit, I've asked Moss to take thee into his company and teach thee how to reap. Get thy rest tonight and meet him at the north wall at dawn."

"Toughened me up," Sherlock thought as his head hit the pillow that night, and he thought no more until he was being shaken awake.

Moss' harvest company was an independent group of harvesters who came from the cities and the towns to the north and east of Yorkshire and worked their way south with the harvest. They were fifteen men and their families. They had been coming through Mycroft Manor for decades and Sherrinford had renewed their contract at the Lammas Day Fair.

Moss didn't mind training Sherlock and he was always glad of an extra hand, especially one that would not be sharing the pay. Moss showed Sherlock how to hold the scythe and sweep it around and cut and gather the grain under his arm.

"When thy arm gets full, drop the sheaf. That's when the womenfolk take over, and tie and stack the sheaves. I'll loan thee a pair of my daughters to stack behind thee."

This brought a giggle from the pair of ladies mentioned, and Sherlock smiled.

"Thank you, ladies," he said to Moss' daughters.

There was some discussion among the company about whether to cut with the grain of the plow or against it. They drew lots to determine the strips each would reap. Then they began. Each man swept his blade around a clump of grain while gathering up the clustered ears in his left hand.

The stalks were severed and bunched up under the left arm. Down the rows the men worked leaving a trail of sheaves in their wake that their families fell upon and stacked up to dry. Sherlock soon fell into the rhythm of the work, but the girls behind them were fast workers and he pressed harder to keep ahead of them.

The sun rose higher in the sky and the women pulled their kerchiefs and hats down over their faces. Still the company worked on. Finally, cursing at the dullness of his blade Moss called a halt. Then out came the stones to sharpen the blades and a barrel of ale was rolled up.

This was part of the company's harvest pay, but they shared it with Sherlock. As warm as it was it seemed cool and sweet to his parched throat. Sherlock brushed some of the straw from his shirt and his blistered and scratched arms. He stretched his right arm that had held the scythe so long. It ached now. He had not noticed it before. Then he whetted his blade and the ale was rolled away and the company went back to work.

The break for lunch was also short. The harvest cannot wait. As the sun sank towards the west, sweat ran in streams down the men's faces and over their backs stinging the blisters and scratches and attracting biting insects. But no breath is spared for complaint nor hands for swatting. Chests heaving and backs stooped the men pressed on. Upward glances told them that the field was nearly cut, but the sun was low as well.

The hares that made the field their home all summer long had drawn back from the advancing line of harvesters. Now trapped between the men and the stone wall, some attempted to scurry over the wall while the rest made a dash across the stubble. As the hares burst from the grain like a shotgun blast, shouts went up and boots and sticks and stones flew. Some escaped, but many lay stiffening in the sun as the harvest continued. They would make nice stew for the harvest families. As the sun sank below the horizon the last clump of grain was cut and a shout went up. Men slapped each other on the back and rolled out the barrel again to drink to a good day's work. Then they helped the womenfolk tie up the last of the sheaves and stumped away to their camp.

Sherlock was left standing alone, his back aching, and his arms scratched and sore. The dusk was cool and fragrant. His body was tired and it felt good just to stand up straight and drink in the night air. But he was hungry as well, so he reached up, and wincing as his blistered hands grasped the saddle, threw himself onto his horse.

Sherlock worked with Moss' company for several weeks. He admired the hard work that they put in and the gusto with which they greeted each new day. He enjoyed their camaraderie. Whatever they might say when they were alone in their camp, during the day they treated him as an equal. If his father thought to shame him, then the plan had failed, for he shared the company's pride in the work they did. The company seemed to forget his name was Holmes; and though he never did, he did not encourage them to remember.

Early one morning as he rode up to the assigned field, he saw that Sherrinford and Eston had arrived there before him. They were discussing the harvest.

"I need 50 more bushels by the end of the week. You say that Moss' company will have this field cleared today. How much will it yield?" Sherrinford was asking Eston.

"30 bushels; give or take a peck," a voice answered from behind them.

Sherrinford turned.

"Sherlock," Sherrinford cried with mixed surprise and embarrassment.

"I believe the lad's correct. Though I'd best quit calling thee a lad. Thou'st been doing a man's work and doing it well, so's I hear. But how did thou come by that figure so quick?"

Sherlock shrugged and ran his horny hands up an ear of wheat.

"I have become well acquainted with the subject matter. I know the volume that an average plant produces, the average number of plants per acre, plus the size of the field. The calculation is elementary."

"Sharp as a tack, that one," Eston said as Sherlock left them to join Moss' company as they were arriving. "But Mr. Holmes, thou art far more embarrassed by thy brother's situation than he is."

"I don't believe the squire is treating him fairly," Sherrinford said.

"Eh, well, whether he is or not, thy brother is taking it well. He has a great skill for adapting and blending in. I think he'd be as comfortable taking tea with the Queen as sharing swag with highwaymen."

Sherrinford laughed.

"I suppose you're right," he said.

"Things will sort themselves out, Mr. Holmes. As I always tell thee: work hard and keep smiling and things will always sort themselves out."

Moss' company worked on through the sun and the wind and when an occasional shower hit them they kept on going silently thanking God for the cooling relief. Even the thunder and lightning did not stop them. Once lightning struck a tree next to the field and the tree toppled over and killed a man. The company stopped their reaping and freed the dead man and his family took him away, weeping and wailing. Then the company went back to work, each contemplating, perhaps, how another Reaper had come to claim their comrade.

Then as the last of the reaping was done, Moss' company prepared to move south but before they did they took part in a grand feast to celebrate the harvest. All the harvest companies were there and the regular farm hands of the manor and the tenants and their workers. The feast was held on the manor grounds and the squire came out and received a small sheaf of wheat as token of the acceptance of the harvest and turned over the wages to the itinerant companies. Sherrinford lead the first toast before he and the squire retired to the Hall. Sherlock was there among the company because Moss had asked him. If either his brother or his father had seen him they had shown no sign of it. Suddenly he felt out of place, caught somewhere between the manor and the field and not belonging to either. Moss approached him.

"Sherlock, thou'st done well and we'll miss thee. I don't know how things are with thee, but if thou'st a mind to travel south with us, we'd gladly take thee on, full wages."

It was a kindly offer, but Sherlock thanked him and declined. He wandered out beyond the harvester's tents and leaned against tree. The full moon lit the night and Sherlock contemplated his future. He hadn't had much time to think in recent weeks but now he did.

While he had shared their labours and mingled his sweat with theirs, he knew he was not one of them. Going with them now would mean committing himself to a life of labour and giving up the life of a gentleman. Working one manor harvest was one thing, but going off with a harvest company was quite another. His father, he was certain, would never allow him to return. It would be giving up any hope of going to the university and would be a final admission that the professor was correct. It would mean leaving Violet behind. Even if he did return, how could he hold his head up to her when he had run from his troubles and left the dale in shame? How could he live with himself?

Sherlock heard footsteps crunch on the dry grass and looked up. Eston was walking towards him.

"Out counting stars, Master Sherlock?" Eston asked.

"Just thinking," Sherlock replied.

"Ah, been doing a bit of that myself. Thou'st done well. No man would be ashamed of the work thou'st done, but thou aren't meant to be a farmhand. Thou art too smart for that."

"Little good it does me," Sherlock said.

Eston chuckled.

"We'll see. Wait a week till the gleanings done and I'll speak to the squire and let him know my mind. Meantime, well, I understand thou said some pretty nasty things about that the professor. But he's still here and thou might want to be thinking about what thou want to say to talk him into taking thee back. I donna say it'll work, but thou might want to be thinking about it."

Suddenly the path cleared that had seemed to be blocked. Sherlock knew now what he must do, and he knew why his elder brother had always praised Eston's wisdom.

"Thank you, Eston, I will think about it very carefully," Sherlock responded with the new light of a plan in his eyes.

The itinerant reapers moved off to the south and the regular farm hands finished with the pitching and hauling. When the fields were clear of the stalks they were opened for gleaning. The gleaners were local folk: wives and children from the village, the cottages, and the small farms came for their traditional share. The gleaning bell was rung at a cleaned field at dawn but the gleaners would be there earlier and rush into the field with the tolling of the bell. With backs bent and eyes on the ground the gleaners moved down the field, the fingers of one hand probing among the rough stubble while the other held their pickings in a bundle on their back. An ear here; an ear there; quickly they moved along stopping rarely and briefly for refreshment. At dusk the bell would toll again and the field would be cleared for the night. A lucky woman with a horse or ass could pack her gleanings on the animal but most tied them up and carried them home upon their heads.

Sherlock saw all this going on around him from a perspective he had never had before. As he began his day pitching he would hear the gleaning bell in some other field. Then as they were finishing up for the day he'd hear the bell ring again and know the women were trudging home, but they'd be back tomorrow to glean this field. Then as the week drew near its end and the last stalks were on their way to the granary, Eston rode into the field Sherlock was working and called him aside.

"They can finish without thee. Get thy horse and come along with me. I'm going to close up a field for gleaning and we can talk on the way," Eston said.

"That field that thou were working on is the last to be cleared. The gleaning will end tomorrow. Hast thou thought over what I said about talking to the squire?"

"Yes, sir, and I'd appreciate anything you could do," Sherlock said.

"Twon't be much. More will depend on what thou do," Eston said.

"Yes, sir, I've thought it over very carefully and I know what I must do. Thank you for your advice," Sherlock said.

"'Tis nothing but an old farmer saying what to wind plows in his head. But here we are."

A cluster of women was gathered near one end of the field. Eston and Sherlock rode up to them and dismounted.

"Wot's this, wot's this?" Eston cried out as they approached the women.

"Lass fainted," one woman said.

"Get back thou biddies and give her air," another protested.

The circle drew back and Sherlock saw who it was. The women's chatter receded to a distant clucking as Sherlock rushed forward and knelt by Violet's side. A bucket of water was passed from somewhere and he dipped his handkerchief in it and wiped her face.

"Ladies, you'd best be about your business. The field will be closing soon," Eston announced.

Violet opened her eyes. She drank the water that Sherlock offered her.

"Are you ill?" Sherlock asked.

"No, no, tis only the heat," she said.

"Then we should move you out of the sun," he said.

Before she could say anything Sherlock scooped her up and carried her to the shade of a tree by the edge of the field. She rested silently there. Sherlock watched her anxiously, but she did not look at him. The bell began ringing, signaling the time to clear the field. Violet tried to rise again, but Sherlock gently pushed her down.

"No, stay here and rest a while until you are stronger," he said.

"But my pickings," she protested.

"I believe Eston is seeing to them," he assured her.

The field slowly cleared and Eston shut the gate. Then he walked over leading Violet's horse. Two large bundles were tied behind the saddle.

"Thou art looking a bit perkier now, Miss Rushdale. I took the liberty of tying thy gleanings to thy horse," Eston said.

"Thank ye," Violet said. "I mun be getting home."

She began to stand up but she was still a bit shaky, and she staggered and held on to the tree.

"Violet!" Sherlock said, reaching for her.

"I'm alright," she said waving him away.

"You are still too weak to ride! I will take you home," he said.

"No," Violet said.

"Yes," Sherlock insisted.

"Eston," he said as he mounted his own horse. "Hand her up to me and I shall ride her home."

Violet protested but eventually allowed Eston to pass her up into Sherlock's arms. Muffin's lead was tied behind Gale's saddle and Sherlock turned the horses out of the field, leaving Eston behind. Violet's face was still pale.

"Are you sure you are not ailing?" he asked.

"Nay, twas just the sun. Tis warm for the season," she said.

Did he imagine it or was there a tension in her voice?

"True enough," he responded.

Her head lay against his shoulder, rocking gently as they rode. Her dark hair tumbled down over his arm that held her tight in his lap. It was pleasant having her so close again.

"I have missed you," he whispered.

She was silent, but her heart pounded close to his. What was it saying? It seemed to flutter like that of a trapped animal, as if she were afraid.

"Violet?" he began.

But she interrupted by reaching out her hand and pulling on the reins, and sliding down from the horse.

"What is this?" he asked.

"Where I'm going on my own," she said.

There was her old flippancy back but it seemed to hide a tremor.

"No, I'll take you home," Sherlock said.

"And cause a peck of trouble. No, thank ye," she said, then she took his hand. "Goodbye, Sherlock," she said firmly, but her hand was trembling. She dropped his hand and turned to her horse. Sherlock could stand it no longer.

"Violet, what is wrong? If you are not ill, then what are you afraid of?" he asked.

"Me? Afraid? I'm merely afraid that thou'd be fool enough to follow me home, and my papa would make good on his threat to send thee home in a box," she tossed at him with almost an angry tone. She tugged on Muffins lead and began walking home.

Sherlock smiled.

"Then I won't follow you, but must you go?" he asked.

She looked back at him.

"Aye, and, of course, I mun be going. I thank ye most kindly for the ride, but thou mun knowst, sir, that the bountiful days of summer are gone and I've no time for blathering." She snorted. "I've no servants to store my grain, to winnow it, and to grind it, or to bake my bread. I've work to do if Papa and I are to eat this winter. Fare thee well," she said, and with a toss of her proud head she turned about and marched off towards the farm gate.

Sherlock was left smiling and shaking his head. She was the same wild and independent Violet he'd met in the spring. And yet... she had been different during the summer. Women were a bit like the weather, Sherlock mused, they warm to you in the summer and grow cooler in the autumn. He turned his horse about and headed home.

Two days later Eston and Sherlock had an audience with the squire. At their request Professor Moriarty was also invited.

"Eston, I believe you wished to say something regarding Sherlock's performance of his duties," the squire said.

"Aye, sir, that I do. The lad here is a fine worker. Of course, he's not used to such work and some of the men are tougher, but he worked hard and fast and never once complained. But I really donna believe he's meant to be a farm hand. He's too smart for it, sir. Once he figured exactly how long it would take the men to clear a field and how much wheat they'd get out of it. Now, ah usually have a good idea, but it took me years to get the knack, and he did it right off to top of his head."

"A simple matter of mathematics," the professor said.

"Yes, sir," Sherlock agreed.

"But sir, all I'm trying t' say is that it would be a waste to leave him doing farm work. I believe the lad should be given another chance to go back to his schooling."

"That is for me to decide. Do you have anything else to add, Eston?" the squire asked.

"No, sir," Eston said.

"Sherlock, Eston has spoken in your behalf. Do you have anything to say on the matter?" his father asked him.

Sherlock drew in a breath and swallowed. He knew it would seem to be from nervousness, but in truth it was his pride he was swallowing as he prepared to play the role he knew he must.

"Yes, Father, I would like the opportunity to return to my studies," he said, occasionally looking down from his father's piercing gaze to the desk top, the proper penitent son.

"However, I understand that Professor Moriarty may not be willing to take me back as a student without an apology," Sherlock said.

Sherlock turned to faced Professor Moriarty, first looking up at that snaking head, then hastily looking down at his shoes.

"I admit, Professor, that I have no evidence of any wrong doing on your part. I was hasty in my judgment and I'm sorry to have falsely accused you."

"Oh, my dear boy, all is forgiven!" Moriarty said clasping Sherlock by the hand. "I can see that you have learned a valuable lesson from this experience. One you must not forget. But perhaps now we can be friends, and with your father's kind permission we could resume your lessons."

"Then let it be so," Squire Holmes said.

"Come then, lad, let us recommence our work," Professor Moriarty said.

But as they turned to leave and Professor Moriarty had his back to the squire, Sherlock saw the gleam of triumph in Moriarty's eye and he wished to pluck it out.

Chapter 20
Lessons Resume

Sherlock looked up from his work. The lamp light was being rivaled by the growing dawn. From his window he could see blushing clouds sailing about the moors now livid with the purple of the heather and the rust of the bracken. He knew the moors in autumn. The crisp chill of the air heightened the rich scent of the heather. The bracken crunched underfoot. How he'd love to be up there now with Violet at his side.

Sherlock drummed his fingers on the desk. It had been several weeks since the gleaning was over. He had not seen her in all that time. He had spent all his time at his studies and had not dared ask for permission to do anything else. He did not want to give the professor any reason for rescinding his decision to take him back as a pupil.

The professor had seemed somewhat lenient of late as if to reward Sherlock for his surrender, or perhaps to lull him into false confidence. Sherlock knew it was only a game. Professor Moriarty played the congenial tutor and Sherlock played the obedient student.

But more and more his mind wandered to Violet, and he wondered what she was doing and how she was faring, especially that. He remembered how pale she had looked that day and how she had staggered when she stood up. She had denied being ill. What if she had been wrong? Or if she had lied to him? But then she had walked off towards her farm seemingly as well as ever.

Yet she had not come on the last day of gleaning. Sherlock himself had opened the gates and closed them again that evening. He knew she had not been there. If it was as important to her as she had said, why had she been absent? These questions haunted Sherlock. They plunged in when he was about to go to sleep and they intruded into his studies.

"Master Sherlock," the soft voice said, "your mind is not on your work."

"I am sorry, sir," he replied.

"Is this work so boring? Perhaps I should provide you with something more difficult?" Professor Moriarty suggested

"No, sir, it is not that at all. I will try harder to concentrate," Sherlock said.

"What is it that distracts you so?" Moriarty inquired.

"Nothing, sir," Sherlock responded.

That had been yesterday. Again that evening when he had been studying, Sherlock had found himself worrying about Violet. Then he had risen early this morning to complete his work and again his mind wandered to Violet. She could be ill, he thought.

He stared up at the moors in the direction of the Rushdale farm. How could he see her, he wondered. Then a flock of geese flew over and as he watched the v disappear to the south it came to him. It was prime grouse shooting season! The birds were fattened up for the winter on the rich berries of the moor. He put away his books and wound his way downstairs to the kitchen.

"Ah, lad, has been a long time since thou'st come to visit ol' Tessy. Thought perhaps thou'st forgotten her. Oh, but I hear thou's back at thy books. Too bad, that. Whilst thou was working the fields thou wast eating proper. Ah, look we put some meat on thee," Tessy teased Sherlock. "No, in truth, lad, I'm right glad for thee. But now thou lookst as if thou wanst me to close my lips for a piece so thou can cram a word in. What's on thy mind?"

"The grouse are fattening for the winter," he said.

"Aye, and I've been missing those fattened fowls but I know thou hast thy books to see to. Mr. Sherrinford said he'd bring me some if he found the chance but there is so much to keep a body busy. Eh, if I was onny good with a shotgun and a horse, I'd go and shoot them myself but I'm as like to shoot off my own toe

163

and the horse would probably be so tickled with the idea of me on his back that he'd just sit down and laugh. Certainly lad, I'd welcome them if thou had the time."

"Then I shall ask my father," Sherlock said.

But Sherlock's father denied the request.

"You must concentrate on your studies and put everything else aside. You lost valuable time earlier. You have been given a last chance to redeem yourself. You must not forfeit it," the squire said.

"I am asking for only a few hours. I have been working hard at my studies. Things have been going well and Professor Moriarty and I have had no further conflicts," Sherlock said.

"That is not what the professor reports to me. He says that you are far behind and he doubts whether he can get you prepared in time to be accepted to by the university. He has agreed to make his best efforts but he is doubtful," the squire said.

"I don't understand this, Father. The professor has said nothing about this to me. I've done everything he's asked without complaint," Sherlock protested.

"Professor Moriarty says you are still not working hard enough," his father responded.

"I've done nothing but study for weeks. I spend nearly every waking hour studying," Sherlock argued. "I do work hard. Eston told you that I was a hard worker when you sent me out into the fields."

"Yes, he did," the squire agreed. "It would be a pity if it turned out that was the only type of work you are fit for. But until you are accepted into the university, that is still a possibility. I don't want to hear you asking to do anything else until then."

"Yes, sir," Sherlock said and walked out in despair.

Did it matter what he did? Professor Moriarty was bound to twist anything against him and even complete obedience was rewarded by lies. He went to his room and gathered his books and met with the professor. Throughout the day of lessons, Sherlock brooded. When Moriarty released him before supper he stopped in the kitchen again.

"Tessy, could you tell Pearl that I would like to speak to Jonathan again after supper?" Sherlock asked.

"Aye, lad," the cook responded.

Throughout supper Sherlock was silent as the professor sat across the table engaging in witty conversation with the squire, his wife, Sherrinford, and Amanda.

"You are very quiet this evening, Sherlock," his sister-in-law said. "And you have hardly touched your supper."

"I'm sorry, Amanda, but all I can think of this evening are Greek epigrams and they aren't very appetizing or amusing," Sherlock said.

"I'll admit that there are some that I can neither swallow nor spit out," Sherrinford said.

After supper Sherlock found Jonathan by the back door. He asked him to go and speak to Violet.

"I need to know if she is all right," Sherlock said. "I need to see her. But they won't even let me leave the house. Ask her if she will come here so I can speak to her."

The boy agreed and hurried off in the dark. An hour later Sherlock stood by the back door again. Jonathan ran into the yard and stopped breathlessly before him. Jonathan shook his head from side to side, trying to convey the message before he spoke.

"She won't come," he gasped at last.

"You spoke to her?" Sherlock asked.

Jonathan nodded.

"Her father was out front so I crawled over the back wall. I threw some stones and she came to the window, but she wouldn't come down, so I went up the backstairs."

" 'What art thou doing here?' she asked. I told her what you said, but she said she couldn't come."

165

"Did she say why?" Sherlock asked.

"She gave no reason," Jonathan replied.

"How did she look?" Sherlock asked.

"She was looking a bit on the peaked side," Jonathan answered.

Sherlock bit his lip. Then he patted Jonathan on the back.

"I suppose that's all you can do. Thank you for trying, Jonathan," Sherlock said and started back into the house. Then he turned around again.

"Wait," Sherlock said. "If I could ask one more thing of you.... when you go by the stables tell them to saddle Gale first thing in the morning. I might be wanting her."

Then Sherlock returned to his room and worked on his lessons.

Chapter 21
A Proposal

The clock chimed and Professor Moriarty looked up. His charge was late. Five minutes later he rang for a servant and requested that Master Sherlock be reminded that the time for his lessons had come.

The servant returned shortly and told Professor Moriarty that Master Sherlock was not in his room. Moriarty dismissed the servant and paced the room. He paused at the window. His eyes lit upon one figure in the yard. It was the boy Sherlock used to fence with. Now he was here and Sherlock was late. Something was afoot. The clock chimed quarter past and Moriarty decided to investigate.

As the professor came out of the back door, Jonathan drew back towards the stables and the barns. There among the comings and goings of the stable hands and other workers he felt less conspicuous.

Then a voice called out to him, "You there, boy!"

Jonathan's first impulse was to run, but it was a kindly sounding voice and he turned and looked up at its owner. It was a tall, balding man with a pale face.

"You are the lad Master Sherlock used to fence with, are you not?" Professor Moriarty said.

"Aye--yes, sir," Jonathan said.

"I am Master Sherlock's tutor and I am afraid he is late for his lessons," the professor cooed softly. "When I saw you out in the yard, I thought to myself, there's a smart lad who will tell where my pupil's gone."

Jonathan pressed his lips together.

"You do know where he is, don't you?" Moriarty asked.

"N-no," Jonathan lied.

"Eh, what's thou doing here?" a high-pitched voice squawked in surprise. "Oh, thou mun forgive him, sir. Tis my little brother. Not a brain in his head, sir," Pearl said rapping Jonathan on the head with her hand. "Now get on home and stop bothering the gentleman."

Jonathan took the opportunity and dashed off.

"He was no bother, really, Miss," said the professor. "I was just asking him if he knew where Master Sherlock was."

"Well, I saw that one taking off on his horse a while back. Stable hands said it was about time. They'd had his horse saddled since dawn," Pearl said.

"I wonder where Master Sherlock is off to? He is late for his lessons," Professor Moriarty pondered aloud.

"Well, I don't exactly know, but I've my own idea," Pearl said, with a twinkle in her eye. "But I don't suppose thou'd be interested in that."

"Why, yes," said Professor Moriarty in a very soothing, confidential tone, "I certainly would be interested in any idea a bright lass like you may have."

Sherlock rode up to the Rushdale farm. Godfrey Rushdale sat upon the front porch. The man grabbed up his shotgun as Sherlock entered the gate. Sherlock dismounted.

"Thou'd best get back on thy horse and ride out of here," Godfrey said.

"I've come to see Violet," Sherlock responded.

"Thou don't need to be pestering my daughter," Godfrey said.

"I won't leave until I've seen your daughter," Sherlock said

"Then they'll be carrying thee off," responded Godfrey.

"Violet!" Sherlock called.

Violet appeared at the door. She did not look ill, a bit tired, perhaps, but as strong as ever.

"Sherlock! Thou shouldn't have come!" she said as she saw him.

"Violet, I must speak with you," Sherlock said.

Violet hesitated. Did he know?

"I don't think my daughter wants to talk to thee," Godfrey said.

"Violet, please," Sherlock pleaded.

"It's alright, papa. I'll speak to him. Leave us be," Violet said.

Godfrey reluctantly withdrew.

"If he gives thee onny trouble I'll be right here," he said before disappearing into the farmhouse.

Sherlock reached out to hold Violet, but she drew away.

"I've missed you," he said. "I've been worried about you."

"There's no need," she said. "I've been doing for myself since afore thee came back from France."

"Violet, I love you. I don't want to be away from you. I- I--" Then the words came tumbling out: "Violet, will you marry me?"

Violet was silent. She turned away from him.

"What of thy plans of going to the university?" she asked.

"Oh," he sighed, "I'm not sure anything will come of that. The professor has nearly convinced my father that I'm not fit for the university or much of anything else. But what does it matter?"

"Thy father will disown thee if thou wast to marry the likes of me," she said.

"He might. He might throw me out without a penny. Or he might give me this farm. In his eyes that might be punishment enough, to making me sweat for a living. But I could accept that if you would accept me," Sherlock said.

But she turned almost fiercely and challenged him.

"Why should I want to marry thee? The youngest son of a country squire, disinherited, uneducated, without fortune or future-- What dost thou have to offer?"

Sherlock was thunderstruck.

"Violet, I--" he began.

"No, Sherlock, I think this has gone on long enough," Violet said.

She unfastened the chain around her neck. She held out her arm and there swung the silver heart.

"Here," she said. "Go and don't return."

Sherlock did not reach out his hand. He looked at her, but her eyes would not meet his. He bowed his head.

"I will go if you want me to," he said softly. "But, please, if you have any regard for me at all, then keep the locket."

He looked up and searched her face but knew not what was written there.

She withdrew her arm with the locket still in her hand and said, "Go."

Sherlock turned and walked off the porch and gathered Gale's reins. Violet watched as he walked the horse through the gate and down the lane, then she sank to her knees and cried. Godfrey came out and put his arms around his daughter.

"Did he hurt thee child? I'll--" Godfrey said.

"No, Papa, no. He didn't hurt me. Leave him be. He won't be coming back, Papa," Violet responded.

"Stop thy crying then, lass, and come inside. Mama'll be home soon," he said.

She looked up at his grizzled face and knew that he still believed it.

"I love thee, Papa."

"I love thee, too, lass."

Slowly Sherlock withdrew. He turned at the gate and walked his horse down the lane. A whirlwind of emotion churned within him. Just as he was about to turn towards home, he stopped, mounted his horse and headed her toward the moor road. They mounted that winding road like a raging tornado, shoe ringing loudly against stone. On and on they raced as Sherlock tried to run from the hurt and anger, from all of his feelings for Violet, and Violet herself, and the professor and the squire and all that waited for him below.

But even as he rode, he remembered watching Violet ride with him, her hair bouncing in the wind, and he wished she were there. Then Sherlock groaned and brought his horse to a stop. Never again would she ride with him. Never again would they walk hand and hand across the moors. Yet he could not escape her. His senses were full of her. Everywhere he looked he saw that flowing hair and those teasing brown eyes. Each breeze was filled with the ringing of her laughter, first with joy then that mocking laugh he had heard when he had last seen her.

She had seemed so cold, as distant as she had been that first morning in spring when they had met on the moor. Had she merely grown tired of him or had she found another? Gale nudged him. Oh, if women only had the consistency of a horse, he mused rubbing the horse's forelock.

"Bah! Who needs them!" he said aloud.

But he didn't mean it. He missed her now. He leaned against the horse's shoulder and stared out at the purple waves of heather beneath the dark autumnal sky. He did not know why Violet had changed her mind towards him. Perhaps his father was right and a woman was not to be entirely understood. Yet he knew he loved her still.

She had kept the locket. Why? To sell it, perhaps? No, she had offered it back and had kept it only at his request. She was, if nothing else, an honest woman, and a forthright one, too. He could imagine her flinging it at his feet if she truly hated him. If she kept it, it was because she still had some kind thoughts for him. Then perhaps there was hope. Perhaps someday this wall which had risen between them would fall away. Until then he had to face Professor Moriarty. He mounted and sent his horse homeward.

Sherlock carried his books into the room over an hour past his usual time. Professor Moriarty looked up from the book he was reading.

"You went riding in direct disobedience of your father's instructions," the professor said.

"Yes, sir. I'm sorry, sir," Sherlock said, reluctantly taking up his role as submissive student.

"This will not do, Master Sherlock," Professor Moriarty said.

"Yes, sir," Sherlock said. "It won't happen again, sir."

"No, it will not," the professor said firmly, but softly. But then Professor Moriarty set his book aside and stood and walked over next to Sherlock's work table.

"What is it that draws you up there, boy?" The professor asked in a soothing confidential way.

"Nothing, sir, just the moors," Sherlock said.

"There is something you are not telling me, Master Sherlock," Professor Moriarty said.

"No, sir," Sherlock said. "I went riding up the moor road and turned around and came back."

"Then what of these evening visits with that boy from the cottage?" Professor Moriarty asked.

"He wants me to fence with him some more," Sherlock said. "But I told him I have no time."

"That is good. But you would do better, young man, to confide in me," Professor Moriarty cooed.

"There is nothing more I have to say, sir," Sherlock said, wondering what the man was up to.

"Well, well, and what do you expect me to do as punishment for your tardiness today?" Professor Moriarty asked.

"I do not know, sir," Sherlock responded honestly.

"Your father would not be pleased if he were to hear about it," Professor Moriarty pointed out.

"No, sir, he would not. I would appreciate it if you would not tell him, sir," Sherlock said.

"Yes, I believe you would," Moriarty said with a gleam in his eye.

"Well, we shall see. Let us not waste more time," Moriarty concluded before beginning their lessons for the day.

Chapter 22
In Search of Evidence

Sherlock studied harder, concentrating with all his effort to distract his mind from his final encounter with Violet. From the professor he received no word of praise. A raised eyebrow was Moriarty's only reaction before he increased Sherlock's assigned work. Sometimes after Sherlock had been kept through tea, the squire would call the professor into his study to inquire as to the reasons therefor. When his tutor would return with the hint of a twinkle in his eye, Sherlock knew that the extra time had been attributed to some false dereliction of duty on Sherlock's part. But still Sherlock worked on in silence.

Sherlock knew that there was no argument that he could make now that would salvage his character in his father's eyes. Either he had to manage to continue this silent war of wills until he was actually accepted into the university or else he must find some way to impeach Professor Moriarty's character. No theories would be enough. Sherlock needed proof.

Hastings had said something about a publication. Perhaps there was something in Professor Moriarty's room that would provide a clue. Sherlock watched the professor carefully for several days. He studied his habits and found a time one evening when the professor was occupied elsewhere. Sherlock opened the door to Moriarty's room quickly and closed it cautiously behind him.

He had not been in this room since the professor had come. They had always met elsewhere for lessons. It was very much like his own room, though it was much more sparsely decorated. There was a fireplace with a fire burning in the grate. There was a bed, some tables and chairs, and a desk. The only lamp burning sat on a table beside an upholstered chair near the fire.

Sherlock searched quickly. The drawers of the tables were all empty. Most of the papers on top of the desk were Sherlock's own work. He tried the desk drawers, but they were all locked. Just as he was checking the last desk drawer footsteps stopped before the door. Quickly, Sherlock pressed himself to the wall next to the door. There was a knock. It wasn't Moriarty. Sherlock waited silently. Perhaps they would go away, he thought. Then slowly the door began to open and a hesitant step was heard. As she came past the edge of the door he saw that it was only the little maid, Michelle, with a duster. Before she could turn he wrapped one hand over her mouth and closed the door quietly with the other.

"Pas un mot, comprendrez-vous?" Sherlock whispered in her ear.

Michelle had tensed with fright when he had grabbed her, but she relaxed when she heard his voice. She nodded her assent. He released her.

"You must do two things for me. First, you must promise that you will tell no one that you saw me in here. Will you promise?" Sherlock asked.

Again she nodded.

"And now you must look out to see if anyone is in the hall."

Michelle peeked out and shook her head.

"Merci, Michelle," Sherlock whispered before he slipped out into the hall.

Back in his room Sherlock looked at his own desk. It was very similar to the desk in Professor Moriarty's room. It, too, had locks on the drawers, but he did not remember ever having had a key for them. He went looking for his brother, Sherrinford, whom he found working at his own desk.

"Ah, Sherlock, you have crawled out of your den of study for a moment?" Sherrinford said. "How can I help you?"

"I want to be able to lock my desk drawers. Do you have the key to them?" Sherlock asked.

"Someone been pilfering things from your room?" Sherrinford asked.

"There was that one paper that disappeared, nothing since. I just want to be able to lock things up if necessary," Sherlock said.

Sherrinford pulled out his own keys and unlocked a lower drawer in his desk. From that drawer he produced a wooden box that contained a number of keys on different rings. Sherrinford prodded around in the box for a moment and pulled one set out and handed it to Sherlock.

"Here. It should be one of these on this ring. Bring the rest back to me after you figure out which it is," Sherrinford said handing the ring to Sherlock.

"Thank you. I will," Sherlock said.

This was better than Sherlock had hoped. He had hoped merely to be able to understand the locks on Moriarty's desk by studying the locks and keys for his own desk. However, there was a good chance that one of the keys on ring he now held in his hand would open the professor's desk drawers. That would simplify things. But he could not wait long to try them or his brother would miss the keys.

First Sherlock found and separated from the ring a key that fit his desk drawers. Then he watched for his opportunity to return to Moriarty's room. He waited impatiently, but in the first twenty-four hours he found no convenient time. At supper on the second evening, Amanda was commenting on how pretty the stars looked.

"Now you are talking about Professor Moriarty's specialty," Sherlock said.

"Indeed?" Amanda said. "Professor, I knew that you were a genius at mathematics, but astronomy as well? How fascinating!"

"All astronomy is mathematics at its root. We calculate how big, how far, how fast, how bright," Professor Moriarty replied.

"But that sounds so unromantic!" Amanda protested.

176

"The romance is still there," Moriarty disagreed. "To some of us the numbers themselves are beautiful. But knowing the names of the stars and their intrinsic brightness or distance does not detract at all from the glory of a starlit night, but rather adds to its wonder!"

"Oh! Could you just show me a few, Professor?" Amanda said.

"Certainly my dear, if you would like to step out on the porch after supper," Professor Moriarty offered.

As his sister-in-law and his tutor donned their coats after supper for a bit of stargazing, Sherlock approached Moriarty's room and entered. The room looked much as it had before and was again lit only by the fire and the single lamp upon the table. Sherlock crouched next to the desk and began trying the keys one-by-one. It was a frustrating process but at last the lock snapped. The first drawer was nearly empty. Another contained the professor's cheque book and some others contained correspondence of no importance. At last Sherlock came to one drawer containing a four inch tall stack of papers bound with string. Sherlock took the papers over near the lamp to read them better. He untied the string and began to look through the stack quickly. It was an odd assortment of papers from the last few years including mathematical notes, letters, conference notes, stray invoices, and a few telegrams. But buried amongst them was one letter that caught Sherlock's eye.

It was a letter on Westgate University stationery. It was addressed to Professor James Moriarty and read: "Due to the sudden, and, we must presume, accidental, death of Arthur Stanwick, as well as the disappearance of all his papers, we are unable to continue the inquiry into his claim that your publication, "Dynamics of An Asteroid," was plagiarized from his work. However, in light of the circumstances, the Trustees of Westgate University believe it that would be in the best interest of the university if you were to resign your chair and seek employment elsewhere." The letter was signed by Charles S. Winthrop IV, Chancellor.

Quickly Sherlock stuck the letter inside his shirt and retied the rest of the bundle. He was just placing the bundle back in the drawer when he heard footsteps in the hall. He closed the drawer, dropped the ring of keys in his pocket, and crouched down beside the dresser as the door knob turned and the door slowly opened.

Footsteps came into the room and stopped. He heard the sound of a chair creaking and then another sound of something being taken out of a drawer.

"I'd suggest you stand up, Master Sherlock," Moriarty said in his softest voice. "I believe that you will find that position much less cramped." Then there was a click, the click of a pistol being cocked. "Oh, and I don't suggest you try to make a run for it."

As Sherlock stood up he saw the professor sitting in a chair across the room calmly pointing a gun at him.

"Ah, that's better," said the professor. "We seem to have underestimated each other again. But if you plan to take up a life of crime I suggest that you learn to be a bit more careful in your searching. It was obvious to me that someone had been in here looking for something. I suspected the servants. Thieves among the help are not that uncommon. But then that maid apologized for having knocked things about while she was dusting, so I let it pass. I should have realized it was you, and that you were not as submissive as you have been acting. You've done a good job of playing the obedient student recently. I must grant you that."

Sherlock did not move or speak. He thought of the distance to the door. Professor Moriarty could surely get a shot at him before he got there, if he dared.

"Now kindly come over here and hand that slip of paper to me," Moriarty cooed.

"Oh, don't pretend," he continued. "I know you have it stuck in your shirt. And don't think that I'll hesitate to shoot you if you head for that door."

"You can't shoot me," Sherlock responded defiantly.

"Oh, can't I? It would be a terrible accident if I caught an intruder in my room, shot him in my fright, and it turned out to be my charge. I had a student who had an accident once...." Moriarty said sweetly. "Of course, I wouldn't have to kill you, though that's more efficient. There are ways to maim or disfigure a man so he'd wish he were dead. I'd still be able to get the paper from you and your father still would believe you were at fault. But let's not speculate. Just come here and hand that paper to me."

Sherlock walked slowly across the room.

"Close enough. Give it here," Moriarty said reaching out his hand.

Sherlock drew the paper out of his shirt. He paused a moment and then handed it over to the professor. Moriarty glanced at the paper and smiled.

"You were right to remind me of this letter," Professor Moriarty said, then tossed it into the fire where it curled and burst into flame. "I should have taken care of it long ago."

"Of course, I could still shoot you. The intruder story would still hold," Moriarty continued.

There was another click as he uncocked the pistol.

"But I don't think I shall," Moriarty said in mock benevolence. "I will, however, have to inform to the squire of his son's prowling activities."

Moriarty smiled broadly and Sherlock winced at the message behind that grin.

"Now run along, lad," the professor said. "I'm sure you still have work to do."

Sherlock left silently seething with anger at himself for failing. He was filled with dread over what Moriarty would make of the incident. Back in his room he tossed the ring of keys upon the desk. He was in no mood for lessons. He picked up his violin and played it until he was ready to sleep. In the morning he rang for a servant and requested that his breakfast be brought to his room.

After Sherlock left, Professor Moriarty thought about the encounter and pondered how best to use it. He realized now that the maid must have been covering for Sherlock. That could be more damning evidence. He decided to speak to her before breakfast the next morning. When morning came he considered ringing for her, but decided to seek her out downstairs instead. However, in the back hallway he heard voices coming from the kitchen and paused to listen.

"We'll be bringing them in early this afternoon," Pearl said. "Ol' Cyril's saying twill be a blow tonight."

"So I heard. Now be a good lass, Michelle, and bring that to Master Sherlock," Tessy said. "Poor lad's been looking a bit down, and could use the sight of a pretty face."

Pearl tittered.

"I know whose face would please him!" The milkmaid grinned sheepishly as she continued. "And the winds are whispering that's more than her face that's been pleasing him."

"Cackling hens," Tessy scolded. "Thou donna know nowt, lass."

"Ah do! Word is she's pretty far along. And there haven't been onny other bulls in her pasture."

"Whisht!" Tessy admonished. "Such blethering around here will bring nowt but trouble. If thou'st nowt better to do, get thee out of my kitchen."

Moriarty heard another door to the kitchen slam.

"Gwon, Michelle, donna listen to that wench," Tessy said.

Michelle passed through the door to the hall with the tray and nearly bumped into Professor Moriarty.

"Excusez-moi! Excuse me, sir!" Michelle said.

"Oh, no, not at all, it was my entirely fault," the professor said looking thoughtful. "I should have been paying more attention. I had a question for you, but now I've forgotten what it was. Go on your way. Don't mind me."

Professor Moriarty headed back up to his room to think over this new information. After breakfast he wandered out to the stables. He had rarely been beyond the Hall itself. Some of the hands gave him sideways glances or a "g'd mornin'" but most ignored him. Moriarty had a feel for character and he soon found a likely stable boy for his purposes. He drew some silver from his pocket and jingled it in his hand.

"What is your name, boy?" Professor Moriarty asked.

"Sam," the boy responded.

"How would you like to earn a little extra silver, Sam?" said the professor with a smile.

"For wot?" Sam asked looking interested.

"A very simple task. I just need someone to take a note to one of the tenant farms later today," Professor Moriarty said.

"That's simple enough," Sam replied.

"There's a good boy," said Moriarty flipping him a coin.

"Thank ye sir."

"I will bring the note by later."

When Sherlock arrived at the usual hour for lessons, Professor Moriarty was not in attendance. This was unprecedented. Sherlock's initial thought was that the professor was meeting with his father. However, Sherlock realized that was not possible since his father had passed him heading towards his own room as Sherlock had come out with his books. Before Sherlock could speculate further Professor Moriarty appeared.

"Please excuse my tardiness. I was involved in a bit of research," Professor Moriarty said brightly.

The professor was unusually cheerful as they commenced their work. He made no reference to the incident the night before. The morning lessons proceeded as usual and then they recessed for lunch.

In the afternoon Moriarty handed Sherlock some written problems on orbital dynamics to solve. The irony of the assignment was not lost on Sherlock, but he took it silently and worked at it the best he could while he worried when and how the blow would fall. While he was doing this he noticed that the professor himself sat down to write on a piece of paper. Professor Moriarty looked at his paper thoughtfully for some time after he wrote on it then folded it and placed it in his coat pocket. He stood up.

"You will need to excuse me, dear boy," Moriarty said. "I have something to attend to. I will be back shortly to check your work."

"Yes, sir," Sherlock said with his stomach in knots. This must be it.

Professor Moriarty descended the staircase of the old house slowly, savoring the moment. He had no doubt that the game was at its climax and total victory was at hand. The note in his pocket was gratuitous, the final blow to demoralize the opponent. But somehow that made it even sweeter. He knocked on the door of the squire's study and was invited in.

"Squire, I always hate to be the bearer of bad news, but ethically, perhaps, morally even, I feel that I am left with no choice," Moriarty said timidly. "You entrusted your son in my care and thus I feel I have an obligation to keep nothing from you regarding him. Perhaps I have been lax in fulfilling that obligation and I should have come to you weeks ago. But after what happened last night I don't feel I can protect him any longer."

"What happened last night?" Squire Holmes asked.

"When I returned to my room after pointing out a few stars to your lovely daughter-in-law, I perceived that there was someone in there. In my fright I caught up a small pistol I keep for such situations. But then I discovered that it was Master Sherlock."

"I will have him down here immediately," the Squire said.

"Oh, please, sir, do not," the professor begged. "The more I learn of your son the more a confrontation with him frightens me. That is why I did not haul him before you at the moment last night. I merely told him to leave. Your son is much stronger than I, and I feared what he might do. I've been doing much thinking over it since and I believe if you hear me out you will understand why I would much prefer if we could speak alone and that I not be present when you confront him with it. He is currently occupied with some calculations and I can send him down afterwards."

"Then speak sir," the squire said.

"There are also other more delicate matters that I feel I must tell you that I am sure you would wish to be kept within the family. They are not something that an outsider such as myself need be party to, but which I feel obliged to report," Moriarty continued.

"Tell me of these other matters," the Squire said.

The professor and the squire spoke for sometime and as he left the study Professor Moriarty promised the squire that he would send Sherlock down to the study shortly. But first the professor returned to the stables.

"There you are, Sam!" Moriarty said. "Here is the note and a little something extra for your trouble. I need you to take this note to a girl named Violet Rushdale."

"The Rushdale farm?" Sam objected. "Thou'st wanting to get me killed? Her ol' man's barmy."

"Just be quick about it and you should be perfectly safe," Moriarty said somewhat impatiently. He had not anticipated this factor. After he offered a bit more silver, Sam agreed to deliver the note.

Professor Moriarty returned to the manor house and reentered the room where Sherlock was working. Sherlock looked up as Moriarty closed the door behind him. The professor said nothing, but he was looking far too pleased with himself. He gazed out of the window for a few minutes. Then he asked to see Sherlock's work. Sherlock handed it to him and watched Moriarty as he read it over. The professor wandered about the room as he studied the calculations. Periodically he looked out of the window again. At last he smiled and turned to Sherlock.

"Your father wishes to speak with you in his study," Professor Moriarty said.

Chapter 23
Deception

Professor Moriarty walked slowly down the stairs as the door to the squire's study closed behind Sherlock. He smiled a smile that the squire would not have attributed to the meek professor. The butler, Thomas, approached him.

"May I help you, sir?" Thomas asked.

"No, thank you," Professor Moriarty said. "I was just thinking of taking a walk."

The professor exited by the front door, but skirted the drive and walked along the path that curved around the north side of the manor house. He had seen the rider coming down the road from the window above. He stepped back between the bushes to await her.

Violet had been startled by the knocking at the door. No one ever came to their farmhouse any more -- except -- but not him any more either. She rushed to the door before the knocking woke her father who was snoring in a chair. She pulled her shawl close around her before she opened the door.

"Violet Rushdale?"

"Aye," she said.

"I've a note here for thee," the boy said as he thrust it forward.

As she took the note, the boy turned and ran towards the gate and was gone.

Violet opened the note and read it. She was not accustomed to reading script and it was slow going. It said: "Dear Miss Rushdale: Please come to the manor house at once. I need to speak to you regarding Sherlock's well-being. It is most urgent." It was signed by the squire's wife.

Violet was puzzled as to why Mrs. Holmes would be writing to her. She had never had any dealings with the squire's wife. She read the note through a second time. "Well-being"? What did she mean by that? How come these folks couldn't just speak plain? Then fear ran through her. Perhaps Sherlock was ill? Her hand went to the locket that she still wore around her neck. He seemed healthy enough when she'd-- when she'd last seen him, but that was three weeks ago. She had heard nothing of him since. He could be ill. He could be dying. He could be asking to see her. It was the least she could do to visit if he were ill.

She went upstairs and opened the chest of her mother's things. She took out her mother's dark blue traveling skirt and jacket. They were a little large for her but that's what she needed right now, she thought running her hand over the curve of her belly. She donned them over her dress. She tucked the letter in the pocket of her skirt and put on her heavy hooded cloak. She saddled Muffin and mounted her. It had been weeks since she had last ridden and it felt strange. Violet rode slowly towards the manor house.

It was cold and the sky was grey. The air was still, as if it was holding its breath in anticipation of something. The road was busy. The herdsmen of the manor were bringing in the cows for milking and the shepherds were bringing their flocks in. They merely glanced in her direction as she rode by and went on about their business.

Violet rode past the stables and dismounted near the side of the manor house where she usually tied up Muffin. She wrapped her long grey cloak around her carefully. As she looked up a tall man stepped forward and greeted her. He was a stranger to her.

"Good day, Miss Rushdale, you seem in a hurry," he said.

"Aye, I've had a note from Mrs. Holmes to come at once," she said.

"Yes, indeed, Mrs. Holmes asked that I discuss the matter with you," he said gently.

Violet was puzzled.

186

"Who art thou?" she asked.

"I am Professor Moriarty, Sherlock's tutor," the man said.

Violet was suddenly wary. Sherlock had not spoken well of this professor.

"The note says Mrs. Holmes wished to speak to me concerning her son Sherlock's well-being. See?" Violet said drawing the note out of her pocket. "I thought him ill."

Moriarty took the note he had written and looked at it carefully.

"No, no, the lad's quite healthy and doing well enough in his studies," the professor said brightly as he stuffed the note in his own pocket. "And his mother wishes him to continue in that way. So she's authorized me to make arrangements with you," Moriarty continued.

"Arrangements?" Violet asked. "What art thou talking about?"

"I have been authorized to offer you a sizeable sum-- enough for you to live off comfortably for some time I might add-- if you will leave the dale and make no claims against her son," the professor said in a kindly fashion.

Violet backed away in disgust.

"I've made no claims on Sherlock," Violet said.

"Come now, Miss Rushdale. There is no need to play games. The whole dale knows you carry his child," the professor said drawing closer to her.

Violet gasped in surprise and backed away further.

"I donna believe thou speak for Mrs. Holmes," she retorted, her mind a jumble of shock and fear.

"Does it matter whom I speak for? Perhaps the squire? Perhaps Sherlock himself?" The professor said coming towards her again.

"Thou art lying. He doesn't know," she insisted.

"He does now. Look," Professor Moriarty said grabbing her and spinning her around to face the manor house. "See him there in the study window? See him bow his head in shame. See him beg his father's forgiveness. If you could hear his words, you would hear him renounce you as a plaything, a childish fancy."

"No!" Violet cried turning her head away. She could not believe that.

"How do you know it wasn't he who sent me to speak to you?" the professor asked.

"No!" Violet cried.

She would not believe it. She remembered their last encounter. Sherlock would have come to her if he had known.

"If you don't take this generous offer," said the professor in a gentle voice that was far more convincing and thus far more terrifying than an angry shout, "they'll lock your father away and throw you out to give birth to your child in a ditch."

Violet did not-- she could not-- believe his words yet they brought all her fears into bloom and she saw her whole world crashing in around her.

Professor Moriarty turned her around to face him. His grip was firm, his voice was still soft, but there was an insinuating edge to it.

"You know what kind of a man the squire is. Do you think a mere boy could stand up to him? You need a man to protect you."

Professor Moriarty pulled her close. She struggled in his hold and avoided his eyes. There was an icy malevolence in their depths, cold, yet mocking. It terrified her.

"I have an offer of my own. Marry me. We'll leave the dale. I'll claim the child as my own," he said with mock sincerity.

Empowered with a fresh wave of fear and panic, Violet freed one arm from his grasp, slapped his face, twisted the other arm free and ran. Moriarty caught her again just before she reached her horse. His grasp was painful. In her struggles the locket had worked its way from under her clothes. Moriarty saw the silver heart and grasped it between his long thin fingers with one hand while holding her in an iron grip with the other.

"What is this?" Moriarty asked, but as he did a growling sound rose up behind Violet, and Sherlock's dog, Sandy, launched herself at the professor's leg.

As Sandy bit into the professor's ankle, Violet wrapped her fingers around the locket and pulled it from his hand. Professor Moriarty cursed the dog and loosened his grip on Violet's arm as he tried to free his leg. Violet wriggled free from his grasp again. She tucked the necklace back under her dress as she ran toward her horse terrified that Moriarty would catch her again. She mounted Muffin quickly and rode off in a panic, not once looking back.

Chapter 24
Accusation

Sherlock walked slowly down the hall and down the front stairs. His mind was racing. He had no doubt that Professor Moriarty had told his father of the encounter last night. Exactly what the professor had said and what lies he might have embellished it with were things Sherlock would soon learn, but he knew it mattered little. The naked truth was damning enough. He could imagine his father's reaction. Sherlock was not expecting his father to punish him with manual labor this time. He was expecting to be banished from the manor. So he walked slowly like a man on the way to his own execution.

On the other hand, he felt he had no more to lose. He would go down fighting. He knocked at the door of the study and entered at his father's invitation.

"Please be seated," the squire rumbled. "I have some very serious matters to discuss with you."

"Yes, Father," Sherlock said sitting down as he had been instructed.

"I believe I have been very patient with you, Sherlock. You have been repeatedly warned that your behavior has been unacceptable. Yet you have failed to mend your ways. Instead you seem determined to go beyond all boundaries of civilized conduct!" Squire Holmes thundered.

"Sir, if you would let me explain," Sherlock said.

The squire's dark eyebrows lifted and his steel grey eyes grew wide.

"You, sir, are to listen!" Siger Holmes roared. Then he paused and continued on in a less voluminous, though no less menacing, tone. "When Professor Moriarty first mentioned that you were being distracted from your studies by your outings upon the moor, I felt that was easily mended. However, then you progressed to bickering with your tutor, flagrantly abandoning your lessons, and insulting the professor with wild accusations. The man's a saint to have struggled to teach you anything. Yet rather than following the professor's patient example you seem determined to be his antithesis, and you continue to sink to new depths."

"Father!" Sherlock protested.

His father shook his head, like a great black lion shaking its mane.

"I never imagined that I should raise a son to be a thief," Squire Holmes said his voice laced with disappointment.

"I am not a thief!" Sherlock insisted.

"Do you deny that you entered Professor Moriarty's room, searched through his possessions, and even broke into a locked drawer?" his father inquired.

"No, sir, but--" Sherlock began.

"Yet you deny that you are a thief," his father continued in his cross-examination.

"I took nothing," Sherlock said.

"Only because the professor caught you," his father rumbled with a scowl.

"I found a letter-- a letter from the Chancellor of Westgate University--" Sherlock said.

"What did you propose to do with this letter after you stole it? Add blackmail to your list of crimes?" the squire interrupted in an accusatory tone.

"No, Father, it was proof," Sherlock insisted, "proof that Moriarty is not all that he seems. He plagiarized the paper that he called *The Dynamics of an Asteroid*. One of his students wrote it. Westgate was investigating the charge of plagiarism, but then the student died. There was no direct proof that Moriarty had anything to do with the death. But the student's papers all vanished as well. The trustees of Westgate asked Moriarty to resign his position."

"Great heavens, Sherlock, do you really believe that you can mask your own black deeds by attempting to impugn Professor Moriarty's character?" the squire roared "I will not sit here and listen to any more lies about that man!"

"But, Father, I had proof. I had it in my hand," Sherlock protested, holding out his hand as if he could see the paper there.

"This letter you spoke of?" his father said.

"Yes," Sherlock said.

"Then what's become of it?" Squire Holmes asked.

"Professor Moriarty made me give it back. He threatened to shoot me if I didn't. Then he burned the letter," Sherlock said.

There was an awesome silence after Sherlock finished speaking. In Sherlock's mind it was more terrible than the shouting that had preceded it. His father's frosty eyes burnt into his. Sherlock dared not turn away, and he knew not what to say. Finally his father looked away.

"I cannot believe that you are my son," Siger Holmes said. "I cannot believe that any son of mine would make up such lies and expect me to believe them. Professor Moriarty has told me about discovering you in his room. He told he was frightened when he perceived that there was an intruder in his room and pulled out a small revolver. He said that when he realized it was you, he let you go."

"After he threatened to shoot me," Sherlock insisted.

"I cannot imagine Professor Moriarty threatening anyone," his father said in disbelief.

"He did," Sherlock said.

"Why?" the squire asked.

"To force me to give up the letter so he could burn it," Sherlock said.

"He mentioned no letter."

192

"Of course not. Father, Professor Moriarty is an evil and cunning man," Sherlock said.

"I have heard enough of that! Do you deny that you entered his room when he was not there intending to remove something from that room?" his father said.

"No, sir," Sherlock responded.

"Then you are a thief! The matter is settled. We will discuss it no further."

"Father--" Sherlock appealed.

"No. There is another matter we need to discuss. It is my understanding that you have been having clandestine meetings with Miss Violet Rushdale, is this true?"

"Y-yes, Father," Sherlock said, taken aback by the question. "I-I had been meeting with her."

"Did you tell anyone in this household that you were meeting her?" the squire asked.

"No, sir," Sherlock said suddenly fearful that his actions were going to backlash on Violet and her father.

"Did you avoid telling anyone in this household about these meetings?" his father asked.

"Y-yes, sir," Sherlock said.

"Why?" Squire Holmes inquired with his dark eyebrows drawn down together.

Sherlock looked down at the desk between them.

"Because I felt that you would not approve," he said.

"I do not approve. I also do not approve of your sneaking around to avoid my authority," his father said.

Sherlock was silent.

"What are you intentions towards this girl?" the squire asked.

Sherlock looked back up at his father.

"Well, sir, I-I don't know," he said both puzzled by the question and embarrassed to admit his rejection. "She doesn't want to see me any more."

"What claims does she intend to make against you?" his father asked.

Sherlock's bewilderment deepened.

"Claims, sir? I don't know of any," he said.

"Do you deny that you are the father of the child she carries?" his father inquired.

Sherlock gaped at his father. He could think of no words to say, but suddenly many pieces fell into place.

"Oh, what a fool I have been!" Sherlock exclaimed burying his face in his hands and shaking his head from side to side. "How could I have been so blind!" He murmured. "Of course," he said looking up, but talking more to himself than to his father, "that must be why she sent me away. She didn't want me to know!"

"You were not aware that Miss Rushdale was with child?" his father asked.

"No, sir, I--" Sherlock began, but a movement outside the study window caught his eye. He looked out the window, cried, "No!" and jumped up and ran from the room.

Siger Holmes, startled by the suddenly transformation of features on his son's face, also turned to look out the window. He saw Professor Moriarty holding Violet Rushdale roughly with one arm while his other hand seemed to grasp a chain around her neck. Then he saw her break free of Professor Moriarty's grasp and run.

Chapter 25
The Pursuit

Sherlock ran out of his father's study, banged open the heavy front door of the manor house, and raced around the side of the house. Violet had struggled free from Moriarty's grip and run to her horse and mounted. Sandy stood barking between Moriarty and Violet. The professor kicked at the dog as he attempted to run after Violet. Sherlock caught Moriarty from behind and spun him around with his left arm and swung with his right. Never before had Sherlock been so glad of his boxing lessons. It was not just training that powered the blow, but Sherlock's built up resentment and new born anger at what he had seen. Moriarty was completely unprepared for it and went sprawling upon the ground.

Sherrinford appeared from somewhere at that moment. He saw Moriarty lying on the ground clutching his face and Sherlock running from him.

"What is this now?" Sherrinford asked as he approached Moriarty to help him to his feet. But Sherlock ignored his brother as he raced off after Violet. Sherlock could see Muffin flying off down the back road and knew he had no hope of catching her on foot.

"Violet!" he called, but the there was no response. He ran to the stables and whistled.

He often called Gale in this fashion when they were upon the moor, but never had he called her thus from the stables. But come she did. There was a crash as she broke free from her stall and stable hands scattered as she came out. Sherlock leapt on her bareback, and knitting his fingers in her mane, he urged her on after the other horse. Sensing the urgency felt by her rider, Gale stretched out her legs to the task.

Labourers returning from the fields and shepherds herding
in their flocks had drawn to the side of the road as the first horse
had thundered past. They now stood shaking their heads as a
second followed.

As the distance between them slowly decreased, Sherlock
once again called out to Violet, but she did not turn or seemed to
notice in any way. As they passed the outlying cottages, Sherlock
thought to cut across the meadow and catch her on the road
to the Rushdale farm. But she did not turn towards the farm.
Instead she headed straight up towards the moor.

Sherlock called to Violet again as his own horse mounted
the moor road. It was then that he felt the first icy sting upon his
cheek. Then another and another. He did not look up to see parts
of the matted sky break loose and crystallize, but felt them as they
hit his cheeks like needles. Violet still rode away at a frantic pace.
Again he called to her but his shout was lost in the wind. Flakes
were soon flying all around him. Some melted to icy tears upon
his cheeks. Others caught about his hair and clothes to swirl off
again in the wind. The snow fell heavier and heavier befuddling
his vision. He could just make out Muffin in the distance. He
pleaded with Gale to close the distance as they charged across
the moor. Now he lost Muffin and Violet. No, there they were
again. Gale began to let up her pace as the snow-covered ground
became slick. Still Sherlock begged her to go on, even as Violet
vanished completely from view.

"Violet!" he cried in desperation. He could no longer see
Violet or her horse at all. All he could see was white. Moor and
sky merged in every direction. The grey of the sky and purples
and golds of the moor had all faded to white. Obstacles rose up
before them unexpectedly and Gale whinnied in protest when
Sherlock still ordered her forward. She halted. At Sherlock's
appeals she merely shook her head and snorted. The fog of the
horse's breath mingled with the flakes for a few seconds before

vanishing. Gale pawed at the ground and refused to go further. Sherlock shouted Violet's name repeatedly but there was no answer but the howl of the wind. He had lost her. Sherlock shivered as the wind cut through his coat. He had not noticed the cold before.

He dismounted and brushed the snow from his hair and coat. He leaned against the horse's heaving body for warmth. He had lost all sense of direction. Even the horse's hoof prints had rapidly filled with snow. He shivered again and sneezed, and knew he must seek shelter. He called out once more for Violet. Then laying his arm upon the horse's shoulder, he turned her around and urged her back the way they had come. Gale moved slowly and reluctantly and Sherlock hugged close to her. He searched in vain for some landmark, but all the world was a shrieking wilderness of white. If the sun had shone, however faintly, through this blizzard Sherlock would have rejoiced. But the lighting was diffuse and seemed to be growing more faint. They wandered about blindly stumbling over rocks, and scraping their legs in shrubs, without determining where they were.

Suddenly the ground gave way under Sherlock's feet. He found himself sliding down an icy slope. He grasped about wildly for any hold, but found none. Then he rolled and rolled until he struck ice, water and stones in succession. Sherlock lay there for a moment stunned by the fall, then picked himself up and shook himself. He shivered. The water into which he had fallen was running water. He had ventured too close to some gill crossing the moor and fallen down its steep banks. Better than a mire, he thought, at least there was solid ground beneath his feet. Above he could see Gale's nose as she looked down at him. Sherlock attempted to climb back up the icy bank but each time he gained a few feet he slid back down. Then he gained a purchase on a lip of stone sticking out in the bank. Looking up he saw Gale above him. If she had worn a bridle he might have been able to reach her lead, but he knew she was unbridled. But perhaps, if she would let him, he could catch hold of her foreleg hoof and pull himself up. He reached up his numb fingers, but Gale snorted and drew back. He lost her in the snow and called to her, but she did not return. Thus abandoned, Sherlock made one last effort to climb the bank. He slipped again and splashed once more into the stream below.

His hands dug into the streambed as he pushed himself shivering to his knees. As he drew his hands out of the water he looked at them half-frozen as they were and covered with sand and gravel. Then he paused before he wiped them on his trousers. For there in the final dim glow of the twilight, he saw red flecks like fire among the grains of sand. Suddenly Sherlock knew where he was. This was the very gill that ran past the hut before crossing the road and plunging into the dale! He scrambled to his feet and stumbled downstream. He kept to his feet the best he could but he slipped now and then on smooth stones or patches of ice he could not see. Night had fallen suddenly as it does in winter, but the snow still fell.

At last the banks widened and flattened until Sherlock could find a place to crawl out upon his hands and knees. Still the snow fell. Sherlock could feel it accumulating upon his hair and back but he was so cold by now that it no longer chilled him.

The storm and the night combined to create a darkness so complete that if his eyes had been gouged out he could have been no blinder. He had to rely totally on his hands and feet to guide him and they were so numbed by the cold that they were of little use. Somehow he made his way, groping with his hands, through the invisible tors to the stones he knew must be at the entrance to the hut. He pushed at them and his frozen hands screamed with pain at the effort and they did not budge. Sherlock leaned his whole weight and strength against the rocks. Then slowly, the rocks, which seemed frozen to the ground, slid to the side.

Sherlock panted with the effort. Sweat rolled down his brow to freeze upon his cheeks. Then he pulled down the flat rock that was the door and tumbled into the hut. He fell, exhausted and half-frozen, upon the mat.

Chapter 26
Sherrinford's Search

Sherrinford was up long before dawn. Sherlock's bed had not been slept in. No one had seen or heard of him all night. Sherrinford dressed warmly. The snow had stopped falling, but it was bitterly cold outside. He had no idea when he would be back.

"What are you going to do?" Amanda asked.

"I'm going to find my brother," he said. "I'll be back as soon as I can."

"God be with you," she said and kissed him.

The wind whipped about Sherrinford as he left the house. He pulled his muffler tighter. At the stables he made inquiries. None of the stable hands had seen Sherlock or his horse since they had ridden out of the yard the previous day.

"Just as well the horse ain't back yet," one said. "We're still mending her stall."

"Ask Ben," one of the stable boys suggested. "He says he was driving his flocks down from the heights when thy brother and the farm girl came riding past him like thunder."

Sherrinford hunted up the shepherd, Ben, while the stable hands saddled his horse.

"Eh, first that lassie, Farmer Rushdale's daughter, goes by looking like the devil's on her tail and then I be thinking it's safe and here comes thy brother nearly trampling my sheep."

"Did you see which direction they took?" Sherrinford asked.

"Aye, and I reckoned them both crazy riding up to the moor when it's setting to snow."

"They both went up the moor road?"

"Aye, that's wot I said."

Sherrinford returned to the stable. Sandy scurried out from somewhere and yapped at him. He ignored her and mounted his horse. He rode eastward, and hesitated at the crossroad before turning his horse towards the Rushdale farm.

The blanket of white had not improved the look of the farm, but had deepened the silence about it. The only sound Sherrinford heard was the hissing voice of the wind sweeping the snow around. There were no tracks, he noticed, as he rode into the yard. But if there ever had been the drifting snow would have covered them long ago.

"Hello!" he shouted, but there was no response.

The place seemed abandoned. Was this how it was for the prince in the fairy tale when he entered Sleeping Beauty's enchanted castle? Sherrinford mused. But it was no beauty he found sleeping and it would take more than a kiss to wake him up.

Godfrey Rushdale was sprawled back in a chair beside the hearth. His snores puckered out his lips and ruffled his beard. The reek of the place told Sherrinford more than that Godfrey could use a bath. He shook the man and called his name, but Godfrey Rushdale only stirred and brushed him away like a fly. Some garbled speech came out of him but that was all. Try as he might, Sherrinford could not get any sense out of the man. So he left him to his drunken stupor and searched the house. He found neither Sherlock nor Violet nor any sign that either had been here since yesterday afternoon.

Sherrinford left the house and searched the barn and the surrounding buildings and found nothing there either. He remounted his horse and rode out through the gate again. He paused for a moment and looked down the road. There were other farms along there. But why should they have gone to any of them and not the Rushdale farm? There was also the road into the village. It branched off south of here, but would they have tried to go into the village in the storm? No, none of these choices made any sense, but neither had what Ben had told him. Ben had seen them heading up the moor road.

Sherrinford turned toward the moor. It loomed large and white behind the farm he had just left, like a cloud that had come to rest upon the ground overnight. He knew that was where he must go.

As he headed back towards the crossroads he heard another little yap and saw a ball of gold plowing its way through the snow. It was a comical sight and Sherrinford had to smile.

He dismounted and scooped the dog up from the snow.

"How did you get out, girl? Do you think you can find your master, hmmm?"

He remounted with the dog on one arm and settled her in front of him on the horse.

"Hold on, girl," he told Sandy as they ascended the moor road.

The fickle winds swept the snow about the moor, first building a drift here then gusting it away to be rebuilt somewhere else. Some places the ground was bare and in some spots the snow was three feet deep. The going was not easy and Sherrinford pondered the sanity of his mission. Where was he to find them up here, he thought as the wind swept up a swirling column of snow that engulfed him and tore at his eyes and stung his cheeks.

There were legends Sherrinford had heard as a boy of folks being lost on the moors in blizzards such as they had the night before. The tales told that those folk's spirits still wandered about the moors and that their hopeless cries could be heard in the bitter winter winds, such as those that gnawed at him now. Sherrinford shook off such thoughts. Then the wind shifted wildly again and the dog before him perked up. Sandy barked and then pounced from the horse's back. She dashed across a bare space and barked again before tackling a drift. This time she was answered by a horse's neigh. Sherrinford followed after the dog and found Sherlock's horse standing amongst the brush near the gill. But Sandy only paused a moment near the horse and then dashed on along the banks of the gill. Of course, Sherrinford thought, the hut is near here. He had nearly forgotten it. He quickly dismounted and dashed after the dog with renewed hope.

When he came near the entrance he saw that the stone "door" to the hut was open and snow had drifted into the entrance. Sandy dashed inside and Sherrinford followed. There in the dim light he saw Sherlock on the heather bed where he had thrown himself the night before. His hair was matted and frozen against his head. His face was pale and his eyes were closed.

Sherrinford reached out to touch his brother and recoiled. Sherlock felt cold to his touch. Sandy barked. It seemed sacrilegious, like desecrating a tomb. Before Sherrinford could stop her, Sandy pounced and began licking Sherlock on the face. Sherlock stirred. Sherrinford pulled the dog back and grabbed his brother by the shoulders.

"Sherlock!" he cried.

Sherlock's eyelids fluttered open. He stared blankly up at his brother for a moment then his eyes slowly closed. Sherrinford shook him again, and his eyes opened. This time there was recognition. His lips parted in a hoarse whisper.

"Violet?" Sherlock whispered, "Where is Violet?"

Sherrinford began wrapping a blanket about his brother.

"I don't know, Sherlock," Sherrinford answered. Then he took off his own great coat and threw it over Sherlock who was shivering now. As he did, Sherlock caught his sleeve.

"Find her," he begged, "promise-"

"Yes, Sherlock, I promise. Now--."

But with that assurance, Sherlock fell limp.

"First, I need to get you home," Sherrinford said aloud to no one at all.

Sherrinford carried his brother's limp body out to where the horses stood. He secured Sherlock to Gale's back, threw a rope around her neck to lead her, and mounted his own horse.

As they rode past the stables, Sherrinford shouted to Eston who stood in the yard. Soon hands came running up.

"Send one of the hands to the village for Dr. Thompkins," Sherrinford told Eston. "Here, help me get him down."

Sherrinford carried Sherlock through the back door of the manor house. Tessy looked up as he passed the kitchen.

"Lord preserve us!" she cried, "He's found Master Sherlock. Hurry lass!" she called to the maids, "Get some more towels and take them upstairs. Go and see to Master Sherlock's fire. Susan, thou go and tell the missus."

As Sherrinford lay Sherlock upon his bed, their mother appeared in the doorway followed by Amanda and several of the maids.

"Take those wet clothes off," Mrs. Holmes commanded.

Sherrinford helped the women and servants tend to Sherlock until the doctor came. Then Sherrinford turned and picked up his great coat that he had wrapped Sherlock in from the chair by Sherlock's desk. As he did he spotted the ring of keys he had given Sherlock two days before lying on the desk. He picked them up and returned them to his own desk. Amanda intercepted him as he headed downstairs with his coat in hand.

"I must go out again," he told her. "I promised Sherlock I would."

Professor Moriarty was near the front door as Sherrinford went out. Moriarty's boxes were being loaded on the sleigh to be taken to the railway station in Thirsk. The squire had dismissed Moriarty the night before, shortly after Sherrinford had helped him to his feet.

"I will not tolerate such treatment of women regardless of their station," the squire had said to Professor Moriarty. Sherrinford did not know what his father had seen, but he was certain it was what had sent Sherlock out after Violet in the storm.

"You had best be gone before I return or I might forget I'm a civilized man," Sherrinford told Moriarty with his hand on the door.

Sherrinford opened the door and turned back to Moriarty whose face was swollen and discoloured from Sherlock's blow of the night before.

"And if my brother dies you'd best hope our paths never cross again," Sherrinford added before shutting the door behind him.

Sherrinford gathered a handful of men from the yard and headed back up into the moors. They grouped in pairs and fanned out. They searched the bare rocky places and frozen marshes and streams. They searched on horseback and on foot. They suffered frostbite and bruises and one man sprained a wrist in a fall. But they found nothing.

The vast frozen wasteland seemed to taunt them as if it hid some secret. But all they found hidden in the snow were rocks and brush which seemed especially placed to deter their search. The winds clawed at them with frozen fingers and threw snow in their faces. Still they searched.

But they found no sign of Violet or her horse, nor any sign that anyone or anything had ever been here in the last thousand years. The shifting snows like the shifting sands of time held no footprint for long. Even their own vanished behind them. It was only their knowledge of this beastly place and the guidance of the coquettish sun, which often promised, but never quite came through the clouds, that led the men home again.

As the day wore on the seed of hope which had propelled Sherrinford shriveled and faded, and the seed of fear that he had brought with him from Sherlock's room grew and grew. He had come out to fulfill his promise to Sherlock. Was he wasting his time while his brother lay dying? But if Sherlock was dying what could he do? No, he had promised Sherlock, and as long as there was any hope of fulfilling his promise he must strive on. But the bitter winds snatched hope from him and at last Sherrinford and his men descended from the moor cold, tired and discouraged.

Chapter 27
The Illness

No sooner had Sherrinford entered the house that evening then Amanda ran to him.

"You look tired, dear," she said.

"I am," he replied as he shed the last of his outer garments.

She threw her arms around him and he kissed the top of her head.

"How is Sherlock?" he asked.

She shivered.

"He is very ill. After you left his shivering subsided as he became warm, but then he began coughing and retching. We had our hands quite full with him. Then he began shaking horribly all over. The doctor had the servants bring packs of snow and we placed them about Sherlock's head and the shaking stopped. But I've never seen anything more frightening in my life. He's in a terrible fever. He tosses and turns and mumbles and cries out and has these terrible coughing fits that wrack his whole body. Oh, the poor boy!"

Amanda sighed and buried her face against Sherrinford's chest. Sherrinford stroked Amanda's hair.

"Perhaps you should visit your parents for a while, Amanda," he said.

"My place is here with you, Ford," she protested. "This is where I wish to be. If I can be of any help in caring for your brother, I wish to try."

"But I'm afraid Sherlock's illness will be to upsetting for you. In your condition, I--" Sherrinford said.

"Sherrinford, I will be fine," Amanda said.

"Well, I will ask the doctor. Come now, I wish to see Sherlock," Sherrinford said.

As they entered Sherlock's room a dry, hacking cough tore through the air. For a moment Sherlock was bent double with pain. Then the doctor gently pressed him back down against the pillows which kept him in almost a sitting position. Sherlock's eyes were closed and his cheeks were flushed.

Dr. Thompkins wiped the sweat from Sherlock's brow.

"How is he, doctor?" Sherrinford asked.

Dr. Thompkins shook his head.

"Your brother is very ill. Worst he's ever been. He is so restless that it is tiring to watch. Can you tell me what happened? He's covered with scrapes and bruises as well."

Sherrinford told the doctor what he had seen and how he had found Sherlock.

"I presume that he must have fallen after becoming lost in the storm," Sherrinford said.

"Well, that would explain it. He must not be left alone. I have suggested that the household take shifts watching over him," Dr. Thompkins said.

"Yes, Doctor. Is there anything we can do for him?" Sherrinford asked.

Again the doctor shook his head.

"Just keep his body warm and his head cool. He breathes easiest if he is propped up on the pillows. The kettle on the hearth should be kept full."

Sherrinford sat down beside his brother. Amanda stood beside him. Sherlock was quiet now.

As Dr. Thompkins prepared to leave, Sherrinford stopped him and said, "Doctor, I want to send Amanda away to visit her parents. I don't believe that it is good for her to be here. The atmosphere in this house is far too upsetting for one in her condition."

Dr. Thompkins smiled.

"Sherrinford, do you really believe that she would fare better away from here, where she would have nothing to do but wait and worry? It will not prevent her from sharing your concerns. Here, at least she feels useful. Let her stay if she wishes."

"Thank you, Doctor," Amanda said.

Sherrinford sat with Sherlock again after supper. Sherlock was delirious again and called out for Violet. His struggles became so violent that he threatened to throw himself on to the floor, and Sherrinford had to hold him down. Sherlock grabbed his brother's arms and clung to them. His hands were hot. As Sherrinford held Sherlock, his brother's fever seemed so great Sherrinford thought it must heat the room even if the fire were to go out. He tried talking to Sherlock but the boy did not seem to hear him and only continued with his babbling. That night, before tumbling into an exhausted sleep, Sherrinford sank to his knees and asked the Lord to forgive all of them for their folly and to help his poor brother.

The following day Sherrinford rose early again. He sat with Sherlock for a while then set out on his search again. He and his men swept up and down the dale, knocking at every cottage and farmhouse, asking everyone they met for news of Miss Rushdale. No one had seen her since she had set her horse upon the moor path two days before. No one knew of any friends that she might be visiting. She had lead a fairly lonely life since her mother had died, what with her father and all. She wasn't known to have any friends at all, except-- and here they would hesitate but Sherrinford would draw them out, to his great surprise --except, of course, they would tell him, for his brother, Sherlock. Some had seen them walking together along the road; others had seen them riding together on the moor; still others had heard only talk. The tale of how Sherlock had taken her home after she fainted at gleaning had traveled up and down the dale, though Sherrinford had known nothing of it before this day. He was amazed at how much the common folk of the dale knew of his brother's romance when he himself had been totally ignorant of it until a few days ago. And the rumor came to him as well that Violet carried his brother's child, adding both light and mystery to the events that had unfolded.

No one knew of any kinfolk of Miss Rushdale's living, except perhaps a sister of her mother's who had married a man from the south of England years before and moved away. No one knew where. At last Sherrinford came back to the Rushdale farm. He saw no change in the farm as he rode through the gate, but as he neared the house, the front door opened. Godfrey stood there with his shotgun leveled at Sherrinford.

"What thou be wanting, Mr. Holmes?" came Godfrey's thick shout.

"A word with you, Mr. Rushdale."

"That be all? Thou's not come to put me out?" Godfrey asked.

"Not yet," Sherrinford had to reply. He knew it was only four weeks until the next quarter day. With Violet gone the rent was not likely to be paid, and his father was determined to have a new tenant in by spring.

"I'm looking for your daughter. Have you seen her?" Sherrinford asked.

Godfrey scowled.

"No," he responded. "Been looking for the lass myself."

He squinted at Sherrinford.

"But why art thou int'rested in where she be?"

"My brother Sherlock asked me--" Sherrinford began.

Godfrey spat on the ground.

"Thy cursed brother!" Godfrey exclaimed. "Shoulda knowed he'd be innit. Tell thy brother to leave my lass be!"

Sherrinford could get no further information out of the man. He also knew it was not wise to stand too long at the end of Farmer Rushdale's shotgun. Godfrey Rushdale could not be trusted not to pull that trigger, whether due to accident or anger, and there was no telling whether the man would hit or miss. So Sherrinford left the farm and returned to the manor house. Sherlock was much the same as he had been in the morning.

That night Sherrinford composed a telegram to Mycroft in London. He informed Mycroft that Sherlock was ill and requested that Mycroft "come if convenient." He sent a stable boy off to Thirsk with it in the morning with instructions that he wait for a response before returning.

Sherrinford went into the village that day. He had a lengthy discussion with the village constable and then together they walked from house to house and shop to shop asking everyone they encountered what they knew of Violet Rushdale.

The constable filled his notebook with odds and ends, but not much of it was useful. The shopkeepers felt kindly towards the poor lass who had struggled so gamely, but she had spoken little of herself. Widow Hadley was a tight-lipped woman but she told them how the girl had collected herbs for her upon the moors.

"Aye, she learned them well. Twas rare thing she mistook an herb."

"Where'd she collect them?" the constable asked.

"Upon the moor. I don't know precisely where," the Widow said.

"Mother, didn't she collect some by the old abbey?" Will Hadley suggested.

"Suppose she did," said Widow Hadley looking cagey. "But I don't know t'will help thee."

"Where's this abbey?" the constable asked.

"Tis some ruins, nowt much of it left, back a ways on the moors. I've been there," Will said.

"So thou could lead us there if need be?"

"I believe so, though I've never gone that way in winter," Will replied.

Mrs. Ross crossed herself as they came in, for, of course, she had seen them at the Widow's house across the street. When they inquired about Violet Rushdale, she lectured them for sometime on the girl's dealings with that witch across the street and how she had little doubt that Satan himself had sprung up to claim his own or the good Lord had struck her down as a sign of warning to them all. When they asked if she knew of any friends or relations that the girl might have had, she poured forth all the gossip she knew about the girl and her family, annotating with her own extrapolations and moral judgments. For more than an hour she went on about how saintly Mary Rushdale had been-- "a blessing on this earth" and how she had been delivered from the insipid evil around her that had blossomed forth when her saintly presence had been removed.

"Godfrey showed his true colours then. An evil man, possessed, I'd naught hesitate to think. Lord knew his decline from drink was coming and delivered the angel afore it. That daughter of his was no better, dealing with that witch and carrying on so with the squire's son--" then realizing her audience, she said, "Begging thy pardon, Mr. Holmes, but I do believe that thy brother strayed a bit further than he aught with that girl. Not that I ever saw them together myself. No, they were careful of that. But the things I've heard!"

"Mrs. Ross, my brother is extremely ill, near death even," Sherrinford said quite red in the face. "Since he cannot defend his actions at this moment, I do not believe it fair that we judge him."

"Just keep to the facts, Mrs. Ross," the constable said.

"Well, it's a sign, I say, a sign," Mrs. Ross said shaking her head. "When thou hast dealings with the devil's own.... But the facts, yes, the facts...." Then she gossiped on for another twenty minutes before they determined that they had heard all that was useful and a great deal more.

By the end of the day they had gathered little useful information, but decided to organize another search of the moors for the following day.

Mycroft's reply telegram was waiting for him when Sherrinford returned home: "Not convenient. Will come at your word. Mycroft."

Sherrinford sat with Sherlock again that evening as he stewed over Mycroft's response. Mycroft was leaving the decision to his judgment at a time when Sherrinford was not sure his judgment was still intact. But as his youngest brother raved Sherrinford wrote, "Come when you can" and added "He would not know you were here."

That was one fact that Sherrinford was certain of: Sherlock had shown no sign of recognizing anyone since he had spoken to Sherrinford in the hut. The trip from London was a full day's journey and he could not say with any certainty that Sherlock would be alive the next evening. He sent the stable boy back to Thirsk the following morning with the same instructions as before. As the boy left, the constable arrived with a wagonload of men and a pack of hounds.

"I'd like to see thy brother first, if I may," the constable said.

"Come, then, my wife is sitting with him," Sherrinford said.

Sherrinford and the constable mounted the stairs towards Sherlock's room. Sherlock was in the midst of a coughing fit when they entered. Amanda gently wiped his brow as the fit subsided.

"He's been in a fever since I brought him in," Sherrinford said.

The constable shook his head.

"Does Dr. Thompkins think he'll pull through?" the constable asked.

"He doesn't say," Sherrinford said.

"Thy brother has said nothing about Miss Rushdale?" the constable asked.

"He asked me to find her, and he hasn't made any sense since," Sherrinford said.

Squire Holmes and his wife were coming out from breakfast as Sherrinford and the constable returned downstairs.

"Mornin', Squire," the constable said.

"Good morning, sir. What is it that brings you out from the village?" the squire asked.

"Sherrinford is helping me organize a search for Miss Rushdale. We've rounded up some hounds and some men from the village and we're just about to head up to the moor," the constable responded.

"Do you feel it wise?" Squire Holmes asked.

"Well, sir, there's a lass missing. We mun do what we can," the constable responded.

Squire Holmes nodded.

"Yes, I suppose that is your duty," the squire said.

Then he looked at Sherrinford.

"When you are out there, just remember that you have other responsibilities," the squire said.

"Yes, Father," Sherrinford responded.

Sherrinford lead the party first to the hut where he had found his brother.

"My brothers and I used to play here. We kept the entrance hidden, so I'm not sure if anyone else knew of it," Sherrinford said.

"Would thy brother have told Miss Rushdale about it?" the constable asked.

"I don't know. I don't know that it matters either. She wasn't here when I found him. I don't even know how he found his way here in that storm," Sherrinford responded.

"Well, I'm just trying to cover everything. Now thou said thou'st had men all over this region?"

"Yes, we covered it quite thoroughly without finding anything," Sherrinford said.

"Well, then I guess nothing would gained by looking around

here. The dogs haven't shown interest in anything, have they, Mac?"

"No."

"Then Mr. Hadley, lead us to that abbey thou wert talking about," the constable said.

Will Hadley lead them out towards the ruins of the old abbey. He was confused a few times because snow covered landmarks, but finally they arrived there.

The constable shook his head and said, "I was hoping that there was some kind of shelter here. I can see there ain't, but let's look around."

Man and dog searched the surrounding area. Finally the constable stopped and scratched his head.

"Where else could she have been heading for?" the constable asked.

Each of the men shook his head.

"There is nothing out here, Constable," Sherrinford said. "The road near here heads south and doesn't get to anywhere for a half a day's ride."

Will Hadley said, "The other fork continues to the east. The terrain there is rough. Then a couple of miles on there is a steep cliff. The road winds down the cliff on a narrow ledge. I've driven a wagon on it, but, lord, I donna do it when the weather's foul."

"No, sir. Constable, thou'd know if thou had ever been on the moor when it's snowing. Thicker'n flour. Canna tell right from left nor up from down," said the miller.

"Wot's beyond that cliff?" the constable asked.

"The road meets another road in the valley," Will Hadley said. "Nearest house is a shepherd's cottage set high on the moors about ten miles back north on the other road. Nearest village is thirty or forty miles to the south. But, sir, I wouldn't even try to make it down that cliff on a clear day like today. With the snow and ice, it isn't sane."

"She's not likely to have gotten that far either," the miller agreed. "No, I wager we find her in one of the gillies or marshes we passed `tween here and the dale."

At last it was decided that nothing could be gained by continuing further across the moor. So they fanned out and headed westward again, searching as they went. As the sun slid to the brink of the frozen sky the men stood overlooking the dale they called home.

"It doesn't mean she's not there, Sherrinford, only that we can't find her," the village constable said. "There are places here where a man donna go in winter without risking his own life."

"I know," Sherrinford responded, as he watched the sun vanish. "But I've got to keep looking. I'm going to search the dale again tomorrow."

"I'll give thee all the help I can, but for now we'd best be heading home," the constable said.

Back at Holmes Hall, Sherrinford sent the men into the kitchen to warm themselves and fill their bellies before they went home. As he was about to enter the main foyer, he heard his mother's voice.

"Oh, Doctor, thank God you've come back. Quickly please," she said.

Then footsteps clattered up the main stairs. Sherrinford followed quickly. In Sherlock's room he found the womenfolk huddled together in great distress and a few of the servants trying to be useful. Dr. Thompkins was leaning over Sherlock who was coughing savagely. The doctor was holding Sherlock's head to one side. As the coughing subsided and the doctor released Sherlock, Sherrinford saw Dr. Thompkins wipe something from Sherlock's mouth. It was reddish brown and gritty like the mud of the moors after a spring rain.

"Oh, my God," gasped Sherrinford.

Dr. Thompkins looked around at Sherrinford.

"Have them clear the room. I don't need an audience," Dr. Thompkins said.

As Sherrinford began to follow the others, Sherlock was struck with another spasm of coughing. Dr. Thompkins said, "Stay, Sherrinford. I may need you."

"He's coughing up blood, isn't he?" Sherrinford said.

"Yes," the doctor confirmed.

As Sherlock relaxed again, the doctor said, "Now hold him down, Sherrinford. I'm going to give him something that I hope will stop this."

Dr. Thompkins pulled a case from his bag and after some preparation he drove a needle into Sherlock's arm.

"You can let him go now," Dr. Thompkins said sitting down next to the bed.

The doctor watched Sherlock very carefully.

"You are an educated man, Sherrinford. You know about the changes going on in the world at large, the factories, the machines. The same is true with medicine. Doctors are offered new gadgets and new drugs with amazing claims and little information. Maybe the doctors in the hospitals down in London can experiment on a few hundred patients and discover which drugs work best and how best to use them, and if a few patients die that's the price of progress. Here in Yorkshire all I have is one very ill boy and the hope that this drug will indeed stop the bleeding in his lungs, and not cause some other unwanted effect."

"We understand that you are doing your best," Sherrinford said.

"I'll stay with him for a while. Perhaps you should say good evening to that pretty wife of yours," Dr. Thompkins said.

Sherrinford found Amanda alone in the sitting room. She jumped up when he entered and they hugged each other in silence. When they broke embrace she picked up a piece of paper from the table.

"The stable boy brought this back while you were out."
Sherrinford ripped open the telegram and read it.
"Understood. Keep me informed. Mycroft."

That night Sherrinford sat down and wrote a long letter to Mycroft, explaining all that had happened in the last four days. The letter would take several days to reach Mycroft, Sherrinford knew, but he could not say all he wanted in a telegram.

The next day the constable and Sherrinford and a few men from the manor searched the dale once more. They looked in the ditches alongside the roads. They scoured the fields of snow-covered stubble, the pastures, and the woods. They searched every barn and stable and hayloft.

While they were out, the vicar came and anointed Sherlock's perspiring head and convulsing hands and said the appropriate prayers, then he bowed his head. When he raised it again he said, "It's so sad. I remember Sherlock standing at the rail at his brother's wedding. Was it six months ago? So tall and straight and full of life and I thought that it wouldn't be long until he was joining a bride up there himself."

Suddenly the house rumbled, and rumbled again. Dr. Thompson and the vicar sprang to the door of the room as hurried footsteps headed for the front door. Again and again the pounding on the front door resounded through the building even as the door was opened. The squire emerged from his study and the ladies from their rooms as the offender tumbled in as he made another attempt at the door as it was opened. He began shouting even as Thomas grabbed him up from the floor.

"Where is she? Where is my daughter?" Godfrey Rushdale roared.

"Your daughter is not here," the squire rumbled in return.

"Eh, then where be that scoundrel son of yours. He's to blame for this, to be sure. I'll know wot he's done with my daughter!" Godfrey shouted.

"Sherlock is very ill, Godfrey," Dr. Thompson responded from the top of the stairs. "You cannot see him."

"Thus you have no business here and should take your leave," the squire said.

"I've come for my daughter and I'm not leaving till I knows her whereabouts," Godfrey growled.

"Sir, you will leave this house and the grounds around this house, or I shall send to the village for the constable and have you locked up," Squire Holmes announced.

Godfrey made no motion to leave.

"Remove him," the squire ordered with a wave of his hand and withdrew once more to his study.

Godfrey struggled gamely. Some of the maids joined the butler in dragging him to the door way.

"Oh, Farmer Rushdale, don't do this!" The vicar pleaded as he rushed down the stairs and through the door following the throng of servants aiding Godfrey Rushdale's exit from the Hall. Dr. Thompkins returned to his patient.

Sherrinford came home early that afternoon. The clouds were settling down on the moors and the flakes were beginning to fall. They continued to fall for the next two days. Sherrinford tried to attend to the business matters he had been neglecting. But he was restless. When he couldn't stand it any longer he went and sat next to his brother, and when he couldn't stand that any longer, he returned to his work.

Sherlock was growing quieter. His coughing was less violent and his bouts of delirium came less frequently. His pulse rate was still high, but his breathing was slower. Sherrinford had thought these good signs, but Dr. Thompkins shook his head.

"Some's due to the injections I've been giving him. But mostly he's growing weaker. All we can get into to him is a little honey water."

If he would only wake up... Sherrinford began to think... if he

219

would only wake up.... It formed a chorus that drummed through Sherrinford's brain until he could stand it no more. One night as he sat with Sherlock, he suddenly stood up and grabbed his brother by the shoulders and shook him as he had done in the hut. He called his brother by his name and Sherlock opened his eyes and looked at Sherrinford.

"Violet?" Sherlock whispered, "Where is Violet?"

"I don't know. I don't know," Sherrinford cried. "I have tried--"

"Find her-- promise," Sherlock whispered and closed his eyes again.

"Oh, my God, Sherlock," Sherrinford said wrapping his arms around his brother and holding him. "If I knew she were half the world away, I'd go and get her, if that would bring you back to us."

But Sherlock was limp in his arms and said nothing. Sherrinford knew he had not really reached him. He had only triggered some part of Sherlock's delirious brain into repeating their conversation in the hut. Sherrinford released his brother and sat with his head in his hands until his mother came and sent him off to bed.

The next morning the sun peeped over the moor through broken clouds to find Sherrinford was already working his way on horseback across the moor. Three other men from the manor followed on horseback. They made slow progress through the deep snow. The snow was so deep that sometimes they would lose the road altogether until some visible landmark set them right again.

At last they stood on the brink of the escarpment at the place where the road began its winding descent.

Eston looked down.

"I wouldn't want to be going that way with a full sun over me, much less in a snowstorm in the glooming. Thou thinks she came this way?"

Sherrinford sighed.

"I don't think anything anymore," Sherrinford said. "I just keep looking. To go anywhere to the east she must have crossed this, and that is the only road that makes the descent."

They stood in silence for a while looking down at the frozen cascade of ice and snow on the cliff below them.

"I'm going down there," Sherrinford announced.

Eston had a scowl on his craggy face. Then he shook his head. Sherrinford thought he was going to tell him he was crazy but Eston turned to his horse and said, "Then we'll be glad of these ropes I brought along," as he untied the rope and hoisted it on his shoulder.

"You don't have to come," Sherrinford said.

"Ach. I'll follow thee down. We'll leave these two up here," Eston said.

As their horses followed the road down they seemed to enter a whole new world. Icicles hung over the edge of the cliff gleaming in the morning sunlight. Some places the ice formed large spikes and daggers and in others it had formed into glassy columns of winter's temple. The horses did not like the road, alternating as it seemed to between fluffy snow and ice. No matter how wide the road was the edge of the cliff always seemed too close. Still they made it halfway down with no incident. Then suddenly a bank of icicles above Sherrinford gave way and crashed down to the road. His horse panicked and backed way to the opposite side of the road. But what had seemed to be a solid part of the road turned out to be but an overhang of ice and snow which caved in under the horse's weight, and the horse began to fall. In the seeming millennium in which Sherrinford felt his horse sliding off the cliff and taking him with it, he realized what his father had meant when he had told him to remember that he had other responsibilities. He also realized how foolish he had been. As he

221

tried to leap free of the horse he realized that it was probably too late to do anything about it. Then he felt a rope tighten about his chest and he grabbed on to it with his hands. He dangled there for a moment, half off the edge of the cliff watching his horse careen off the rocks and land far below. Then the rope pulled him up onto solid ground and Eston helped him stand. A shaken Sherrinford tried to thank him, but the stoic Yorkshireman brushed it off, as if nothing unexpected had happened.

"I couldn't let thy wife become a widow ere she was a mother," Eston said. "Not to think what thy father would do to me if I lost his heir over a cliff. Oh, the wigging thou art gonna get for losing that horse twill be light by comparison. But I'm thinking it time for heading home."

"Yes, let's go home," Sherrinford agreed.

Sherlock continued to grow weaker over the next few days. His raving stopped altogether. The only sound he emitted was an occasional low moan. His pulse was irregular and he drew each breath slowly and with great effort.

"It's the worst case of pneumonia I've ever seen." Dr. Thompkins said. "I've seen old folks die of it before this. They don't fight it like he's been doing." The doctor shook his head. "I don't think he can keep it up much longer. I'll be back first thing in the morning."

The following morning Dr. Thompkins found that Sherlock's fever had risen dramatically. He ordered the snow packs brought back. "I don't want to worry the womenfolk but as high as his temperature is now, I fear there's brain fever, too."

The doctor was silent for a moment. Sherrinford looked down at his brother. Sherlock had grown thin. His cheeks, flushed with fever, were sunken in. The veins of his forehead were swollen and his lips were tinged with blue.

"I think the crisis will come tonight. Either his fever will break or--"

Dr. Thompkins hesitated.

"Or what?" Sherrinford asked.

"Or he will die."

That night the doctor stayed at Sherlock's bedside, wiping his forehead and changing the snow packs, and though he was glad of company, he refused to be relieved. He took the lad's temperature each half hour hoping to see it go down. But for two hours after sunset it continued to rise. Sherlock lay silent now. The only sound being the little puffs of breath he took. His pulse was still rapid-- his heart pounding to distribute what little oxygen it could get from his lungs. Sherlock's cheeks had lost their flush and had taken on a faint shade of blue. The doctor attended each gasp of breath fearing that it would be the last. Suddenly the doctor noted a drop. He checked again fearing error. But the result was the same. A half hour later the thermometer recorded that the fever had dropped further. Close to midnight Sherrinford entered the room.

"You look exhausted, Sherrinford. You should be in bed," the doctor said.

"I can't sleep. How is he?" Sherrinford asked.

"His fever has broken. His temperature is close to normal now," Dr. Thompkins said.

"Then he'll live, doctor?" Sherrinford asked hopefully.

"It's too soon to say. Now go and get your rest."

Two hours later Dr. Thompkins sat up with a start when Mrs. Holmes entered the room and he realized that he had fallen asleep. Sherlock's fever was still low. Mrs. Holmes was heartened by the news and urged the doctor to get some rest. When the doctor returned to Sherlock's room in the morning he found the lad unchanged.

"Has he awakened at all?" the doctor asked Amanda, who was tending him now.

"No, Dr. Thompkins, he just lies there so still it frightens me,"

Amanda said.

Dr. Thompkins didn't admit that it frightened him as well. But he knew of nothing else he could do. He was in and out all day checking on Sherlock between visiting other patients. Mrs. Wald's baby was due at anytime and it was threatening to be a breach. The village baker had broken his thumb and the Taylor boys were down with something, too. Sherlock's temperature remained near normal, but he was quiet, too quiet.

Late that night after Dr. Thompkins had returned to the village, Michelle took her turn watching Sherlock with strict instructions from Mrs. Holmes that she was to be called if anything happened. Michelle took up her place by the bed and stared shyly at the glowing fire for a few minutes. She could hear Sherlock's breathing and slowly turned to look at him. She remembered when she had first seen Sherlock in France. It was over a year ago now. One of the girls who had tended the Holmes' house in Montpelier had gotten married. The Sisters, who had taken her to live at the convent when her family had died, heard of the position and had taken Michelle to the house to apply. Michelle had been frightened even when the Holmes had decided to take her on. Mrs. Holmes seemed nice enough but the squire seemed so gruff. Then when she had been given a tour of the house she saw a tall slim garcon fencing in the garden. Mrs. Holmes had introduced him as her son, Sherlock, and the man with him as one of his tutors. Michelle had curtsied to them both. Sherlock had smiled at her and then she wasn't so frightened any more.

Since she had no family to go back to the Holmes had taken her with them when they returned to England. She had been glad of that even though it meant going to a strange land where everyone spoke a strange language, for it meant she would be near Master Sherlock. And the young master had helped her learn the new language by saying everything to her in both languages. She had liked that and had learned quickly.

But now he lay on the bed before her, so pale and still. So much like... so much like... Oh, the memories of those horrible days flooded back to her. She remembered all too well how her family-- first father, then mother, and her two sisters-- had fallen ill; how she had fetched and carried for them and tended to their needs the best she could. The doctor had come sometimes but he could do nothing. They had grown weaker and weaker and first one then the other had died. Michelle had groveled at their bedsides begging them not to go and leave her alone and when they had all died Michelle had pleaded with the God that her mother had always trusted in that she be taken, too. But she had been "spared." The Sisters had been good to her, but she had not been happy. She could not understand why God had taken them all away and left her behind. Then she had gone into service for the Holmes' and had met Master Sherlock, and things had changed. Though she was but a servant, and a lowly one at that, he was kind to her and just being around him made her happy.

But now... but now, she thought with a fresh wave of panic, he would be taken, too. Her trembling hands engulfed the limp hand that lay before her on the bed, and she pressed her tear stained cheek down upon it.

"Non, Monsieur, pas vous aussi!" she sobbed, "Non, mon Dieu, non!"

She was so overwhelmed with misery that she did not see Sherlock's eyelids flutter for a moment, nor did she hear Amanda enter the room behind her.

"Oh, my poor dear," Amanda said enfolding the little servant girl in her arms. "You are tired and overwrought. Go to your bed. I will sit up with him now. After Michelle left Amanda tossed some more wood on the fire and settled herself in the chair close to it. She could understand Michelle's tears. Despair hung heavy in the room. No mortal can relieve this, Amanda thought. She clasped her hands together and bowed her head.

Chapter 28
Muffin Returns

The first thing that Sherlock was aware of was the weight of his own body. It seemed immensely heavy, especially in his head and chest. It felt as if large rocks had been placed upon his chest, making each breath an effort. And his head, when he moved it slightly he heard a low moan. Was that him? He knew he had been ill. He had been through this before, but he had thought it all behind him.

He forced the weight of his eyelids up. He saw but a dull blur then blinked and the room swam into focus. It was his own room in Yorkshire. There was the stuffed ferret upon the mantel, the boxing gloves hanging in the corner, and his epees upon the wall behind his desk.

He rolled his head to the left to continue his survey of the room, and his head ached and his vision blurred again. Then there was that moan again. This time he knew the voice was his own. There was another voice calling his name. He blinked until the room focused again. Then he saw the doctor from the village sitting by his bed.

"There Sherlock, take it easy. We nearly lost you that time," Dr. Thompkins said.

Sherlock attempted to swallow, but his throat was dry. Next he knew Dr. Thompkins was holding him with one arm and holding a cup to his lips with the other. Sherlock drank. The water was cool and sweet, very sweet, but Sherlock was not surprised. The honeyed water was familiar, too. Then he lay back upon the pillows again and the weight of his eyelids overwhelmed him and he slept.

It was hours later when Sherlock awoke again. It was the voices that he heard first.

"I think he's coming around again. Quick, girl, run fetch that broth from the kitchen," Dr. Thompkins said.

"Yes, sir."

Sherlock blinked his eyes.

Dr. Thompkins smiled at him and helped him to some water again. Then the French girl arrived with the broth and the doctor spoon fed him. Then Sherlock slept again.

When next he awoke, Sherlock felt the weight of his body had receded some. He opened his eyes and surveyed the room again. His eyes fell at last on a young blonde woman who sat beside his bed. He stared at her blankly.

"Good morning, Sherlock," she said.

His brother's wife, Amanda, he realized. He struggled with his voice and managed to croak out "good morning."

Amanda pulled the bell rope.

"Your mother will be pleased to see you. She asked me to send for her when you awoke."

A tray was brought and his mother came with some of the maids, and the women fed him and washed him and changed the linens upon the bed. It was all a familiar pattern to Sherlock, and when they were through, he slept again.

When Sherlock awoke for the fourth time he still felt weak and groggy and his chest ached but the heaviness of his body had left him.

Dr. Thompkins was there and helped him with the pillows. Another tray was brought and it included milk and some scones with the broth. After Sherlock had eaten he lay back against the pillows. He lifted his hand to his brow.

"What is the matter, lad?" Dr. Thompkins asked.

"I can't remember becoming ill," Sherlock said.

"It's not important, lad. All's important now, Sherlock, is that you get well," the doctor said.

"But I can usually remember. It must have been quite

sudden," Sherlock said.

"That it was," the doctor said. "You were burning with fever when I first came. I was told you were caught out in a snowstorm. But you shouldn't worry yourself about it or you'll make yourself ill again. Eating and sleeping is all you should trouble yourself about."

Sherlock watched as the doctor took some things out of his bag and began to fill a hypodermic needle with fluid. This was something new to him.

"Here let me have your arm," Dr. Thompkins said.

As the doctor took his arm and plunged the needle in it, Sherlock noticed that there were a number of needle marks on that arm already. Sherlock thought about the number of needle marks for an instant, but as the drug took effect he forgot about it.

"You should rest," the doctor said.

Sherlock lay back trying to remember anything of the last few days. Sleep came eventually.

When Sherlock awoke the next morning the fragments of a dream tugged at his memory but he could not piece it together. It was morning now he knew from the way the sunlight seemed to give the curtains bright edges without really lighting the room. The heavy drapes were drawn across the large windows that faced the moors, just as they had been each time he had awaken before. The only light in the room came from a lamp on the table and the glow of the fire.

Michelle was kneeling before the grate tending the fire. When Sherlock shifted in the bed, she jumped up.

"Oh, Monsieur, bonjour. You are awake. I did not know it."

Sherlock smiled and said good morning.

"I will bring your breakfast," she said, curtsied and hurried off.

Sherlock was surprised when the door opened again but a moment later. It was his brother, Sherrinford.

"Good morning, Sherlock," Sherrinford said with surprise.

"You are awake early this morning. I was on my way out, but I thought I would look in on you before I left. How are you feeling?" Sherrinford asked, but Sherlock seemed to sense some other question in Sherrinford's manner. There was an unusual timidity in his eldest brother's approach. What was Sherrinford afraid of?

"Good morning," Sherlock replied, "I am feeling better, thank you."

"I am glad to hear it."

Then the door opened again and Dr. Thompkins entered, followed by Michelle with the tray.

"You are looking better this morning, Sherlock," Dr. Thompkins said. "I wager you can handle your breakfast alone this morning."

"Yes, Dr. Thompkins, I believe so. But it is a bit dark in here. Could the curtains be drawn?" Sherlock asked.

"Ah, well, it is quite bright out there with the sun reflecting off the snow on the moor, but surely we could open them a bit," the doctor said.

Michelle was in the process of setting the tray upon the bed when Dr. Thompkins drew back the curtains.

A shaft of bright, white light fell into the room through the parted curtains. It caught Sherlock's eye and mesmerized him. He felt himself surrounded and consumed by whiteness. Images flew through his mind. His hands flew up to his face and his knees drew up so violently that if Michelle had not been there to rescue the tray it would have been thrown to the floor. His breath caught suddenly and then released in a coughing fit.

Sherlock remembered... he remembered what his father had said... what he had seen from the study window... the wild chase across the moor through the snowstorm. It all came alive for him again. He was lost once more in the blizzard hunting for Violet.

"Violet," he whispered and coughed more and the images

faded away.

Then Sherlock realized that someone was calling his name, and that fingers were grasped about his wrists gently attempting to pull his hands from his face. The curtains were closed again and Dr. Thompkins and Sherrinford were bending over him. He let his hands fall and leaned back heavily against the pillows. The vision had drained what little energy he had and still seemed to haunt him.

"I remember. I remember what happened," Sherlock said.

Then Sherlock grabbed Sherrinford by the arm.

"Where is she, Sherrinford?" he asked.

"I don't know, Sherlock," Sherrinford replied.

"I was following her. I was lost the storm. How did I get back here?" Sherlock asked.

"I found you, or rather Sandy found you, in the hut on the moors and I brought you back," Sherrinford said.

Sherlock looked puzzled.

"The hut? I don't remember reaching the hut. She wasn't there?" he said.

"No. We've been doing everything we can to find her. But it won't do any good for you to worry yourself over it. You must work on getting better," Sherrinford responded.

"Yes, I will," Sherlock said. "Promise me that you will tell me as soon as you find her?"

"Yes, Sherlock, I promise. Now I must go," Sherrinford said.

Sherrinford left and Sherlock said a silent prayer that Violet would be with him when he returned. Then the tray was placed before him again. He had less interest in it now, but he ate his breakfast at the doctor's urging.

Dr. Thompkins gave Sherlock another injection and then left to make other visits. Sherlock took short naps in the morning and afternoon, but for most of the day he was awake. In the afternoon Sherlock requested once again that the curtains be opened. This time he blinked at the brightness of the snow and then lay back staring out at the blue sky and wondering where Violet was. Mrs. Holmes and Amanda each stopped in awhile to visit but when he asked them of news of Violet they professed ignorance and were uncomfortable with the subject.

Sherlock was not himself entirely comfortable asking them about Violet for he had kept his feelings for her secret for so long and had spoken of her to no one save that boy, Jonathan, that it was awkward just to mention her name. But Sherlock chastised himself for such feelings. He was not embarrassed by Violet, no matter what others might think. So he asked but the women had heard nothing, and knew nothing but that Sherrinford was looking for her. So they spoke of other trivial things.

When left to himself, his thoughts always turned to Violet. Each time the door opened he turned to it expecting that it was she. But it never was, and no word came.

The next day he asked Dr. Thompkins if he might sit on the window seat.

"I don't see why not. Might do you some good to have something else to stare at besides these walls. But you must keep warm, lad."

So Dr. Thompkins helped him to the window seat and wrapped a blanket about him.

The sky was grey that day, dark and heavy. The snow which covered the grounds and gardens was crisscrossed with the footprints of humans and animals. People were going about their business below, their breath showing as clouds trailing behind them, and the cold white moors brooded above it all. Sherlock searched the scene earnestly as if here from his perch he could spy Violet where others had failed. But the day wore on and he saw no sign of her.

In the afternoon he lifted his violin out of its case and occupied some time playing wistful airs, but his arm swiftly grew tired of holding the violin to his chin and he lay it down upon his knees. He drew the bow across the strings as he stared out at the moor. The sounds which rose from the violin were sometimes light and dreamy, full of hope and pleasant memories. Sometimes they were sighs of yearning and impatience, then a gloomy, fearful note would invade. It was while he was so occupied that a wagon came hurrying into the yard from the back road. As he saw it, he heard the door open behind him.

"Good afternoon, Sherlock," he heard Dr. Thompkins say, but Sherlock did not look around. He was intent upon the scene below. The driver of the wagon was Farmer Martin, and the wagon and whatever Farmer Martin was saying was causing a great deal of excitement in the yard. There was something in the back of the wagon covered by a cloth.

Suddenly, the door to Sherlock's room opened and a servant entered out of breath.

"Excuse me, Doctor, but you're wanted in the yard."

Dr. Thompkins brushed passed the servant and left the room. She turned to leave as well, but Sherlock called to her.

"What it is?"

"It's Farmer Rushdale," she said.

"What has the man done now?" Sherlock asked.

"He's dead," she said and was gone.

Violet's father was dead! Poor Godfrey. Perhaps, though, Sherlock thought, it was for the best. He had lived but half a life since his wife had died. Without his daughter's constant vigilance he would have starved or been put away years ago. Poor Violet, she had loved him so. She had dedicated her life to him and sacrificed much. Yet for all the pain her father's life had caused her, Sherlock knew she would feel sorrow in his passing.

It was unlike her to leave her father alone for several days. Where had she gone? Why had she raced away from him on the moor? Why could no one find her? Dark nebulous thoughts crowded the corners of his mind, but he brushed them back and clung to hope desperately.

When Dr. Thompkins returned, Sherlock asked him how Godfrey Rushdale had died.

"Froze to death it seems. Been dead a couple of days, I reckon, but it's hard to tell. Farmer Martin said he found the body in a ditch mostly covered by snow, so he must have died before the last snow." The doctor said as he plunged the needle into Sherlock's arm once more.

Sherlock pondered this as the drug took effect. Before the last snow. So her father had died before that snowstorm, Sherlock thought. Perhaps she had gone looking for him? Sherlock embraced this theory without testing it, and untested it kept his fears at bay and fueled false hope. So when Sherrinford reported no news that evening, he was surprised at how light-heartedly Sherlock took the message. But Sherlock was now certain that Violet had gone off in search of her father and would return.

The following day after breakfast Sherrinford entered Sherlock's room wearing his coat. As he shut the door, something seemed to squirm in the coat.

"I brought something," Sherrinford said, opening his coat. Sandy leaped on to Sherlock's bed and proceeded to lick him joyfully.

Sherrinford pulled her back.

"Now, calm down, girl, your master is not as strong as he's been," Sherrinford said.

"It's quite all right," Sherlock said, stroking the curly haired dog on his bed.

"She is glad to see you," Sherrinford said.

"Has she been ill, too? She's lost some weight," Sherlock said.

"She's been lying outside the kitchen door with her tail between her legs ever since I brought you down from the moor. Tessy says she's hardly touched a thing. Tessy's afraid ol' Sandy would starve herself to death if we didn't show her that you were still around. So I brought her up. She can stay for a bit if you'd like."

"Oh, yes, let her stay," Sherlock said.

"But you have to keep her quiet. You know what father thinks of having an animal in the house," Sherrinford reminded him.

"Yes, but you'll be good, won't you, girl?" Sherlock said to the dog.

"Then I'll be back for her later," Sherrinford said.

Sherlock lay back again on the pillows with the dog next to him after Sherrinford left. He stroked the dog's long hair and scratched her behind the ears. He spoke to her in a low voice.

As Sherrinford left Sherlock's room, Thomas approached him.

"A letter came for you, sir," Thomas said.

It was from Mycroft. Sherrinford had wired Mycroft four days before that Sherlock had awakened, but this letter looked like it had been posted before then. It was full of questions Mycroft had about Violet Rushdale and her family. Sherrinford took the letter to his room and answered it the best he could.

"You are a valiant lady," Sherlock said to the dog as he petted her. "I remember how you tried to defend Violet. Brave and loyal Sandy! Sherrinford told me how you helped him find me. I know you would help find her if you could."

With one arm wrapped around her, Sherlock stared into Sandy's big brown eyes until his eyelids drooped and he fell asleep.

Dr. Thompkins came late in the morning to check on his patient. As he entered a golden head popped up from beside Sherlock to regard him. Sherlock himself was just blinking awake.

"Sorry to wake you. I see you have a friend," the doctor said to Sherlock.

"That's quite all right. Yes, Sandy has come to visit for a little while. But don't tell my father. He would not approve," Sherlock said.

"Not a word," Dr. Thompkins agreed. "But let's see how you are doing."

The doctor examined Sherlock and listened with his stethoscope to Sherlock's chest.

"Definitely improving. I think now we just need to let nature take its course. You need plenty of rest," the doctor said.

"Yes, Doctor," Sherlock said as there was a knock at the door. It was a servant with Sherlock's lunch tray.

"Well, I will leave you to your lunch," Dr. Thompkins said as he gathered up his bag.

"Goodbye, doctor," Sherlock said.

After lunch Sherrinford came back for Sandy and smuggled her down the back stairs again. Sherlock bid her farewell reluctantly. He was going to miss her comforting presence. After the dog left Sherlock slept again until his supper came.

The next morning Sherlock awoke with sense of foreboding. He could not shake the dark mood. He made his way to the window seat soon after breakfast. He scanned the moors again and watched the yard down below. He stayed by the window all day, thinking earnestly of Violet, wishing she were home and worrying.

Sherlock even ate his lunch upon the window seat and when the tray had been taken away, he noticed some disturbance in the yard near the stables. There seemed to be a large group gathered about a horse. Sherlock did not have a good view of the horse and he could not tell what was happening. Then the horse's head turned his direction and Sherlock saw the markings upon its face. Muffin! It was Muffin! His heart leapt with joy and there was nothing that could have held him back. Sherlock sprang from his seat, raced from his room and down the backstairs. But as he passed the servant's quarters Thomas intercepted him.

"Master Sherlock, you shouldn't be out of bed," he said, and when Sherlock attempted to push past him to the door Thomas grabbed him and held him back. Struggle as he might Sherlock was too weak to break free of Thomas' grip. Tessy and the maids were drawn from the kitchen by the commotion.

"Oh, quick, lass, run out back and fetch Mr. Sherrinford," Tessy said.

Sherlock couldn't understand why they were holding him back. He could see out the window of the door. He could see the cluster about the horse. He could see now that it included not only several stable hands and other workers, but his brother Sherrinford and the constable from the village. And the horse! It was Muffin. There was no doubt it his mind now. If Muffin was there then surely Violet must be! Why wouldn't they let him go to her?

Sherrinford ran towards the house with the constable on his heels. Sherlock still looked beyond them as they drew near. The little group drew back from the horse. It was then that Sherlock noticed the horse's ribs sticking out and its haggard look. He did not see Violet in the group as it drew back. Suddenly, a shot broke the icy air of the yard behind them. Sherlock jumped as if the shot had hit him but it was the horse that fell.

"Sherlock! What are you doing out of bed?" Sherrinford cried. "Let Thomas help you back to your room or I shall carry you there myself!"

Sherlock was speechless. As he had seen the horse kneel and fall as its life drained out upon the ground, the energy and hope that had propelled him down the stairs had drained out of him as well. He turned and leaned heavily upon Thomas as they mounted the stairs. He went in silence for he could find no words for the confusion that consumed his mind.

Once in his bed again Sherlock leaned back upon the pillows breathing heavily with intermittent coughing. There was something wrong. All through his youth Sherlock had been quick of mind. Given a set of facts, his brain would race forward separating the wheat from the chaff and soon arrive at a solution, or declare the facts insufficient. He and Mycroft would entertain themselves for hours during the long winter evenings creating word games to challenge each other with. When they were traveling they had a special game. The boys would study a person they saw along the way and try to determine their trade. Then the loser from the last round had to ask the person their business. Sherrinford would soon grow tired of such games. He always lost. Sherlock was sharp, though not as sharp as Mycroft, and the challenge of possibly beating Mycroft each time drove him on. But now Sherlock's mind was in a jumble and the facts refused to sort themselves out. It was as if some part of him did not want him to understand. But he must understand!

"Perhaps, we'd best leave," Sherrinford said.

"No," Sherlock protested. "That was Violet's horse," he stated. Sherrinford cleared his throat.

"Yes, it was," Sherrinford said. "But it came alone."

"But why," asked Sherlock, as he sat up, "Why was the horse shot?"

"It was lame, frost-bitten and half-starved, Sherlock. I am really surprised that it made it here in that condition. It was half-dead already," Sherrinford said.

"Aye, lad, thy brother just had them put it out of its misery," the constable added.

"But surely it would help lead us to her? She was on that horse when last I saw her!" Sherlock insisted.

The constable shook his head.

"Who knows where it's been, lad," the constable said. "Maybe it deserted her somewhere or maybe when she was racing through the snow it struck a foreleg on something and threw her."

Sherlock remembered having seen Muffin throw Violet once before, and the memory stung like a bee, but he clung defensively

238

to his spark of hope.

"Then couldn't you follow Muffin's tracks and find her--" Sherlock began.

Somewhere deep inside a small voice added "body," but he could not say it, and he bit his lip to chastise that voice for suggesting it.

"Oh, no, lad, would take more than a good tracker. We've had men all over the moors. To their own risk, I'll tell thee. But thou knowst the moors. There are a thousand marshes, ravines and gillies where someone could fall and not be found again."

"Then we need a specialist-- We should get a detective from Leeds, or York, or London even," Sherlock suggested.

"No, the searching is over. We aren't going to risk onny more lives up there. I'm sorry, lad, but she's gone and thou must accept it," the constable said.

"No, no, it can't be over. You can't stop. She still could be-- could be--," Sherlock stammered. "Was it-- was it my father who has told you to stop?"

"No, lad," the Constable said shaking his head sadly again. "There's no detective on earth who could find her now. What thou'st wanting is more of a miracle than a work of detection. The snow that night and the two snows in the fortnight since have covered up even the tiniest trace there might have been."

Something inside his brain screamed, 'a fortnight!' but Sherlock just stared at the constable. Finally Sherlock managed to gain control enough to turn to his brother. Sherrinford was sitting on the trunk at the foot of Sherlock's bed. His profile was towards the bed and his head hung low. It seemed to Sherlock that his brother had somehow shrunk from the big man he was.

Sherrinford had known Sherlock would find out eventually, still he was not prepared for the moment when it came.

"Sherrinford?" Sherlock whispered.

His brother didn't move.

"Sherrinford?" Sherlock said louder.

"We did all we could, Sherlock," Sherrinford said.

"A fortnight?" Sherlock choked out the words that plagued him.

"Yes, fifteen days actually," Sherrinford whispered.

"Fifteen days," Sherlock's lips formed the words but he couldn't give voice to them.

"You were ill for a long time," Sherrinford continued. "I was out every day for a week looking for her, not knowing if you would still be alive when I got back. We had twenty other men besides. But there wasn't a trace and then it snowed again...."

Then Sherlock exploded. "You didn't tell me! You let me think--."

Sherrinford turned to look at his younger brother.

"I couldn't. You were so ill. I was afraid it would upset you," Sherrinford pleaded.

Sherlock lay back upon the pillows, wincing as if in pain.

"I'm sorry, lad," the constable said softly and left the room.

Sherlock covered his face with his hands. Sherrinford rose and approached the side of the bed.

"Sherlock--," he began.

"Leave me alone," Sherlock whispered.

"Sherlock," Sherrinford tried again.

"Please!" Sherlock pleaded, and his brother left, closing the door softly behind him as a single tear forced its way down Sherlock's cheek to spread itself out upon the heel of his hand. Then Sherlock threw himself over in his bed, buried his face in the pillows and cried until sleep overcame him.

Chapter 29
Through the Crack

Sherlock awoke several hours later. The constable's words came echoing through his brain: "She's gone... never be found again.... There's no detective on earth who could find her... she's gone...." He tried not to believe the words, but they came back at him and the pain welled up inside.

He pulled himself up from the bed and sat by the window. He stared out at the snow-covered moor where Violet had disappeared. He pressed his hand against the windowpane as if to reach out to her wherever she was, but all he felt was the icy glass. The cold seemed to fill his hand and flow through his veins to be consumed by the searing pain in his heart.

He sat transfixed, his hand pressed to the square of glass. But when at last a noise made him jump and draw his hand away, the sky was dark beyond the glass and the room was only lit by the uneven light of the fire.

It was a knock at the door that had startled him. The door was opened by a girl with dark curls. His heart raced with new found hope. Violet! He wished to call her name. He parted his lips but before they could form the word, he knew he been deceived.

Michelle stood in the doorway with a tray.

"I have your supper, Monsieur," she said.

Despair devoured the false flicker of hope and the pain was more than Sherlock could bear.

"Get out!" he shouted.

Michelle was so startled by this outburst that she jumped and the tray clattered to the floor. Tears welling in her eyes, she bent down to pick up the scattered contents of the tray. With unexpected fury, Sherlock jumped down from his perch. He grabbed Michelle by the arm.

"Get out, I said," he screamed.

With a look of terror, Michelle fled from the room.

Sherlock fell upon his bed exhausted, panting, and coughing. A moment later Sherrinford and Dr. Thompkins appeared in the doorway.

"Sherlock! What did you do to that girl?" Sherrinford asked.

Sherlock stared at the ceiling.

"I don't want her in here," he said in nearly a whisper.

"Sherlock, you're being--" Sherrinford began, but Dr. Thompkins cut him off with a wave of his hand. The doctor studied Sherlock intensely. Sherrinford had told him what had occurred earlier. He reached out and held Sherlock's wrist. Sherlock was trembling.

"Then Susan can bring your supper," Dr. Thompkins offered still gently holding Sherlock's wrist.

Sherlock's whole body seemed to tense at the suggestion.

"No," Sherlock said, pulling his arm from the doctor's grasp. "I don't want any of them in here." His voice was almost a hiss now. "I don't want another woman to enter this room."

Sherrinford started to speak but the doctor took his arm and gave him a warning look.

"All right, I'll have Thomas come and clean up this mess," Sherrinford said and left the doctor alone with Sherlock.

Sherlock had fallen back upon the pillows and closed his eyes.

"How do you feel, Sherlock?" Dr. Thompkins asked.

"Tired," he whispered.

"Are you hungry?" Dr. Thompkins asked.

"No," sighed Sherlock, "just tired."

"Well, I'll leave you and let you rest soon," Dr. Thompkins said as he pulled the quilt back up over Sherlock. "I think you have overexerted yourself today. You need to rest in order to get well."

Sherlock was silent.

The squire was waiting with Sherrinford when the doctor descended the stairs. He motioned them into the study.

"I understand that my son attacked one of the maids this evening," the squire said. "Can you explain this behavior, Dr. Thompkins?"

"Sherlock is upset. He has been very ill and has suffered a great shock. People are often more easily upset in such circumstances," Dr. Thompkins said.

"But unprovoked violence?" Squire Holmes asked.

The doctor sighed.

"Sometimes under strain people do things they'd regret otherwise. Sometimes it is an isolated incident; sometimes--"

"This could happen again?" Siger Holmes asked.

"It's possible that it could happen again even if it is a temporary condition," the doctor said.

"Are you suggesting that my son is suffering from some form of insanity?"

Dr. Thompkins looked uncomfortable.

"Not necessarily, it may be merely the emotional and physical stress has him overwrought, and he may recover fairly quickly," Dr. Thompkins said.

He paused and looked away.

"Then again," he continued, "brain fever has been known to bring on some forms of insanity. It is too soon to tell."

The clock ticked in the silence.

"Dr. Thompkins," the squire said in a business-like tone.

The doctor turned back to meet those piercing eyes.

"If you should decide that the condition is permanent," Squire Holmes announced, "then you are to report to me at once. If the condition persists then I shall consult a specialist. If the boy should be permanently insane then he shall be taken to an asylum. I shall not shelter a lunatic in my house."

Sherrinford stared at his father too shocked to speak.

Siger Holmes rose.

"Sherrinford, supper shall be served shortly," he said and limped from the room.

"Doctor, we can't let that happen," Sherrinford argued. "My father will tolerate no weakness. He has always considered Sherlock the runt of the family and has more than once nearly given up on him, but I know Sherlock better than he. I know that what I saw upstairs was totally unlike the Sherlock I know. But there is a great mind in there and I think if we can give him time he will come to himself."

"Sherlock is lucky to have a brother with such faith in him. I wish I were so certain, but I'll do all I can," Dr. Thompkins said.

"What can I do, Doctor?" Sherrinford asked.

"Avoid upsetting him. That seems to mean keeping the womenfolk away from his room," the doctor said.

"But Thomas is our only male servant in the house. Father would not tolerate taking him away from his other duties," Sherrinford protested.

"Then find some boy, anyone who doesn't upset him. Sherlock must be watched carefully. I must know of any other odd behaviour," Dr. Thompkins said.

"Is that all we can do?" Sherrinford asked.

"I'm afraid so," the doctor said.

After supper Jonathan Beckwith was helping his mother and his sister rearrange the washing on the racks before the fire. Pearl was telling them the news from Holmes Hall.

"As I've been saying word was he was at death's door till a few days ago," Pearl said. "Since then he's been awake and eating and the maids said he was getting better. But today Tessy saw him herself. He was standing on his own feet at the back door she said, but looking a shadow of himself. After arguing with his brother he nearly collapsed and Thomas had to half carry him up the stairs."

The reports of Violet's disappearance and Sherlock's illness that Pearl had been bringing back over the last two weeks had pained Jonathan. But he wanted desperately to know how Sherlock was faring.

"Then as Tessy was telling me this," Pearl continued, "Michelle comes running down in tears half hysterical with a muddled tale more in that furren tongue of hers than onnything. Most I could get out of it was that he'd attacked her. Then they'd called for Thomas and he'd had to pick up the dinner tray off the floor, which he was none too pleased about and said none of the maids were to go to Master Sherlock's room no more. We dinna know--"

Pearl was interrupted by a knock at the cottage door. It was a very unusual thing for anyone to knock at the door to their cottage on a winter evening. Jonathan opened the door with his mother and sister watching. It was one of the manor stable boys.

"Jonathan Beckwith?" the boy asked.

"Aye," he responded.

"A note for thee," the boy said and handed a piece of paper to Jonathan. Then the boy was gone. Jonathan closed the door against the cold night air and carried the note towards the fire.

"What is it?" Pearl asked.

"Let him open it and we'll see," her mother said.

Inside was writing in very neat script.

"Jonathan Beckwith:

My brother, Sherlock, recommended you to me last summer. If you would please come to the Hall first thing in the morning, I have a position for you.

Mr. Sherrinford Holmes"

Jonathan's mother hugged him.

"I always knew. Now we're going to have to get thee dressed up nicely," she said, putting the flatiron upon the fire. "Thou go there in the morning and do whatever Mr. Holmes asks and don't bother about us. Thou stay at the Hall as long as he wants."

The next morning Jonathan entered Sherlock's room quietly and set down the breakfast tray. He stirred the fire, then turned to look at Sherlock as he lay sleeping. Jonathan could barely be certain that this was the same young man whom he'd fenced with weeks ago. Sherlock had always been lean, but now all the color was gone from his cheeks and the skin seemed to hang on the bone. When Sherlock awoke he looked up at Jonathan.

"What are you doing here?" Sherlock asked.

"I am your new manservant," said Jonathan as he took a deep bow.

"Boy-servant, you mean," Sherlock said.

"Yes, sir," Jonathan agreed even as Sherlock's caustic words bit into him. He had been pleased and excited when Mr. Holmes had told him that he was to serve Sherlock himself. He had not expected it to be like this.

Sherrinford had warned Jonathan that he might find Sherlock different. Jonathan did not know what he had expected, but he was shocked by what he saw that day. Sherlock seemed so wrapped up inside himself that he rarely seemed to notice Jonathan's presence. When Sherlock did speak to him, his words seemed mixed with hostility and melancholy. Jonathan, more than anyone, understood how Sherlock had felt about Violet. He had seen them together and had carried messages between them. Yet what he saw was beyond mere sorrow for a lost loved one.

Sherlock picked at his breakfast absently and left half of it untouched. Jonathan took the tray down to the kitchen. When he returned Sherlock was at the window seat staring out at the falling snow that obscured the view beyond. Sherlock did not look up when Jonathan quietly entered, but he began to speak in a whisper to him.

"She is gone, Jonathan. Did they tell you?" Sherlock said.

"Yes, I know, sir," Jonathan replied.

"No," Sherlock cried turning angrily to face Jonathan. "No,

you do not know. You cannot know!" He turned back to the window. "She is there, ever just beyond my reach," he said wistfully, pressing both palms against the glass.

With all his hopes wrenched from him, Sherlock's thoughts dropped with the ever falling snow.

"It was like this, the snow falling all around confusing right and left and up and down," Sherlock continued. "I could not catch her. I lost her and I could not find her. It took all my effort just to stay alive. Had I known she was not coming back I would have lain down in the snow and embraced an icy death."

His anger rose again.

"This is wrong! It is some ghastly trick of fate. It is not right that I sit here now and she is gone," Sherlock shouted.

Just then Dr. Thompkins entered.

"Sherlock," he scolded. "You are getting yourself worked up again." He placed his hand on Sherlock's forehead. "You are going to work yourself into a fever if you keep this up. Come back over to your bed."

Silently, Sherlock obeyed.

Dr. Thompkins stayed for some time, examining Sherlock and trying to talk to him. Sherlock was not interested in talking. He lay staring at the ceiling. Dr. Thompkins was perturbed. Then lunch time came and Jonathan went down for the tray. The doctor encouraged Sherlock to eat and scolded him when he did not. Sherlock ignored him and picked through the food without enthusiasm. He ate little. Finally, the doctor set the tray aside with a sigh.

"Well, I shall leave you now so you can rest," the doctor said.

Sherlock said nothing. Dr. Thompkins left. Jonathan rose and reached for the tray. As he did he saw Sherlock open a drawer in the little table by the bed. He took something out and put it in the pocket of his dressing gown. Jonathan could not see what it was.

When Jonathan returned from the kitchen he quietly opened

247

the bedroom door and was surprised to find Sherlock back at the window seat. Then he saw what Sherlock had taken from the drawer. It was a pocketknife. As he watched, Sherlock open it and watched its blade gleam in the light. Then he ran the edge of the blade along the palm of his hand as if to test its sharpness. Jonathan turned and ran down the stairs. Dr. Thompkins had stopped to speak to the squire in his study and was just now going through the front door.

"Doctor, Doctor!" Jonathan said.

"What is it, lad?" the doctor said turning back to him.

"He has a knife," Jonathan said, keeping his voice low, lest the squire hear, "and he--"

"My God, and you left him alone? Quick, find his brother," the doctor responded and bound up the stairs.

Sherlock looked up as Dr. Thompkins burst in. He said nothing but fingered the open blade of the knife in the pocket of his dressing gown.

"Give it to me, Sherlock," the doctor said.

Sherlock said nothing.

"Give me the knife," Dr. Thompkins repeated.

Sherlock did not ask how the doctor knew that he had it. He merely whispered, "No."

Sherrinford now appeared in the doorway with Jonathan behind him. Dr. Thompkins closed the door. He drew Sherrinford to a corner of the room and whispered to him, but he never took his eye off Sherlock.

Then they approached Sherlock. He drew back, but he had nowhere to go. The window seat was narrow and they had him trapped. Sherlock cried out and struggled as Sherrinford's strong arms grabbed him, but the doctor forced a handkerchief in his mouth which muffled his cries and he was far too weak to resist Sherrinford's embrace. Sherrinford pinned him down to the window seat. Then Sherlock saw the needle and felt it bite into his arm.

Sherrinford remembered holding Sherlock before when it was a disease of the body which tortured him. Was it a disease of the mind now? Sherrinford held Sherlock down until he went limp in his grasp, then he gently lifted him up and laid him out upon the bed.

Hours later Sherlock moaned and Jonathan sprang to his side.

In the recesses of Sherlock's brain Sherrinford was still pinning him to the window seat. He struggled, but was too weak to resist. He looked up to plead with his brother to let him go. But his limbs were numb and even his tongue would not obey him. He could not speak. He could not move at all. He was trapped in this purgatory between life and death. He could see Violet again disappearing in the snow but he could not go to her. His brother was holding him back. Then it wasn't Sherrinford, but Moriarty who was holding him down. Moriarty smiled. Sherlock watched in silent horror as Moriarty plunged his hand into Sherlock's chest, ripped out his heart and held it up before his eyes in his dripping hand. Sherlock could not even scream.

Sherlock's eyes snapped open with a look of terror in them. He was trembling all over. Sherlock closed his eyes again. The memory of the nightmare seemed so terrifyingly real and yet what he had seen in the room was different. He opened his eyes and blinked. Which was real and which wasn't? He closed them again. His head felt heavy and there was something wrong with the wall. He lifted his hands to his head. If this was real, then the other wasn't. His arms ached. His head felt like it was about to explode. He touched the bandage on his arm. Then he remembered being pinned to the window seat and gagged and the sting of the doctor's needle and everything slipping away. That was real.

Anger rose within him as he thought of it. He had been attacked! He had been treated like a criminal. He had been tried, convicted and imprisoned in his own room. Yes, he was guilty: Guilty of breaking the rules; guilty of loving the daughter of a tenant farmer; guilty of fathering her child; and his worse crime yet, guilty of still being alive.

Yet his arms were free. He would not have been surprised to find himself chained to the bed. He was not such a dangerous criminal after all?

Sherlock opened his eyes. The wall over his desk was empty. Why did that bother him? What had been there? The epees! They had taken his epees off the wall. He laughed. It was an angry, derisive laugh. The fools! What had they thought he could do with them? He fumbled for the pockets of his dressing gown. They were empty. The knife was gone.

"No," he whispered and angrily thumped the bed with his fist. They could not do this to him.

"Sir?" Jonathan inquired and drew Sherlock's attention. He had not noticed him before. Now he grabbed Jonathan's arm.

"Where is it? What did they do with it?" Sherlock demanded.

"W-what?" Jonathan asked.

"My knife," Sherlock hissed.

"I do not know, sir," Jonathan said.

Sherlock growled and tossed Jonathan's arm aside. He yanked out the drawer of the little table, dug through it and threw it on the floor. He searched the mantle piece and the bookshelves. He rummaged through the drawers of his desk. No knife. Not even a pair of scissors. He was prepared to slam the drawer when his eyes rested on the leather case inscribed "E.G. Sherrinford." Carefully Sherlock drew it out, his heart pounding. He opened the case and lifted the magnifying lens out. The crack was still there as it had been since June, since that day. That had been the same day he had first kissed her.... Oh, those had been golden, happy days.... And now, and now, he was a prisoner here within this room, within this cell, within this body.... And she, and she..

250

.and this was all he had to remember her by. He lay his head down upon the desk next to the lens and wept.

Jonathan stood uncomfortably watching Sherlock. He wished he could leave or turn away but he had promised.

After Sherlock had slipped into his drugged slumber, Dr. Thompkins and Sherrinford had searched the room. Jonathan had seen them take the knife and several other items as well as the epees from the wall. Then they had spoken to Jonathan.

"He must not be left alone. He must be watched closely and constantly," Dr. Thompkins had said.

"Yes, sir," Jonathan said.

"Someone will have to sit up with him at night as well," the Doctor said.

"I would be most happy to, sir," Jonathan volunteered.

"You might have difficulty staying awake," Sherrinford said.

"No, sir, I can do it," Jonathan assured him.

"It is most important that you not fall asleep," Dr. Thompkins said.

"Yes, sir," Jonathan said.

Sherrinford looked thoughtful for a moment.

"Well, I shall give you the chance, but I shall look in from time to time, in case you should fall asleep. In the morning, I shall relieve you so that you may get some rest," Sherrinford said.

Dr. Thompkins had agreed.

So Jonathan watched uncomfortably as Sherlock cried.

There was a knock at the door. Jonathan opened it. Another servant handed him the tray. He sat it on the small table. He waited.

Finally, he said, "Master Sherlock."

Sherlock lifted his head but did not look at him or say anything.

"Your supper has arrived," Jonathan said.

There was a moment of silence and then Sherlock said, "Send

it back."

"Sir?" Jonathan said.

"I don't want it," Sherlock said.

"But, sir--" Jonathan said.

Sherlock would say nothing else. He rose from the chair and returned to his bed. As he sat down he noticed the violin case by the bed. He opened the case and ran his finger along the burnished surface of the instrument. He drew it out and lay back upon the bed. Hours passed. The tray was untouched. A servant came and returned it to the kitchen. Sherrinford came to see his brother, but Sherlock would not speak to him or even look at him. All Sherlock would do was lie there on the bed scraping the bow across the strings of the violin as it lay across his knees. Sherrinford left again.

Jonathan desperately tried to find a way to occupy his time. He knew that if he merely sat there all night staring at the bed he was sure to fall asleep. Then Sherrinford arrived with a slim volume which he felt the boy might find interesting.

"Goodnight, Sherlock," Sherrinford said, but again his brother ignored him.

Jonathan sat by the fire and began to read. The mysterious nature of the story combined with the mournful sounds emanating from the violin produced an effect on the boy and Jonathan became quite certain he would not fall asleep any time soon. In fact, Jonathan was somewhat glad when the bow slipped from Sherlock's fingers. He laid aside the book and stole over to the bedside.

As Jonathan lifted the violin and bow off of the bed, Sherlock opened his eyes but said nothing. Jonathan laid the violin aside, lit a candle and turned down the lamp.

"Are you leaving?" Sherlock asked.

"No. I have orders to stay," Jonathan answered.

Jonathan waited, but there was no response. Finally he took

the candle to the hearth, settled himself down and blew it out.

Chapter 30
Descent into Darkness

Jonathan had been sitting thus in the darkened room, feeding and prodding at the fire for several hours when Sherlock screamed. Actually it wasn't the scream which first drew his attention, but the laughter. It began as a small chuckle. That startled Jonathan and he thought at first he had imagined it. Sherlock had seemed totally incapable of mirth. But then it continued and grew into full-bodied laughter. There were also some mumbled words, but Jonathan could not decipher them. Sherlock was dreaming, Jonathan thought, and his hopes rose with the thought that somewhere within Sherlock still harbored pleasant thoughts. Then the laughter ended suddenly.

"Violet!" Sherlock called: begging, beseeching, pleading.

Then it was that Sherlock screamed. It began with the word "No!" in ultimate and definitive denial and degenerated into the most heart-rending cry of agony that ever parted the lips of man. It was with trembling fingers that Jonathan relit the candle and rushed to the side of the bed. Sherrinford was at the door almost simultaneously. Sherlock was sitting up in the bed. He was trembling and blinking in the candlelight. As they watched he fell back against the pillows. Sherrinford touched Sherlock's shoulder as he buried his face in the pillow.

"Are you ill? Should I send for the doctor?" Sherrinford asked.

"No," Sherlock responded.

"Well, you don't feel in a fever," Sherrinford said as he pulled the quilts up around his brother again. "What was that all about then?"

"I think it was a dream, sir," Jonathan offered when Sherlock gave no reply.

"A dream? A nightmare? Was that it, Sherlock?" Sherrinford

asked.

"No more than life," was the reply.

Sherrinford sighed. The womenfolk were so much better at this, he thought. What should he do now?

"Is there anything I can do for you, Sherlock?" Sherrinford asked.

"No," Sherlock said.

"I think I can see to him now, sir," Jonathan said.

Sherrinford hesitated, but since he knew of no further way to comfort his brother, he returned to his bed thankful that sound did not travel far in the old building and that the squire's room was in another wing.

Jonathan sat down beside the bed and placed his candle upon the table. He stared down at his hands clasped anxiously in his lap. He was but a boy and knew no great words to comfort his friend and master. So like a child he said just what struck his mind.

"I'm greatly sorry, Sher--sir, I-I..."

The boy's simple words touched some still living spot in the shambles of Sherlock's soul. He looked up at Jonathan and in the light from the candle Jonathan could see warmth and gratitude flicker across those eyes dulled with pain.

"You are not to blame, Jonathan," Sherlock said.

Their eyes held in silent communion. Jonathan felt full force the other's sorrow and yet also sensed that deep inner core where the young man he had known had taken refuge from the pain that had engulfed him. Sherlock in turn fed upon the younger boy's honest sympathy and affection. It calmed him as no words could have. Slowly he closed his eyes.

Jonathan stood and took up the candle.

Sherlock opened his eyes.

"You should sleep, sir," Jonathan said.

"Sleep? And fall prey to such dreams? No, I cannot sleep. I

may never sleep again." Sherlock paused. "Until I join her."

These last words, said with calm conviction, frightened Jonathan more than the terrible scream uttered earlier. They frightened him more than Sherlock's bursts of temper or the dreadful moment he had seen Sherlock draw the blade across his hand. Now he understood his vigil. More chilled inside than out, he returned to the fire and rebuilt it.

Despite Sherlock's protests, sleep finally overcame his weary body. He was resting peacefully when Sherrinford crept into the room in the grey light of dawn to relieve Jonathan.

Michelle was waiting for Jonathan in the hall when he came out.

"Come with me, garcon," she said and led him to the kitchen. She was a pretty girl, Jonathan thought, despite the redness in her eyes and the dark rings around them.

"Ah, lad, thou look done in. A hard night, twas it?" Tessy asked.

"Yes, ma'am," Jonathan said.

"How is our young master?" Tessy asked

"He's sleeping now. Tis good, for last night he had nightmares and was awake for a long while after. The doctor won't it like one bit when he hears," Jonathan responded.

"Ah, the poor lad," Tessy responded shaking her head sympathetically.

"He is main sad most of the time, and all he will do is play with that fiddle of his -- not even proper tunes -- just screeches and moans -- more mournful than dirges," Jonathan said as Tessy set before him the biggest breakfast he had ever seen.

"And he wouldn't touch his supper," Jonathan said.

"Aye, I know that, lad. Sorrows me to see his tray coming back like that. Now thou mun eat," Tessy insisted.

But Jonathan continued to talk between mouthfuls. Once started he felt a great need to speak of the things he had seen.

"Sometimes he speaks to me," Jonathan continued. "Mostly he won't talk to onnyone. Then he has these fits of temper. They're terrible to see."

Michelle sobbed and her eyes brimmed over and tears flooded her cheeks. Tessy threw her arms about the girl and tried to comfort her.

"Now stop thy crying. Thou sees, it wasn't thy fault. Jonathan just told us that Master Sherlock has these fits of temper sometimes. There's no use thou getting all moithered about it. Come on, wipe those tears. That's better. Now, go to thy room and wash thy face. Gwon now, lass."

"Poor lass," Tessy said after Michelle had left the kitchen, "She'd taken a fancy to Master Sherlock, and when he turned on her it broke her heart. Well, eat up there, lad, and we'll find thee a bed for a time."

When Jonathan returned to Sherlock's room several hours later, Dr. Thompkins had just arrived.

"Sherlock, you haven't touched your breakfast." The doctor was saying as Jonathan entered.

Sherlock looked at Jonathan.

"Take it away," Sherlock ordered.

"But Sherlock, you must eat to get your strength back," the doctor said.

"I don't want it. Take it way," Sherlock said.

The doctor shrugged and Jonathan took the tray back to the kitchen.

"Not a crumb!" Tessy sighed as she took it. "Poor lad, he'll glem himself to death!"

Then Jonathan's eyes met hers, eyes too sad and wise for a child of twelve years. Was this the same lad she'd seen playing in the lane but weeks before? He'd aged overnight!

"I think that's what he wants," Jonathan said, and turned and left the kitchen.

He returned to Sherlock's room to find Dr. Thompkins pacing the room.

"Jonathan, Mr. Holmes tells me that Sherlock had a nightmare last night but Sherlock won't tell me about it. What do you know of it?"

Jonathan told the doctor what had occurred the night before. The doctor's face grew dark. He sat down beside the bed.

"Sherlock," Dr. Thompkins said in a soft voice. "Violet's loss is very tragic, and we shall all mourn her, but life must go on. You need to eat and sleep to get well, lad."

But Sherlock gave no response to the doctor's pleadings, and Dr. Thompkins threw up his hands.

"Well, I can't help you, lad, if you won't let me, and I have other patients to see. I shall stop again before nightfall," Dr. Thompkins said.

"Try to get him to eat, Jonathan," the doctor said from the doorway.

But neither Jonathan nor Sherrinford were successful at convincing Sherlock to give up his fast. He merely lay upon his bed scraping on the violin and ignoring all who tried to talk to him. Sometimes it seemed more like he was in a different world, rather than that he was simply ignoring them. Night fell and Jonathan sat next to the fire tending it and listening to the violin hoping that Sherlock would tire and sleep.

A single shaft of moonlight struck Jonathan in the eye and he jumped up awake again. Had someone whispered his name? Had his negligence been discovered?

"Ah, Jonathan, you are awake," came the whisper from the bed so low that only in the quiet of the night could it have been heard.

Blinded by the light, Jonathan could not see Sherlock across the room lit only by the dying embers of the fire and the single moonbeam.

"Yes, sir," Jonathan said, rising to approach the bed.

"Quick! Draw the curtains back," the whisper commanded urgently, and Jonathan jumped to obey. Moonlight flooded the room and Jonathan blinked at its brilliance reflected from the snow on the moor and the ground below. "Look out among the shadows in the garden-- all the blacker in contrast to the moonlit snow! Long and black they stretch themselves across the yard. Look sharp! Does one move?" the strident whisper asked.

Startled, Jonathan fearfully scanned the scene below. The light from the slim crescent moon that had just risen over the moor was magnified and reflected by the snow covering everything. Was there something moving out there? Fear gripped Jonathan as he surveyed the ground below. But his country wisdom comforted him. A fox at most, Jonathan thought, and yet he kept looking. As Sherlock had said long inky shadows lay across the stark whiteness of the snow, but nothing stirred below.

"Perhaps he waits," Sherlock droned on in that whisper that sent chills up Jonathan's back. "Perhaps he waits, stone still, like a shadow, as only he can wait, his ebony hood shrouding the death head beneath. But surely you would see the scythe he carries, curving high over his head as he rests heavily upon the shaft. Waiting, waiting as he has waited for each of our ancestors in turn, as he must have waited for her out there upon the moor!" This last ended in a sob.

Jonathan turned from the window. The moonlight illuminated the bed. Sherlock lay back upon the pillows, the gauntness of his cheeks accented by the deep shadows and silvery light. His eyes were lost in great sunken pits of shadow. He was the very impersonation of Death which he had ordered Jonathan to search for below!

Jonathan stood frozen in fear until he noticed a silvery tear etching its way down the face before him. The illusion collapsed as Sherlock covered his face with his hands and another sob wracked his frame. The form Jonathan watched was human, far too human. Jonathan stood in silent confusion not knowing what would least anger his young master.

"Close them now," came Sherlock's whisper at last. "He will not come tonight. But he will come soon and set me free."

Jonathan needed no effort to stay awake the rest of the night, for Sherlock's words haunted him and would not let him rest. Even in the morning when he was relieved and sent to the servant's quarters to nap, his sleep was fitful and haunted.

Sherlock awoke the next day feeling weaker than before. He attempted to lift the violin from the table next to the bed but found he could not. His head swam with the effort. He lay there comforted by the thought that it wouldn't be much longer. He closed his eyes. Somewhere --it seemed far away-- there was a knock upon a door and distant voices. He didn't try to understand them. Then there was Jonathan speaking to him quite near.

"Wilt thou-- will you eat now, sir?" Jonathan said.

"No," Sherlock replied without opening his eyes.

"The doctor says you must," Jonathan said.

"No," Sherlock repeated.

Jonathan withdrew from the bedside, but Sherlock knew he was still in the room somewhere, waiting and watching, as if it would matter. Sherlock didn't care. He knew it wouldn't matter. It wouldn't be long before he joined her. The room seemed to become even more distant. When he opened his eyes again the room had faded to a white blur and there stood Violet smiling and holding her arms out to him. "I'm coming, Violet," he whispered and reached for her but she faded away and the room came into focus again.

Then Jonathan was there again.

"Are you needing something, sir?" he asked.

"No," Sherlock whispered and consciousness faded away again.

The next thing Sherlock was aware of-- Was it minutes or hours later? He did not know. But the next thing he was aware of was moisture upon his face as from a heavy dew, and someone attempting to wipe it away but his face just seemed to grow damper with each wipe of the cloth. The cloth crossed his parched and parted lips and a few drops of moisture ran down his tongue. It felt good. The next time it crossed his lips he sank his teeth into it and water ran down his throat and he swallowed it. Then there was a cup against his lips and water poured into his mouth. He swallowed it and it seemed to gurgle through his empty frame. Then more came, cool and sweet, and he swallowed again. Then in his semi-consciousness he began to suspect something. When more poured into his mouth he knew for sure. There was honey in the water. They were attempting to feed him against his will. He did not swallow this time but spit the contents of his mouth out.

"Sherlock!" Dr. Thompkins cried reproachfully, as he toweled up the result. "You shouldn't have done that. You need to eat something to get your strength back."

"No," was Sherlock's only reply.

The doctor sighed and shook his head.

"At least allow me to bathe you and have the bed clothes changed," Dr. Thompkins said.

Sherlock did not reply but allowed the doctor to wash him. Was that not how they prepared one for burial, Sherlock thought.

After Sherlock had been washed and new linens placed upon the bed, Dr. Thompkins sat down next the bed again.

"Sherlock," he said, and the boy half opened his eyes. Dr. Thompkins looked into those grey eyes --those eyes which had always seemed so piercing and intelligent and that now seemed so flat and dull.

"Sherlock, I don't like what you are doing. And yet," the doctor said shaking his head, "I know of no way to stop you. Even if we attempted to force feed you, I don't believe we could get enough in you to do more than delay your plan. I shall not advise it."

Dr. Thompkins paused and sighed before he went on.

"You will not eat. You will not talk to anyone except Jonathan, and from what he tells me what you say isn't very pleasant. All you've left for us to do is to watch you die and that is rather painful for us all."

Jonathan watched in silence as Dr. Thompkins sighed again and walked from the room.

Dr. Thompkins found Siger Holmes and his wife in Siger's study. They were discussing the necessity of canceling the Squire's Ball due to Sherlock's illness and Amanda's confinement.

"Please tell us, Doctor Thompkins, when do you think Sherlock will be better?" Mrs. Holmes asked.

The doctor remained standing. He was angry. He was angry with the boy upstairs who was letting the life ebb from his body. He was angry at the parents before him. But mostly he was angry at his own helplessness.

"Your son is dying, madam," Dr. Thompkins said. "He has refused to eat or drink for the last twenty-four hours, and I cannot force him. He grows weaker every hour. It may be a day, or maybe two. I cannot say. But he shall surely die."

Mrs. Holmes wrung her hands. "Oh, dear," she said. "Why is he doing this?"

"Due to his illness he is not thinking clearly," the doctor said.

The squire remained silent. He had not told his wife of the attack upon the maid and did not intend to. If the boy was going to die then she need never know the deterioration of his mind.

"Is there nothing that can be done, Doctor?" she asked.

"Not if the boy continues to refuse food," the doctor said.

Dr. Thompkins knew Squire Holmes and half expected to hear him echo the words of Ebenezer Scrooge: "If they be like to die then they'd best get on with it." But the squire was silent. Even if he thought such thoughts he would not voice them before his wife.

"I have told this to Sherrinford as well. He sent a wire to Mycroft asking him to come at once," the doctor continued.

"Could I see Sherlock?" Mrs. Holmes asked.

"I'm afraid you would only upset him further, madam. Perhaps you could arrange to be called when he is asleep, and look upon him then," the Doctor advised.

Eventually night stole upon Sherlock and no will of his could have kept him awake. That night he rested as much in faint as in sleep. While Sherlock slept there came a dream, or was it? In it his mother slipped softly into the room and held his hand. Another figure loomed for a moment behind her in the doorway then stepped forward. It was his father, the squire, as dark and overwhelming as ever. He stood there looking down at his son with his bushy eyebrows drawn down over his eyes. His eyes were blue-grey like the clay on the moor, but as deep and bottomless as the mires. What was hidden in those eyes? Disappointment? Sorrow? Who could read them? Whatever sentiments had drawn these phantoms here to look upon their youngest son who now sought death so eagerly, they had come too late, perhaps seventeen years too late.

Chapter 31
Away From the Crack

Jonathan shivered and stoked the fire, but it was no earthly chill that made him shiver. It was near dawn and he was glad that he would soon be relieved of his lonesome duty. After the first two nights Jonathan had expected almost anything. But the long silent night had struck Jonathan as more ominous than the eerie nights which had preceded it. Sherlock had lain still all night, too still for Jonathan's liking. Thrice before he had stolen to the bedside with his candle. Now again he could not resist the urge. His candle flared with new life and he tiptoed toward the silent form upon the bed. Sherlock was a ghastly sight by candlelight. He was as near a corpse as Jonathan could imagine (having been too young to remember his own father's death). Yet Sherlock breathed and Jonathan was relieved.

Just then the door slid quietly open and the floorboards creaked as Sherrinford stepped in.

"How is he?" Sherrinford asked in a whisper.

"Very quiet, sir, all night," Jonathan replied.

"But still with us," Sherrinford said as he seated his bulk by the bed. He shook his large head and sighed, "My poor brother."

After a moment Sherrinford remembered Jonathan's presence.

"Run along, lad," Sherrinford said. "See that you get fed and rested."

Sherrinford sat with his brother for several hours until the doctor came back, then he went downstairs and breakfasted with his family. All ate in silence.

Slowly Sherlock became aware of his body again. It still lived. It still held him back. First he felt the rise and fall of his chest. His lungs were mostly clear now, but he was so weak that lifting his chest to breathe seemed an effort. His whole body ached now, increasing his desire to be rid of it. A sharp pain gripped his abdomen and a tightness was stretched like a strap across his lower back. Suddenly, he felt immensely cold and he began to shiver. Dr. Thompkins bent over Sherlock and drew the blankets up. He laid his hand upon Sherlock's cheek.

"Build up that fire, Jonathan," the doctor ordered. "He seems a bit cold."

Jonathan did as he was instructed and then helped Dr. Thompkins spread another quilt upon the bed.

Dr. Thompkins watched anxiously for Sherlock's shivering to end. He hoped that it was just due to some change in temperature and not the forerunner of convulsions. He was relieved when Sherlock blinked his eyes open as the shivering subsided.

"I thought perhaps you had left us for good," Dr. Thompkins said.

"Not yet," Sherlock whispered, as he regarded the doctor through half opened eyes.

"Will you eat now, sir?" Jonathan asked.

Sherlock opened his eyes slightly wider to look at Jonathan. "No," he said firmly.

"Sherlock--," Dr. Thompkins began but he stopped as the door opened.

Sherrinford entered with a yellow paper gripped in his hand. He glanced across at Dr. Thompkins then sat down beside his brother.

"Sherlock, I am glad to see you are awake. How do you feel?" Sherrinford asked.

When Sherlock did not respond, Dr. Thompkins said. "He is very weak. He still refuses to eat."

"Sherlock," Sherrinford said in as gentle a tone as the big man could muster. "I sent a telegram to Mycroft yesterday asking him to come at once. I just received his reply. He is on his way and will be here this evening."

The doctor sighed.

"I just hope that your brother lives that long," he said.

Dr. Thompkins looked at Sherlock. The boy had lost weight enough during the fever. Now the skin hung upon the bones of his face. There were dark circles about Sherlock's eyes and where his skin had been pale it now had a yellowish tinge to it. It was hideous ruin of the cheerful face Dr. Thompkins had seen not many months before. He looked upon it earnestly as if somewhere in it he could find the words to turn its owner from his course. He found nothing there but pain and weariness. So he spoke frankly from his own heart instead.

"Sherlock, you haven't long; you know that. Perhaps a day, maybe two. Eventually you will lose consciousness and not awake again. Perhaps the breath will linger in this body a while longer, but that too shall cease. If you continue on like this I can guarantee you death, but I cannot say when. Listen to me, Sherlock. Your brother Mycroft will be here this evening but I cannot say that you will be either conscious or alive when he arrives. But, Sherlock, if you stay your course for one day then you could speak to your brother, if only to say good-bye. If today you will have some tea and broth, you shall live out the day-- and tomorrow-- tomorrow I shall bring the vicar again."

Sherlock had regarded Dr. Thompkins through his half-opened eyes during this speech and now closed them as the room lapsed into silence. It was Sherrinford who broke the silence.

"Sherlock, you were always closer to Mycroft than to me. I kept you out of trouble," Sherrinford said, a small smile coming to his lips. "But it was with Mycroft that you shared your puzzles and observation games. I was more often the victim than a participant in your little games. But we are both fond of you. I do not want you to die and I am certain that Mycroft does not either. I sent word to him yesterday and he is coming today. Even if you are determined--" Sherrinford began but the words caught in his throat. "Well, surely you could bid Mycroft farewell."

Sherlock's thoughts had come slowly, but Sherrinford's plea had reached some distant place and fond memories had glowed there. Yes, he should say goodbye to Mycroft. The doctor had said but one more day --one more day, Violet! So close! One day until eternity. Surely he could wait a few hours and speak to Mycroft.

"Sherlock, will you do it?" Dr. Thompkins asked.

"Yes," Sherlock whispered.

Dr. Thompkins turned to Jonathan.

"Run down to the kitchen and bring up some tea, milk and honey," the doctor told him.

Bursting with joy, Jonathan hurried out.

Sherrinford took his brother's hand and squeezed it.

"I'm sure Mycroft will appreciate it," Sherrinford said.

"Come, Sherrinford, let us help Sherlock to sit up," the doctor said.

But as Sherrinford put his arm around his younger brother to lift him, suddenly Sherlock's head rolled limply against Sherrinford's shoulder. Sherrinford's eyes went wide with terror.

"Is he-- is he?" he stammered.

"He has fainted," Dr. Thompkins assured him. "In his condition, it is not surprising. Lay him back down. I shall see if I can bring him around."

Dr. Thompkins dipped a cloth in water and wiped Sherlock's face. Finally, Sherlock's eyes blinked open again with a somewhat confused look in them.

"You fainted," Dr. Thompkins explained. "And frightened your brother a bit."

"Quite," Sherrinford admitted.

"Here have a sip," the doctor said, holding a glass to Sherlock's lips. Sherlock drank obediently.

Then Jonathan was back with a tray and they managed the

second time to lift Sherlock into a sitting position.

Sherlock had to be fed for he was too weak to hold cup or spoon. He even had to be reminded that food was before him or else he paid no attention to it. But he did eat as he had agreed to. Dr. Thompkins was heartened by this. While Sherlock was taking food there was always hope, and they had come so very close to losing all hope. Dr. Thompkins spoke to Tessy and gave her a schedule by which Sherlock was to be fed and what she should send on the tray. Then he left Sherlock in Jonathan's care and went on to see his other patients.

With the tea in the morning, Tessy had sent scones. At lunch time she had sent broth with dumplings and fresh milk. In the afternoon there were turnip greens ("Dug them out from under the snow herself.") and some concoction made with apples. At tea time there was more tea with milk and honey and sweet biscuits. True to his word Sherlock ate them all. By the afternoon he found that he had strength enough to feed himself and after tea he lifted his violin into his lap.

It was with mixed emotions that Sherlock felt his strength returning. He welcomed death as a deliverer. But, as in every human being, there was in him the seed of life that fought against encroaching death even as he consciously desired it, and this human seed rejoiced in the reprieve it had been given. Yet consciously Sherlock thought it merely a stay of execution, and intended it to be short. He droned upon the violin as he waited impatiently for his brother Mycroft to arrive.

The doctor returned in the afternoon and was pleased with Sherlock's progress. The sallow tint had left his skin and his breathing was more regular. He was obviously stronger than when the doctor had left in the morning.

"You have done well," he praised Jonathan. "Keep him eating as long as you can and do nothing to upset him."

But as the day wore on Sherlock became more and more

impatient. As the grey day faded to a starless night he began to have doubts concerning his agreement. Seven o'clock went by and half-past and still Mycroft had not come. Soon after there was a knock upon the door but it was only a servant with Sherlock's supper. Jonathan took the tray and brought it to the bedside.

"Send it back," Sherlock said.

"B-but, Master Sherlock!" Jonathan protested.

"I will not eat it," Sherlock said.

"But, thou-- but you agreed!" Jonathan said.

"I have done as I agreed," Sherlock insisted.

Dismayed, Jonathan sent the tray back to the kitchen.

"Why hasn't Mycroft come?" Sherlock asked.

"I do not know, sir," Jonathan said.

Sherlock gave Jonathan a suspicious look then turned back to his violin. Shortly he stopped and listened intently.

"There is some disturbance below. What is it?" Sherlock asked.

Jonathan crossed the room and opened the door.

A chorus of voices drifted into the room.

"God rest ye merry gentlemen. Let nothing you dismay..."

"There are carolers, sir," Jonathan said.

"Carolers?" Sherlock asked.

"Yes, sir, tis but 13 days till Christmas," Jonathan said.

"Indeed? Jonathan, I wish you to find my brother Sherrinford. I must speak to him at once," Sherlock said.

"But, sir, my orders are--" Jonathan protested.

"I must see him. I must know what has become of Mycroft," Sherlock insisted.

"B-but, Master Sherlock!" Jonathan stammered.

"Or am I to suppose," said Sherlock sharply, "that you are part of this conspiracy as well?"

"No, sir, I know of nothing of the kind. But Mr. Sherrinford says I munnot-- I must not leave th- you by yourself!" Jonathan protested.

Sherlock fingered his bow. Then he spoke in a calmer, more friendly tone.

"I am sorry, Jonathan," Sherlock said. "I do not in fact believe that you are part of the conspiracy, if indeed there is one. However, I am anxious to speak with my brother and I give you my word that if you go and find him I shall do nothing while you are gone."

Jonathan thought for a moment. Sherlock had not spoken to him in such a tone since he had come to the Hall. This was a request from friend to friend rather than an order from master to servant. Because he valued Sherlock's friendship Jonathan gave in knowing full well what it could cost.

"I will go then, sir," Jonathan said.

"Thank you," Sherlock said.

As Jonathan opened the door more carols wafted up the stairwell-- "tidings of comfort and joy, comfort and--" just to be cut off again as the door closed.

But Sherlock was not as calm as he had pretended to Jonathan. His appeal to Jonathan's friendship had been the only tact he could think of to override Sherrinford's commands and make the boy obey him. Sherlock was greatly disturbed. Had they tricked him into breaking his fast? Was Mycroft really on his way or were they deceiving him again? They had seemed sincere enough. Yet Sherlock no longer trusted his instincts. Why had Mycroft not arrived?

Then the door flew open and Jonathan rushed back in.

"E's here!" he gasped. "Mr. Mycroft's here!"

"It is snowing again," Jonathan continued, panting between words, but gaining control of his English again. "And I heard that t-the sleigh hit a drift and tipped over."

It was true then, Sherlock thought. They had not been deceiving him!

Shortly there was a knock upon the door and in lumbered Mycroft himself with Sherrinford behind him.

"Good evening, Sherlock," Mycroft said. "You must excuse my tardiness. The train was nearly on time but the sleigh met with a mishap on the way back from the station."

"Jonathan told me," Sherlock said.

"Jonathan is a good lad," Sherrinford said, "but I think right now he should run along to the kitchen and see to his own supper."

"Yes, sir," Jonathan said and withdrew from the room.

"Well, I should offer you my hand, Sherlock, but I'm afraid they're both quite frozen," Mycroft said as he proceeded to rub his large hands together before the fire.

Sherrinford sat and watched his brothers. Mycroft seemed calm, even serene. He seemed more like he was preparing to play a friendly chess match than to talk his brother out of suicide. But Sherrinford did not pretend to understand how Mycroft's brain worked. He merely acknowledged that in many ways it worked better than his own.

On the other hand Sherlock stared at Mycroft blankly through half-opened eyes. He seemed very far away. Sherrinford could only hope that Mycroft could reach him.

"Ah, that's better," Mycroft said at last. With his back to the fire Mycroft regarded his younger brother.

"You do not look well, Sherlock," Mycroft observed. "But you do not seem to be in such dire straits as Sherrinford's wire yesterday implied."

"Sherlock has eaten today," Sherrinford said.

"Ah, yes, such I had surmised," Mycroft said in response, not taking his eyes off Sherlock. "A change of heart then, Sherlock?"

"No," Sherlock said.

"He was quite weak this morning. He fainted in my arms and Dr. Thompkins was afraid he would not live out the day,"

Sherrinford explained.

"I agreed to eat today so that I might have a final word with you. But I have fulfilled my agreement and I shall not eat again," Sherlock declared.

"Ah!" Mycroft said and subsided into the chair before the desk.

Mycroft faced his brother once again.

"I am glad that you have eaten today for whatever reason," he said. "I have not come to bid you farewell and to watch you die, Sherlock. I have come to talk with you."

"There is nothing to talk about," Sherlock replied flatly.

"Isn't there?" Mycroft rejoined.

Sherlock was silent. The bout had begun and Sherrinford knew better than to interfere with intellectual sparring between Mycroft and Sherlock.

"Have you given careful thought to the course you have set out for yourself?" Mycroft asked.

"Thought! I cannot think!" Sherlock cried.

"You should think," Mycroft said.

"What good has it ever done me?" Sherlock groaned.

"What harm has it ever done you?" Mycroft asked.

The room was thick with silence. Then Sherlock spoke, his voice harsh with anger.

"I am not in the mood for word games, Mycroft. I agreed to see you to say goodbye. If you've come merely to badger me then go and let me be."

The room again fell silent, but Mycroft made no sign of leaving. He ran his fingers about in thoughtful circles upon the desktop until they lighted upon the magnifying lens which lay there. He noted the crack and recommenced his finger movements about the instrument itself.

"Sherlock," Mycroft said at last in a soft voice, "I did not know Violet Rushdale well. She was only a child when I came down

272

from the university, but I do remember her. Do you?"

Violet as a little girl? Sherlock had never thought of that before. Always when he had been with her he had been so content with here and now, so full of what she was that he had never thought back to what she had been before. But, of course, he had known her. He had seen her at holidays when all the children of the dale were gathered together. But he had never paid much attention to her until they met again this past summer.

"Yes," Sherlock replied, "I remember her."

"A little thing she was," Mycroft said.

"Yes," Sherlock said.

"But always full of pluck," Mycroft continued.

"Yes," Sherlock said, and a small smile crept across his face and his eyes brightened for an instant. Then he sighed and the clouds returned.

"She is gone," Sherlock said.

"Yes," Mycroft agreed.

"Then, Mycroft, why do you torment me?" Sherlock protested.

"That is not my intent," Mycroft said.

"What is your intent?" Sherlock asked.

"To make you think," Mycroft said.

"Of what?" Sherlock asked.

"Of yourself," Mycroft said.

"There is nothing there to think of," Sherlock protested. "I am nothing."

"Do you mind thinking of Violet then?" Mycroft asked.

"I think of nothing else," Sherlock sighed.

"Sherrinford tells me that Violet grew into a spirited young woman," Mycroft continued.

"Yes," Sherlock agreed.

"She was quite independent in her ways."

"Yes."

"When Mary Rushdale died Godfrey couldn't stand before the blow," Mycroft said. "He let something of himself die with her. He let the farm go to pieces and scared off the help. It was Violet who stood tall and carried the burden. While Godfrey hid in the dark recesses of his mind, she protected him from the outside world and refused to be parted from him. He was weak and she was the protector. He was the burden and she, in her tender years, was the one who carried it. Never did she make herself a burden upon another."

Tears were streaming down Sherlock's face.

"And now--" Mycroft began.

"And now she's gone," Sherlock sobbed.

"And now she is gone," Mycroft agreed. "And Godfrey's gone, too. And you wish to be gone as well."

Silence rose up in the room again like a painful fog and hung there for several minutes until Mycroft's voice rose firmly to pierce it.

"Godfrey Rushdale is gone because he could not live without his daughter's aid and support," Mycroft went on. "What little there was left of him died when she disappeared. Violet--"

"Violet," Sherlock began, but choked on the word and began again. "Violet is gone because that cursed Moriarty used her as a pawn in his game against me. Violet is gone because I was too stupid to realize why she had sent me away. Violet is gone because-- because she was protecting me!" Sherlock sobbed, and the fog of silence descended again.

"And now you would follow Godfrey," Mycroft said softly.

"No, I would follow Violet! I do not want to live without her! I cannot live without her!" Sherlock cried.

"Nor could Godfrey Rushdale. The death of his wife stripped him of his senses and the death of his daughter stripped him of his life," Mycroft said.

"Am I allowed no mourning?" Sherlock interrupted.

"Mourning, yes, but you are headed for self-destruction. A faster route, perhaps, than Godfrey took, but the same destination nonetheless. He did not follow his daughter at all, but went an entirely different way," Mycroft argued.

"What do you mean?" Sherlock asked, puzzled.

Sherrinford was heartened by the fact that Sherlock seemed to be trying to follow Mycroft's arguments.

"If Godfrey had followed his daughter and heeded her example perhaps they would both be alive today," Mycroft responded. "But no, he cast off his responsibilities and wallowed in his misery, never once considering the burden he placed on her. Violet is gone, perhaps, because she tried to carry too many burdens by herself. If those around her had been stronger and shared her burdens then she would have had a longer and happier life. And now you follow her father's example: you are determined that life cannot continue; you are disrupting your household, terrorizing the servants, and closing yourself off from the world. See how complete the analogy is, Sherlock!"

"I'm sure that Violet loved her mother, Sherlock," Mycroft continued, "But she did not allow her mother's death to destroy her as Godfrey did. She knew that her mother would not want that. What do you think Violet would want of you?"

"I do not know," Sherlock said.

"Yes, you do. Think," Mycroft urged.

Sherlock wiped his face and blew his nose on a handkerchief and buried his face again. How could he think?

"She loved you, didn't she?" Mycroft asked.

"Yes," Sherlock admitted. What else could explain what she had done?

"Would she want you to suffer?" Mycroft asked.

"No," Sherlock said.

"Would she want you to die?" Mycroft asked.

"No!" he gasped.

275

The response came out without thought. Yet when he heard it Sherlock knew it was true. It was not for Violet that he did this, but for himself.

"She would want you to live?" Mycroft asked.

"Yes," Sherlock said softly.

"And to go on to the university?" Mycroft asked.

Sherlock was silent.

"You believe she was protecting you?" Mycroft asked.

"Yes," Sherlock said.

"By not telling you she carried your child?" Mycroft asked/

"Yes!" Sherlock responded.

"Why? Because of what Father would do if he found out?" Mycroft asked.

"Yes," Sherlock said.

"Because it would destroy your chances of going to the university?" Mycroft asked.

"Yes," Sherlock agreed.

"Do you wish her efforts to have been in vain?" Mycroft asked.

"No!" Sherlock sobbed.

"She would wish you to be successful?" Mycroft asked.

"Yes," Sherlock agreed.

"And happy?" Mycroft asked.

"Yes-- But how can I?" Sherlock wailed. "I feel empty and lost without her!"

"Then follow her lead," Mycroft said. "Match her strength."

Sherlock looked up at his brother, blinking. Then he shook his head and buried his face again.

"No, I cannot. I can't do-- I can't think of anything but that she is gone!" Sherlock cried.

"Sherlock, you are feeling, not thinking. Your pain warps your thoughts and distorts your view. Your mind is still as sharp as ever, but it is like this lens," Mycroft said, holding up the magnifying lens. "If you look through the crack you see only milky lines and twisted images. To see clearly you must avoid the crack in the lens."

Sherlock Holmes was struck by these words and he looked up at his brother Mycroft as if he had just delivered a message from the grave. Sherlock reached out his hand for the lens and Mycroft handed it to him. Sherlock ran his finger over the glass and remembered the day Violet had dropped it.

"If thou donna look through the cracked part everything is clear," she had said.

Sherlock's hands were shaking and he gripped the lens tighter to make them stop. He leaned back against the pillows. He was silent for some time staring down at the lens in his hand. Then he sighed and looked over at Mycroft.

"I don't know if I can do it, Mycroft," Sherlock said. "I don't know if I have the strength. But I shall try for... for Violet and in honour of her memory."

Mycroft stretched out his hand and Sherlock took it. Sherrinford stood up and gripped Sherlock's shoulder. Sherlock looked up at him.

"Then I can send for your supper?" Sherrinford asked.

"Yes," Sherlock sighed.

Chapter 32
Epilogue

A week later Jonathan was helping Sherlock dress.

"Art thou-- Are you are sure you can do this?" Jonathan asked doubtfully.

"I must do it," Sherlock responded, as he put on his coat. "Now go and do as I asked."

Sherlock sat fully clothed upon his bed gathering his wits and his strength for the task before him. A moment later the door to his room opened silently and a furtive Jonathan entered and closed it.

"Yes, he's there," Jonathan said.

"Good. Now come with me down the stairs, but if he should come out get back quickly. I can't have him see you helping me, understand?" Sherlock insisted.

"Y-yes," Jonathan responded.

Soon Sherlock stood before the door to his father's study. He waved Jonathan back, braced himself, drew himself up straight and knocked firmly upon the door. He entered when the call came. After closing the door behind him, Sherlock said, "Father, I would like a word with you."

Squire Holmes did not show his surprise when his youngest son stood before him when he had been at death's door barely a week before, but Sherlock knew it was there. He knew that his father admired strength and determination in a man, and Sherlock intended to use that knowledge to get what he needed. What he needed was a career so he could gain his independence and leave this place. For that he needed to attend the university.

Siger Holmes told Sherlock to be seated. Sherlock sat slowly, trying not to show how glad he was to be sitting down. They spoke for a long time, but there were many things they did not speak of. They did not speak of their last interview in the study or what came after, or Sherlock's attack on the maid, or Siger's doubts of his son's sanity. Professor Moriarty's name was not mentioned. They spoke of the future, not of the past.

Jonathan waited anxiously outside the door of the study. Thomas, the butler, scowled at him once, but Jonathan ignored him. He was under orders to be where he was and doing what he was. At last the door opened and Sherlock came out, erect as before, but quite a bit paler. As the door shut behind him Sherlock leaned heavily on Jonathan's shoulder for a moment, then straightened up again.

Jonathan started to speak, "Are you--," but Sherlock waved him to silence.

"Upstairs," Sherlock whispered.

But as they reach the staircase, Sherlock's head was spinning and he reached out for the banister to keep himself from falling. He hung onto it for a moment. Just then Sherrinford came down the hall.

"Sherlock!" he exclaimed, but Sherlock motioned him to silence as well.

"Help me upstairs-- quickly now!" Sherlock whispered, fearing his father would appear at any moment and all his efforts would be undone.

So Sherrinford and Jonathan helped Sherlock up the stairs between them. As they approached the door to Sherlock's room, Mycroft appeared in the hall.

"Sherlock?" Mycroft inquired, asking a thousand questions with one word.

Sherlock turn to him. "I spoke to Father," he said.

"Ah!" Mycroft said and followed the three of them into Sherlock's room. Sherlock lay down upon his bed breathing heavily.

"Should I send for the doctor?" Sherrinford asked.

"No, I'll be fine. I just don't have my strength back yet," Sherlock said.

"You shouldn't exert yourself so," Sherrinford said.

"I had to speak to Father," Sherlock said.

"To what end?" asked Sherrinford.

Sherlock leaned back and drew a deep breath. Then he looked up and caught Mycroft's eye.

"He said that he will seek a new tutor for me," Sherlock said. "There is still time to gain admission to the university."

"Oh, Sherlock, that is indeed good news," Sherrinford responded joyfully. "I don't know how you accomplished it, but I am happy for you, just the same. That is all the more reason to rest and gather up your strength. Now, Jonathan, don't you let this brother of mine talk you into any more jaunts around the house until he is strong enough."

"Yes, sir," Jonathan agreed.

"I shall go and tell Amanda this wonderful news," Sherrinford said, giving Sherlock a firm pat on the shoulder and leaving the room.

Mycroft offered his huge hand.

"Congratulations, Sherlock. I know it wasn't easy, but the road ahead of you isn't any easier," Mycroft said.

"Nor was the road easy for her...." Sherlock said, looking away from his brother for a moment. His mind recalled the last dim image of the Violet before he lost her in the snowstorm. He pushed the memory away and looked back at Mycroft. "But I will try to honour her memory the best I can, and match her strength, if I can." He concluded, returning his brother's grip.

In January Andrew Goble did return to take the post as curate at the village church and the squire hired him to tutor Sherlock as well. Sherlock was accepted to the university and began a course in mathematics as his father wished. The following summer a classmate at the university named Victor Trevor invited Sherlock to his father's place in Donnithorpe. Sherlock was glad of the invitation for he dreaded the bittersweet memories that Yorkshire held for him. He avoided returning if he could.

One evening shortly after Sherlock's arrival, Victor Trevor began telling his father of Sherlock Holmes' skill at observation and inference and how Sherlock could tell a man's trade by his hands and something of his history by his features and attire. The old man evidently thought that his son was exaggerating in his description of one or two trivial demonstrations that Sherlock had performed for Victor.

"Come, now, Mr. Holmes," said the elder Trevor, laughing good-humouredly. "I'm an excellent subject. See if you can deduce anything from me."

"I fear there is not very much," Sherlock answered. "You have boxed a good deal in your youth."

"How did you know it? Is my nose knocked a little out of straight?"

"No. It is your ears. They have the peculiar flattening and thickening that marks a boxing man," Sherlock said.

"Anything else?"

"You have done a good deal of digging by your callosities," Sherlock continued.

"Made all my money at the gold fields."

"You have been to New Zealand."

"Right again."

"You have visited Japan."

"Quite true."

"And you have been intimately associated with someone whose initials were J. A., and whom you afterwards were eager to entirely forget," Sherlock concluded.

Mr. Trevor stood slowly up, fixed his large blue eyes on Sherlock Holmes with a wild stare, and then pitched forward in a dead faint. Victor and Sherlock were horrified. They quickly undid the man's collar and sprinkled water on his face. He gave a gasp or two and sat up.

"Ah, boys," Mr. Trevor said, forcing a smile, "I hope I haven't frightened you. Strong as I look, there is a weak place in my heart, and it does not take much to knock me over. I don't know how you manage this, Mr. Holmes, but it seems to me that all the detectives of fact and fancy would be children in your hands. That's your line of life, sir, and you may take the word of a man who has seen something of the world."

"I hope I have said nothing to pain you?" Sherlock Holmes said.

"Well, you certainly touched upon rather a tender point. Might I ask how you know and how much you know?" Trevor said in a half-jesting fashion, but a look of terror still lurked at the back of his eyes.

"It is simplicity itself," Sherlock Holmes said. "When you bared your arm to draw that fish into the boat I saw that J.A. had been tattooed in the bend of the elbow. The letters were still legible, but it was perfectly clear from their blurred appearance, and from the staining of the skin around them, that efforts had been made to obliterate them. It was obvious, then, that those initials had once been very familiar to you, and that you had afterwards wished to forget them."

"What an eye you have!" the elder Trevor cried with a sigh of relief. "It is just as you say. But we won't talk of it. Of all ghosts the ghosts of our old loves are the worst."

Sherlock spoke of it no more. He knew well the ghosts of old loves and they haunted him that night. As he lay in the dark of his room that night old Trevor's words came back to him. He had not put much thought to them at the time, so concerned had he been about his host's health. But now they flooded back full of import.

"...all the detectives of fact and fancy would be children in your hands. That's your line of life, sir..." old Trevor had said.

EPILOGUE

The ghosts in Sherlock's own mind echoed a country constable's stinging declaration: "...there's no detective on earth who could find her now."

The old memories of joy and pain, the memories that he avoided and suppressed, came unlocked and they hit him now like a gigantic wave and submerged him. In his mind he once more looked out the study window and saw Violet fighting to free herself from Moriarty's grasp. Then she was riding away and he could not catch her and the snow was everywhere, but she was gone and he was lost, forever lost.

But they had hidden it from him until they could hide it no more and then they said, "...there's no detective on earth who can find her now." The truth had rent his soul and fractured his nerves. It all lived for him again from beginning to end in his mind this night and tortured him.

He had no concept of time. It could have lasted minutes or hours. Finally, trembling and gasping for breath, he clawed his way to the surface of the wave of hallucinations and emotions. He fought the wave back from whence it came. It subsided again with the words: "...there's no detective on earth who can find her now." The words reverberated through his mind like an aftershock as he lay trembling and staring into the dark room on the bed clothes wet with sweat and tears.

Then old Trevor's words resounded through his brain with the voice of sanity and clarity: "...That's your line of life, sir..."

"...There's no detective on earth who can find her now," the fading ghosts retorted.

"...That's your line of life, sir..." came back again like a spark in the dark and kindled a fire within his soul.

"...There's no detective on earth who can find her now," echoed again.

Sherlock sat up suddenly in bed. "There will be!" he declared aloud.

As Violet's loss had left him empty and at sea, old Trevor's words now filled him with determination and direction.

"There will be such a detective as the world has never known," Sherlock Holmes swore to the darkness.

Acknowledgments

Sherlock Holmes is the offspring of the mind of the late Sir Arthur Conan Doyle. Like most offspring, Sherlock Holmes refuses to stay in the cradle. The exploration of the origins and character of the man Sherlock Holmes dates back over a hundred years, and my own exploration and development of this story reaches back over a quarter century.

I thank Sherlockians everywhere for keeping green the memory of Sherlock Holmes and providing countless resources for understanding Holmes and the world he lived in. In the last 25 years I have also drawn upon the resources of public and college libraries in Poughkeepsie, New York, White Plains, New York, Ann Arbor, Michigan, Norman, Oklahoma and Boulder, Colorado, and in the last five years, many websites available on the Internet. It is not possible for me to list here all the references which helped me understand the time, the places and the people described herein but I am grateful to them all. I have no doubt that Holmes himself wishes he had access to the resources available to me today.

I am especially grateful to the following members of Hounds of the Internet for critiquing the manuscript: Ben Walton, Scott Tate, Richard Sveum, MD, BSI, Cathy Steffen, Al Reneski, Stephanie Nowicke, Laura E. Goodin, and Peter Blau, BSI, and to my sister Diane Kay Zike for her insights and her proofing skills.

About the Author

Darlene A. Cypser was born in Tulsa, Oklahoma, but lived in Poughkeepsie, New York, during elementary school and high school before returning to Norman, Oklahoma for college and law school. In 1987 she moved to Boulder, Colorado where she practiced law until 1999 when she began producing and selling movies, and running other businesses. Darlene is currently producing a movie set in 18th century England based on Alfred Noyes' poem *The Highwayman*.

Darlene became an avid follower of Sherlock Holmes when she was in high school and she attended some meetings of the Hudson Valley Sciontists in her teens. Since then she has corresponded with a number of Sherlockians around the world and been a member of a number of Sherlockian groups including Dr. Watson's Neglected Patients and the Hounds of the Internet. Darlene's first contact with the Baker Street Irregulars was an exchange of correspondence with Dr. Julian Wolff in the 1970s and she wrote two "trifling monograms" which were published by the Baker Street Journal in the mid-1980s when Philip Shreffler was the editor. She is writing sequel trilogy which follows Sherlock Holmes through his years at the university and into his early career.

10206700R0

Made in the USA
Lexington, KY
04 July 2011